NUECES DECEIT

ALSO BY MARK GREATHOUSE

The Frontier Chronicles

Perilous Trails

Wyoming Calls

Longhorns North

Warpath

The Tumbleweed Sagas

Nueces Justice

Nueces Reprise

NUECES DECEIT

THE STRIP GIVES UP ITS EVIL

THE TUMBLEWEED SAGAS
BOOK 3

MARK GREATHOUSE

WOLFPACK
PUBLISHING
— EST 2013 —

Dedicated with love to my wife, Carolyn,
and to our two sons, Mike and Matt.

THE NUECES STRIP

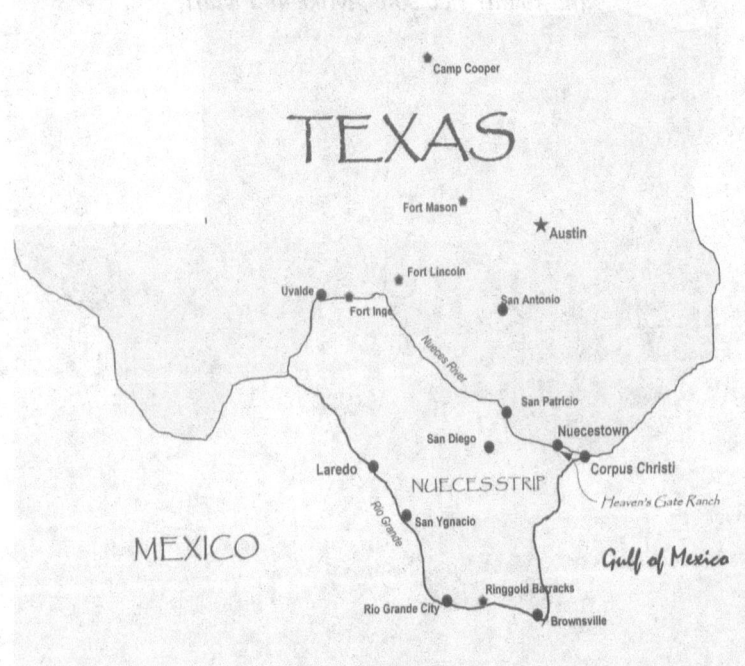

The vast Nueces Strip serves as the primary setting for the Tumbleweed Sagas. The Strip was also called Wild Horse Desert, owing to the millions of Mustangs that roamed its prairies. *(Sketch by Mark Greathouse)*

NUECESTOWN

Nuecestown, Texas, established in 1852 by English and German settlers, was developed by Corpus Christi founder Colonel Henry Kinney along the Nueces River as a ferry crossing. Mostly thanks to the railroad passing it by, it's now a "ghost town" marked only by historical markers. All that remains is a preserved schoolhouse and the old Nuecestown Cemetery. *(Sketch by Mark Greathouse)*

THE CAST

Colonel Henry Lawrence Kinney – *Entrepreneur, rancher, and trader. Founder of Corpus Christi, originally as a trading post, and was a leader in the settlement and economic development of the eastern part of the Nueces Strip.*

John Salmon "Rip" Ford - *Soldier, elected official, newspaper editor, and Texas Ranger, Ford was critically important to taming the Texas frontier. He was a renowned Indian fighter and led a campaign against Mexican rebel Juan Cortina. He would later be intimately involved with secession, fighting in the War Between the States, and post-war redevelopment. He assembled the last great force of Texas Rangers before the War Between the States.*

Sam Houston – *One of the most illustrious leaders of Texas from soldier leading Texas to independence, to politician serving as president of the Republic of Texas, US Senator, and Texas governor. Dreamed of conquering Mexico and becoming US president. His decisions directly impacted formation of the Texas Rangers.*

Benito Juarez – *Part indigenous Indian, he became president of Mexico by the succession mandated by its Constitution when moderate liberal President Comonfort was forced to resign by Mexican conservatives. Juarez remained in the presidential office until his death in 1872.*

Juan Nepomuceno "Cheno" Cortina – *Mexican rancher, politician, military leader, outlaw, and folk hero who did not accept the terms of the Treaty of Guadalupe Hidalgo and fought against settlers, US soldiers, and Texas Rangers on the Nueces Strip.*

HISTORICAL CHARACTERS

Colonel Henry Lawrence Kinney – *Entrepreneur, rancher, and trader. Founder of Corpus Christi, originally as a trading post, and was a leader in the settlement and economic development of the eastern part of the Nueces Strip.*

John Salmon "Rip" Ford - *Soldier, elected official, newspaper editor, and Texas Ranger, Ford was critically important to taming the Texas frontier. He was a renowned Indian fighter and led a campaign against Mexican rebel Juan Cortina. He would later be intimately involved with secession, fighting in the War Between the States, and post-war redevelopment. He assembled the last great force of Texas Rangers before the War Between the States.*

Sam Houston – *One of the most illustrious leaders of Texas from soldier leading Texas to independence, to politician serving as president of the Republic of Texas, US Senator, and Texas governor. Dreamed of conquering Mexico and becoming US president. His decisions directly impacted formation of the Texas Rangers.*

Benito Juarez – *Part indigenous Indian, he became president of Mexico by the succession mandated by its Constitution when moderate liberal President Comonfort was forced to resign by Mexican conservatives. Juarez remained in the presidential office until his death in 1872.*

Juan Nepomuceno "Cheno" Cortina – *Mexican rancher, politician, military leader, outlaw, and folk hero who did not accept the terms of the Treaty of Guadalupe Hidalgo and fought against settlers, US soldiers, and Texas Rangers on the Nueces Strip.*

THEME

DECEIT

The act or practice of deceiving; concealment or distortion of the truth for the purpose of misleading; duplicity; fraud; cheating

INTRODUCTION

The Nueces Strip of 1858 was still mostly a vast prairie of tall grasses and loamy sands that stretched as far as the eye could see and beyond. The grasses grew high enough to reach a horse's withers. The Strip was generally defined as reaching south from the Nueces River all the way to the Rio Grande, its eastern boundary being the Gulf of Mexico. At its farthest point north was the little town of Uvalde. Occasional mottes of live oak or mesquite dotted the prairie. To the western reaches was Laredo and nearby Fort McIntosh.

The often-dry creek beds and arroyos eventually filled with rainwater and emptied into Nueces Bay and…farther to the east…Corpus Christi Bay. Flash flooding was an ongoing fear. Summers? Well, they tended to be hot and humid.

The abundant animal life on the Nueces Strip featured deer, javelina, fox, coyote, and even mountain lion. Occasionally, spotted ocelots and even wolves could be sighted by the practiced eye. Come spring, wildflowers swept across much of the landscape painted like a huge rainbow, with scarlet sage, hibiscus, daisies, poppies, lilies, and the ubiquitous bluebonnets. Groves of cypress, juniper, and palmetto could be found mostly further south toward Brownsville. Cactus along with yucca and agave abounded.

No discussion of the Nueces Strip can ever be complete without mention that much of the most significant fighting of the Texas War for Independence was fought on and just north of the Nueces Strip back in 1835 and 1836, and it was scene to the first fighting of the Mexican American War of 1846. The Strip was officially ceded to the United States by the Treaty of Guadalupe Hidalgo in 1848, though Texas had already laid claim.

The plentiful and accessible longhorn cattle could be called the "low-hanging-fruit" of the Nueces Strip economy. They were a hardy breed that could withstand the South Texas heat, fend off disease-carrying pests, and carry just enough meat on their bones to make them reasonably profitable to raise. Originally brought from the Iberian Peninsula by early Spanish priests, the longhorns eventually escaped the mostly failing missionaries, proliferated, and roamed wild and free across the prairies. Millions of the beasts soon covered Texas and especially the excellent grazing lands of the Nueces Strip. They competed with the wild mustangs that had also been introduced by the Spaniards and with the huge herds of indigenous buffalo. The Texas prairies provided plenty of feed for all its hoofed residents.

Many who came to this harsh and often unforgiving land sought fame and fortune. Permanent residences weren't part of their destiny. Many were what some folks called "second-chancers," seeking a new start on their lives. The early migrants to Texas were seekers and entrepreneurs, often profiting outside the boundaries of the law before moving on to the next opportunity. The factor that would ultimately win the west was the family, the larger the better, as children grew up facing all manner of lurking dangers. Families established the ranches and farms popping up, not only throughout the eastern portions of the Nueces Strip, but across Texas as a whole. The territory east of the 98th meridian that sliced through the very heart of Texas was fast becoming an economic juggernaut, and the Strip was no exception. The economy was mostly based on growing cotton and raising longhorns and horses. Cotton was bundled and hauled to port for markets in Louisiana and points east, while cattle were driven to the Kansas and Missouri railheads to be transported to the packing houses of the Midwest.

The far reaches of the untamed Nueces Strip beckoned to principled men like our protagonist, Luke Dunn. While the frontier grew ever westward, there was ongoing worry about the threats posed by Comanche, Kiowa, and Lipan Apache, as well as the rogue marauding bandits from south of the Rio Grande. This all served to keep early Texans on the wild frontier ever vigilant. It was easy to make the case for calling up companies of Texas Rangers to patrol the Strip, as they took it upon themselves to go where the military found it politically undesirable. On the other hand, the legislators in the state capital in Austin did not have the financial means to fund the necessary companies of Rangers. They had to rely on the US Army, which could be chancy at best, as it was subject to the politics of whomever was in power and perceiving real or imagined threats.

Toward the end of *Nueces Reprise*, Texas Ranger Captain Luke Dunn had been seriously wounded. Thus, *Nueces Deceit*, the next of the Tumbleweed Sagas, begins with him recuperating under the care of his wife Elisa at their Heaven's Gate Ranch near Nuecestown. The ranch had begun to grow both in terms of landholdings and livestock, and the Dunns had added twin boys to their family.

Deceit colored by vengeance and violence looms large in *Nueces Deceit,* as the obsessive mastermind of a government fraud is revealed and a revenge-driven Mexican rebel must be brought to justice. The Nueces Strip had already become a haven for drifters, criminals, and rustlers in the region. Little surprise that folks came to power by means fair and foul, and wealth begat power and often corruption. Luke is ever conflicted over his roles as rancher versus Texas Ranger. Danger lurks, whichever Luke chooses. Prairie fires, blizzards, floods, stampedes, desperate killers, rustlers, and savages are part and parcel, whether lawman or rancher. Just about anywhere he rides, death could be reaching for his bridle reins. While he built considerable notoriety that made him a target, he also established reliable allies. He's determined to bring justice to the Nueces Strip. When John "Rip" Ford calls to form companies of Texas Rangers, Luke is pressed into making a future-altering decision. But, as 1858 yields to 1859, there's the beginnings of a sense of future troubles lingering in the air.

Much has been written about the Texas Rangers over the decades of Texas history. They served as lawmen and militia, with their primary mission being peace on the Texas frontier. They were well-armed and underpaid. Their character spanned the gamut from honest and God-fearing to the dredges of society. Such diversity demanded strong leaders like Jack Coffee Hays, John Salmon "Rip" Ford, and many others. Texas Rangers were certainly a breed unto themselves. The best of them exhibited resourcefulness, harbored valuable innate skills like tracking and marksmanship, were ever alert, loyal, and often possessed uncanny powers of observation. The vast majority were proud to be Texas Rangers. Often outnumbered, they were unquestionably brave. *Nueces Deceit* protagonist Captain Luke Dunn embodied the higher character and purposes of the Texas Rangers. His sense of justice as delivered with an iron hand could—as necessary—be tempered with a caring redemptive spirit.

While the "Cast of Historical Characters" provides some helpful true-to-life framework to the life and times on the Texas Nueces Strip, woven into the Tumbleweed Sagas are actual settlers of the frontier as drawn from the author's family ancestry. Peter Dunn immigrated from Ireland in 1850 and established a blacksmith shop in Corpus Christi, John Dunn ranched and grew many acres of cotton, and Nicholas Dunn was a rancher, drover, livestock speculator, and Comanche fighter of some repute. Such real-life characters, coupled with actual events, have served to reinforce the historical setting for the Tumbleweed Sagas.

Poet and novelist cousin of mine, Mary Maude Dunn Wright (pseud. Lilith Lorraine), in writing the preface to her father's biography back in 1932, posed the question, "Not in the spirit of judging their actions by artificial standards which, in their day, had no existence, but by asking ourselves if we were in their places, should we have acquitted ourselves as well, and by putting to ourselves the still more potent question: how well have we kept the birthright they have given us, how well have we safeguarded the liberties they purchased through untold privations, how courageously are we meeting the problems that confront us today? In short, when we stand before the tribunal of remote posterity, to whom shall the laurel be awarded...?"

Y'all might think on that.

NUECES DECEIT

PROLOGUE

LUKE SLEPT FITFULLY those first few nights. The gunshot wound seemed to hurt every time he moved. Combined with a fever he'd run for a couple of days early on, he'd actually experienced bouts of delirium. This frightened Elisa, as much as by what he said, as by her fear that he'd tear out the stitches Doc had used to pull together his torn flesh. It had taken a week before the fitful nights finally seemed to be behind them.

Elisa's nursing was crucial. Despite a ranch to run and twin boys to care for, she tenderly cared for her wounded husband. Days ran into weeks, as she labored to restore his strength.

From his perch on the gallery he'd built across the front of their cabin, Luke relaxed in one of the chairs he and Elisa had acquired a few months back on one of their trips to Corpus Christi. He soaked up the rays of the rising sun, allowing their curative warmth to course through him. The wound in his side was healing, and he was itching to get back to working the ranch. He watched as half a dozen longhorns ambled past the corral. His gray stallion, Big

Horse, trotted around inside the corral, absorbing those very same sun's rays as his owner. He was surely itching to have Luke saddle him again and head out to search for stray longhorns, or whatever other mayhem could be found.

ONE
HEALING

LUKE'S SIX-FOOT-THREE height had earned him the nickname "Long Luke" from some folk, but he was partial to the name the Comanche had given him: Ghost-Who-Rides. His ruggedly handsome Irish face framed a well-tended fiery-red mustache. Six years had now passed since he'd immigrated from County Kildare back in his native Ireland. Luke had joined rebellious clan factions back in his homeland, learned the use of claymore and firearms, and developed a quiet self-righteous sense of right and wrong. It seemed natural that he gravitated to the lawman profession upon his arrival in Corpus Christi. Having a few cousins who had already immigrated to South Texas, Luke had the advantage of being introduced to Colonel Kinney, the founder of Corpus Christi. Thus, his law enforcement career had gotten underway, first as a security guard at the colonel's cockfights, then as a deputy sheriff, and finally, as a Texas Ranger under the notorious Indian fighter Captain James Callahan.

Luke became increasingly familiar with the landscape and people of the Nueces Strip. He had quickly gained a reputation as having scouting skills any self-respecting Comanche or Kiowa would respect. He generally wore a weather-beaten, broad-brimmed tan hat with a simple leather band. He usually wore a buckskin vest or a coat over a blue shirt with gray trousers stuffed into well-worn cowboy boots. His gun belt accommodated his newly acquired Colt 1851 Navy revolver plus plenty of ammunition.

Luke had replaced the Walker Colts he'd previously carried. Seems that the cylinder of the revolver Elisa had used to kill the murderous Berne Culthwaite had nearly ruptured, likely due to metal fatigue. It was a heavy revolver in any case, so the Colt Navy was much preferable. When on duty as lawman, he pinned the Texas Ranger badge to his shirt, where it stood out so as to be impossible to miss. Today...well...none of that mattered...he was still recuperating.

So, Luke sat for now, soaking in the warm golden rays of the morning sun and trying to get well. Long Luke Dunn, erstwhile notable Texas Ranger captain and now rancher, had been ambushed at his own home. Right on the gallery of the cabin, just as he'd stepped from his front door! His reputation as a lawman bringing justice to the Nueces Strip brought with it the sort of notoriety that made him a target of men of unsavory character seeking to make their reputations by killing him. By the same token, his effectiveness as a lawman was deeply appreciated by those who sought to fight lawlessness. Luke's success in ridding the Strip of the likes of Bad Bart Strong, Dirk Cavendish, and Carlos Perez had solidly established his reputation. Coupled with those experiences back in 1855 riding with Captain Callahan's Texas Rangers in chasing the Lipan Apache out of Texas, the powers that be in the Texas state capitol deeply valued the tall, red-haired Irish immigrant.

He was the toughest hombre on the prairie when he had to be, yet had a certain human compassion that salvaged some folks who had flirted with the wrong side of the law. And, in the case of the Comanche Chief Three Toes, Luke was open to building the sort of mutual respect that turned to friendship.

Luke found himself waylaid, a frustrating situation for a man used to bringing lawbreakers to justice or performing chores on his ranch. He had to heal from a serious wound inflicted by that ne'er-do-well hired gun named Berne Culthwaite. Culthwaite had been known in certain shadier circles as the "fixer." His clientele had included many of the rich and powerful in Austin who tended to stretch the law. This included Horatio Thorpe. Luke had survived Culthwaite's assault—barely. The ambusher's 50-caliber Sharps rifle was favored as a buffalo gun for its effectiveness in bringing down those beasts. On a human, its effect was potentially devastating. Luke had been fortunate that his rifle had caught the primary impact of the bullet, but it still tore up his side pretty badly. Had it not been for Elisa's quick thinking and the marksmanship and fortuitous presence of Horace Rucker, a friend and retired Army colonel, Culthwaite might have succeeded and Luke would likely have been pushing up bluebonnets from six feet under. And Elisa hadn't yet told him how she'd had to take his gun and put the final two slugs into Culthwaite.

Elisa, Luke's wife of little more than a year, was carrying the burdens of caring for the ranch, their newborn twins, and this bigger-than-life husband who'd nearly died in her arms.

"How you feeling this morning, Lucas?" She handed him a cup of coffee and joined him in the chair alongside. "Have you thought about my idea?" She'd proposed building a new cabin…no…not a cabin…a house. It would have more than one room and even a second floor.

Luke nodded. "I think that's a wonderful idea, Lisa. Maybe a bit of carpentry would hasten my healing." He looked out at the ranch spread before them. They'd built it to nearly five hundred acres with a modest herd of one hundred fifty longhorns. Another piece of land adjoining theirs had recently come available and could be theirs if they were able to get a couple of longhorns to market to raise cash to make the purchase.

"You'll have to take it easy at first." She knew as the words left her mouth that he was tired of hearing them and would ignore them. As wife, mother and, more recently as nurse, her words came naturally. Of course, he'd push himself as hard as he could. It was a quality bred deep within his Irish heritage and bigger-than-life Texas Ranger persona.

"You still like putting it up there on top of the hill?" It was a bit of a joke, as hills on the Nueces Strip barely qualified as such. "I think we might see my cousin John's spread from up there." His cousin, who'd immigrated from Ireland back in 1850, worked a ranch that he'd built to a few thousand acres, raising longhorns and mostly cotton. In fact, a couple of his kinfolk were aggressively expanding their landholdings. Of course, none matched up with the hundreds of thousands of acres Richard King was putting together a few miles to the south. The Dunns, like King, were a strong family, and family was vital to settling the Nueces Strip. Luke's and Elisa's Heaven's Gate was a far more humble undertaking than King's ranch, but no less a vital contribution to the settlement of Texas.

"Yes, Lucas. Yes, I love that hill." She smiled dreamily. "Maybe we can build a white picket fence around it." She looked at her husband. Despite his still-healing wound, there was no mistaking the life energy that resided within him. Aside from the physical attraction, it was Luke's strong spirit and honest character that had captured her heart. To her way of thinking, no woman could ever ask for more. And there was no question of his undying devotion to her, regardless of whatever challenges ranching and Rangering might bring.

"Dan said he'd help with construction and, likely as not, we'll get some help from Horace." Dan had learned the farrier trade in Corpus Christi and now operated his business from the livery in Nuecestown. He'd taken Elisa's advice to make himself woman-worthy by developing a trade and was even sparking a local young lady. Horace, formerly Colonel Horace Rucker, had become a preacher upon retiring from military service. This choice of taking up the cloth had likely begun as a sort of penance for having been associated with a group that had been defrauding the military and the Indian agencies. Now, he was assuaging his own guilt while professing his newfound faith by building a church in Nuecestown. Horace had been intimately involved in saving Luke's life from the attack by Culthwaite.

Luke felt he needed to get started on the house sooner rather than later. There was no telling when he might be called back to duty. That would be especially so once word got out that he was healed. For the moment, he eased back in the chair. His thoughts turned to his personal conflict over being a rancher and family man versus a lawman. Ranching beckoned. He'd begun to understand the nature of the longhorns. As his ranching skills developed, he couldn't help but appreciate how the qualities of being a Texas Ranger paralleled those of being a cowboy. Both professions demanded special skills, the powers of observation, alertness, loyalty and, most important, resourcefulness. In addition, he'd become an excellent marksman, fine horseman, and was considered intelligent. He thought on the psychology of managing longhorns and likened dealing with those sometimes unpredictable beeves to wrangling with lawbreakers. Indeed, the similarities he brought to ranching and bringing justice to the Nueces Strip made his conflict between the two roles all the more challenging to choose between—if in fact a choice was necessary. But, for now, Luke yearned to be up and about.

With fencing virtually nonexistent, he could only imagine how far and wide his beeves had wandered. He'd resigned himself to eventually having to mount up and round up as many of the beasts as he could find. Among the longhorns he'd round up, it was likely he'd discover five or six brands other than his –HG (Bar HG) brand. Since all brands were registered in the Stock Records of Nueces County, any beeves Luke sold that were not –HG had to be recorded with credit to their owners. He was entitled to a one-dollar fee for each of those heads he sold.

It was a great system so long as folks were honest about selling and registering. There were hundreds of brands in South Texas, so naturally there were a few ne'er-do-wells that couldn't resist the temptation to modify them and make a few dollars. It was theft, and perpetrators were dealt with harshly. For many, it was worth the risk. Such was the sinful nature of many men. The lawman side of Luke dwelled on that problem, especially since he could appreciate it as both a Texas Ranger and a rancher.

Bullets had taken pieces from him over the past few months. The Texas Ranger business was highly dangerous in this wild territory. He felt Elisa's eyes on him as though she knew what he was thinking. Hell, the very first day they'd met at Doc's office, he was there to have his hand pieced back together from a bushwhacker's bullet. Later on, there was the wound from the raid on Roy Biggs's Twin Creeks hacienda. Now this.

"You've got to make the decision yourself, Lucas," Elisa said. Indeed, she knew his thoughts.

"Lisa, I'm up for a ride into Corpus. Maybe I can order up some lumber to get us started." This recuperation business needed to end.

Lisa smiled impishly as she pulled a piece of paper from beneath the folds of her dress. She extended it to Luke. "Lucas, do you think it might look something like this?" She stood back, pensively awaiting his reaction.

He studied the lines she'd carefully drawn with a stick of charcoal. How could he refuse? "Do you think it's big enough?" The implication wasn't missed. Big families were part and parcel to life on the frontier.

"You feeling frisky, Captain Dunn?" Her hand gently stroking his arm caused an all-too-familiar urge to course through his body. He wasn't that tired. If he felt up to riding to Corpus Christi...well. "Peter and John are sleeping." She led him inside, and they quietly pulled back the bed covers.

He carefully shed his shirt, revealing the still-raw scar running from armpit nearly to his waist. Doc had done a fine job of sewing him up, but it would ever be a reminder. He drew Elisa to him. She'd slipped from her dress, and the warm softness of her breasts pressed against him unleashed feelings in him that had lain dormant for too long as he'd recuperated. He couldn't contain his passions as he fully absorbed her...deeply...to her very core. His utmost urges having been spent, he resisted the urge to pull away. He knew Elisa needed to satisfy herself with his masculinity. Soon enough, they lay together exhausted.

"Lucas Dunn, I think you've healed just fine." She sighed and lay her head on his chest.

They lay for a few moments before Elisa turned to him. "Lucas? I've something I've been wanting to ask."

Luke wondered at her hesitation. "Of course."

"The first few days after you were wounded, you ran a fever and said some things you'd never mentioned before. You seemed fearful in your ravings."

Luke stroked his mustache. Had he some inner conflict that he was unaware of? "Ravings? What did I say, Lisa?"

Elisa was almost embarrassed to repeat the words. "You said 'damned redcoat bastards,' Lucas. You said it many times."

He reddened a bit at what was apparently a painful recollection. He shook his head as though ridding himself of cobwebs somewhere deep inside. "Oh my, Lisa, I expect I'll never rid my head of those memories."

"Of what, Lucas? Memories of what?" She could see he was visibly struggling to recollect the memories.

"Back in Ireland…in County Kildare…the clan was rising up…we were attacked by British soldiers. A couple of thousand, at least. And dragoons. They slew many of my friends…ran us off…and then they killed all of the wounded."

Elisa could sense Luke's deep pain at the memory.

"The British wore red coats, Lisa. Bright scarlet coats they were…with gold buttons and braids. They marched at us row upon row. They outnumbered us, but were such cowards. They were worse than evil." Luke looked away in deep thought. "After the slaughter, the redcoats chased those of us who'd escaped. They hunted me for days. My friend Connor was captured and tortured to death. I could see it from afar, but was helpless to save him. It was all I could do to escape, wend my way through forest and heather, and cross the Irish Sea in a small boat. I found my

way to Liverpool, snuck aboard a sailing ship, and jour-
neyed to a new life in Texas."

"Your words seemed so desperate, Lucas...like they
were from yesterday. It was frightening to hear you cry
out so."

Luke gazed tenderly at her. "When I rode with Callahan's Texas Rangers to drive the Apache from Texas, the
horrors from Ireland and the redcoats all came back. We'd
driven the Apache into Mexico, but the savages joined with
Mexican soldiers to counterattack us. The Mexican
dragoons wore scarlet red coats, Lisa. I saw them and am
told that I turned into a wild man. The raw memories of
those days back in Ireland exploded in my head. They say I
showed no quarter, that I killed at least three...one with my
bare hands."

He sighed regretfully. "I wasn't in my right mind. From
somewhere deep within, I was driven to kill them. In the
heat of battle, my innermost being sought to deliver justice
for what the redcoats had done to me and my countrymen.
Justice? Revenge? Which of those twin impostors was it?
Afterward, after I'd found my way back to Callahan's
defensive line, I found myself fully dismayed at what I'd
done. I had killed mercilessly. I had taken life...but I'd done
it brutally and personally. It was much more than the heat
of battle."

"Oh, Lucas...what a burden to carry."

"Perhaps what was worse was that I buried it all away in
the deepest innermost recesses of my mind. I never wanted
to think of it again. Alas, we don't forget those sorts of things.
I expect it's why I'm so intent on delivering true justice to the
Strip, Lisa. I want to stop wrongdoing, to see lives set right. I
don't want justice confused with revenge." He paused,
looked deeply into her eyes, and kissed her softly. "I guess,

too, that I'm conflicted in those old recollections of the British horrors. Some souls are salvageable, after all. I feel driven to find opportunities for redemption where I can." He rose slowly from the bed. His nearly healed wound protested at being stretched. "I'm sorry you had to learn all this in so scary a' way, Lisa. I thought I'd pushed it from my mind."

"I'm so glad to know, Lucas." She felt blessed, grateful that she had uncovered an insight to her man's soul that few wives could ever hope for.

"Maybe it's part of what drew me to you, Lisa. The Comanche you fought off...the ones that attacked your family. That wasn't so different from fending off the British. We both have a fighting spirit."

Elisa watched Luke slowly pull on his pants. She admired his strength yet appreciated his vulnerability. "I love you, Lucas Dunn."

"You'd better." Luke smiled. "Let's go see whether Big Horse is ready for a ride."

TWO
BOUNTY COLLECTION

ROY BIGGS and his gang of cutthroats boldly rode toward Fort Mason. They had a dozen Comanche scalps to prove their prowess at killing the savages—that is, if massacring defenseless women and children was measured as prowess. Five men mowing down children and women. Some of the women were even pregnant. As wicked as Biggs was, the sheer blood lust of the men he'd surrounded himself with revolted even him. Theirs was a very loose confederation, having been built on these men that had sprung him from the Uvalde jail. Biggs had little confidence in loyalty built on the opportunity *du jour*. In this case, these men needed his considerable financial resources to carry out their vigilance activities. Biggs had lost his hacienda to the combined forces of Luke Dunn's Texas Rangers and the US Army, but he still had his fortune stashed away safely.

The men were still laughing and carrying on at the havoc they'd wreaked on the little Comanche encampment. Biggs would have thought they'd tire of their banter, at least, he'd hoped.

Biggs pulled up about a half mile from Fort Mason.

"You men go ahead and collect your reward. I'm going to hang back here and do some planning." He was a wanted man, and it wouldn't do to show his face in so public a place as a military fort. It was a bit too close to San Antonio in any case.

Bert, Ty, and the others looked quizzically at Biggs, shrugged, and headed on down the trail to Fort Mason. They had bounties to collect.

Biggs rode up to the top of a nearby hill, where he could dismount and relax while staying ever vigilant for anyone following. He had a sense that they hadn't killed all of the Comanche in the encampment. Neither of the two warriors resembled the Comanche that had slain Cutter John a few weeks back when they'd apparently strayed close to the encampment and grown careless. He'd only had a fleeting glance at the Comanche attacker, but was confident he hadn't been among those massacred. He wasn't thrilled with the thought of what a revenge-minded savage might do.

Biggs had built an empire from success in the gold fields of California. He managed to be one of the lucky ones and struck it rich. But the experience netted him trouble, too, as he got caught up in gambling, boozing, whoring, and the like. It was a short leap to cheating at cards, some gunplay, and a stint in a local jail for shooting an itinerant miner. He managed to escape and thence began a crime spree that took him ever further eastward. He was street-smart with a malevolence-tinged sophistication that colored his lawbreaking. Despite his reputation and the bounty on his own head, he'd been careful with how he spent his fortune. That having been said, his mind became ever more numbed to the killing of living things, whether animal or human. He fell in love twice, but both times wound up killing the women's jealous husbands. He shunned relationships and sought solitude. The fact that he found this recent massacre of the Comanche offensive was inherently contradictory. Biggs was a man who'd shot and killed his very own wife as she stood strapped spread-eagled to a wagon wheel under threat of torture. He didn't kill her to save her from any misery. He figured they were merely threatening to torture her. No, he killed her simply to take away his opponents' bargaining power. And his children? He couldn't have cared less. Such was the evil mind lurking within the man.

He watched as Bert and the others rode across the vast expanse surrounding Fort Mason and approached the gate. As they entered, he saw a lone uniformed rider leave. Likely as not it was a courier of some sort. In any case, he was riding at a pretty fair pace and heading toward the Pedernales River from whence Biggs had come.

Lieutenant Belknap was about a half-day ride behind Biggs. They had followed the meanderings of the Medina River. A couple of his Army nags had gone lame, and it slowed their progress from the scene of the massacre of Three Toes's people. Belknap felt a true sadness in his heart for Three Toes. The lieutenant had already come a long way from his early days of looking to kill every Comanche on the planet. He'd seen the aftermath of Comanche attacks and been under attack himself. He couldn't permit himself to forget that the chief was a savage and might kill any man at a seeming whim, yet there was a certain nobility that the lieutenant had observed. He'd learned that the very name of the tribe translated as enemy. The Indians' behavior contrasted to the savagery he'd witnessed in the White men who massa-

cred Three Toes's people. The contradictions were illogi-
cal, but then, such incongruities usually were. He
lamented that humans couldn't simply all live peacefully
together.

★★

Bert and his three companions were escorted to the
commandant's cabin. They waved their hairy trophies to
the few soldiers they saw as they passed the tents that
served as temporary barracks.

"Come in, gentlemen." The major was being generous,
as he found it personally distasteful to deal with men who
sought money in exchange for killing others, whether
White, Indian, or Mexican. It was one thing to engage an
enemy in battle, and quite another to kill for a bounty. "My
adjutant tells me that you men fought some Comanche up
on the Pedernales River."

"Yessir, General. We done that alright. We're here to
collect our due."

The major smiled patronizingly. He appreciated their
awarding him a brevet field promotion, but didn't think it
worth his while to correct the men. Had he known these
were the men that sprang Roy Biggs from the Uvalde jail,
he'd have slapped them in irons. "How many, Mr....?"

"Bert Smith, General. We have twelve scalps." Bert laid
the scalps out before the major.

The commandant noted that only two of the scalps
appeared to feature hair cut in a way that was typical of
Comanche warriors. He quickly deduced that the others
were women and children. "Any of these women pregnant,
Mr. Smith?"

Bert laughed nervously. He sensed the major was seriously disrespecting him. "A couple, General, but hell, the

Injuns in their bellies don't count none." He almost revealed a look that asked whether they might count.

The man's expression revolted the major. He turned to his adjutant. "Lieutenant, give these men their due and escort them out of my fort." He uttered the last phrase with a tone of total disdain.

As Bert and his men were escorted from the commandant's office, they noted the wanted flyer pinned to the board just outside the entrance. There was no mistaking the image or description. There was a three-hundred-dollar reward on Roy Biggs's head. That was a lot of money in frontier Texas.

Three Toes had nearly caught up to Lieutenant Belknap's patrol, but realized that he was drawing ever closer to Fort Mason. The burial of his people had taken longer than he'd expected, owing in part to his own grief over the murder of his wives. The loss of Moon Woman was especially painful and the fact that his other two wives had been murdered while well along in their pregnancies was nearly overwhelming. A weaker man would have turned bitter and angry, yielding to vengeance. The chief had learned that revenge was never truly satisfying, that feasting on it was a very sparse meal.

He considered whether it was really worth his time to catch up with Belknap. If Biggs was going anywhere in the region, it would eventually bring him to the Nueces Strip. It was territory the man was familiar with. Yes, that was where Biggs was headed. The chief decided to turn south. As he rode along and meditated on it, he trusted that the Great Spirit would lead him to his quarry.

As he further considered trekking south into the Nueces

Strip, he wondered about his friend Ghost-Who-Rides. He hadn't seen the Ranger since the attack on Roy Biggs's hacienda. Three Toes thought back on the respect they had found for each other. Perhaps Luke would help him in his hunt for Biggs, the snake-headed man. He expected that Luke would want to capture or kill Biggs, but for different reasons.

He assessed his personal situation. He no longer had family or a tribe to lead. He'd once owned nearly a hundred horses but now had just three. The trappings of being a Comanche chief seemed ostentatious with no warriors to lead. He carefully folded his elaborate buckskin shirt and war bonnet into a blanket and added it to the pack on one of his horses. If they were lost, so be it. His bow and arrows he kept at hand, and he still had the Colt revolver he'd acquired.

Three Toes decided to seek his Texas Ranger friend.

"Roy, we have our prizes. Whatcha got in mind next?"

Biggs recognized that Bert had switched from the respectful address of "Mr. Biggs" to the more casual "Roy." It was easy to figure that they'd seen a wanted poster about him. Now that they knew he had a price on his head, he'd have to be careful. It certainly changed the tenor of the already shallow relationship among the gang members.

"Find anything useful at Fort Mason, men?"

"Just that you're a popular man, Roy."

That quickly confirmed Biggs's suspicion. There were no nuances among these men. "Y'all sprung me from that Uvalde jail. You expecting me to be some Bible-toting preacher?" He narrowed his eyes and stared them down. Squinting made him appear more snake-like, more evil.

"I've killed twenty-seven men and a few women." He said it as though the women didn't count. "You men looking to be added to my total?"

The math was easy. Bert decided that it wouldn't be wise to test any man who would kill that many folks and not get hung or otherwise killed himself. "You're in charge, Roy." He looked at the other three men who nodded their acquiescence. "Where we headed?"

"Let's have an understanding. You do exactly as I say, and you'll get a far greater reward than you did for those scalps." He acknowledged their nods. "First, we're going to clean up a little matter down near Corpus Christi."

"That's a long ride, Roy."

"And you can call me Mr. Biggs." He said it in such a way as to imply that complaining wouldn't be tolerated.

From the cover of the trees, they watched as Lieutenant Belknap's patrol arrived belatedly at Fort Mason. Biggs smiled. It was a good sign. He turned to Bert. "Any idea where that courier was headed in such an all-fired hurry?"

Bert pondered for a moment. "Heard something about the Indian agency. Don't know no more."

It was to be expected that word of the killing of Comanche would get out. Biggs nodded. "Let's head to Corpus Christi, boys." He figured the courier was likely headed to other forts to let them know of the massacre of the Comanche encampment. It would likely incite fear of Comanche retaliation.

"Sir, Lieutenant Belknap reporting." Belknap saluted as smartly as three long, chilly weeks on the trail allowed.

The major returned the salute. "You just missed some men collecting bounty on a bunch of Comanche scalps."

"Been following them, sir."

"Following? Please explain, Lieutenant." He eased back in his chair. "You can stand at ease."

"Those men massacred a small village of Comanche up on the Pedernales River. Two warriors and a few women and children. No bravery there, sir. Three of the women were pregnant. The encampment was what remained of Chief Three Toes's band." He hesitated. "And the attack was led by Roy Biggs."

"Biggs wasn't with the men who collected the bounties, lieutenant."

"I expect he wasn't far off, sir. We'd found Biggs near frozen to death along the Sabinal River, revived him, and parked him in the Uvalde jail while we completed our patrol. When we went to fetch him, he'd been sprung by those men." He shook his head resignedly. "We weren't able to catch them before they massacred the Comanche."

The major's face flushed with just a hint of anger born of frustration. "The Indians are no great loss, lieutenant, but it'd have been great to have captured Biggs."

The implication of disappointment in his failure wasn't lost on Belknap. He inwardly cursed the inadequate Army nags his men had to ride. If only, he'd been able to travel at a faster pace. "Sir, I'm sure those men have met back up with Biggs. I'm confident that my men would be up for pursuit. Just need fresh rations and decent horses."

Belknap's implication about the horses wasn't totally lost on the major. He sighed, as he knew the lieutenant was right. The Army's habit of buying less-than-adequate horse-flesh was widely known. Even the dragoons' mounts were hardly any better. "I'm not certain the horses will be much better, lieutenant, but you have my permission to go after Biggs."

"Is that an order, sir?"

The major nodded. "Yes. Requisition what you need. Dismissed."

"Yes, master. That's what I been told."

Samuel had just finished telling Horatio Thorpe that he'd heard about Roy Biggs's exploits up on the Pedernales River. Thorpe for his part had given up on more work from Biggs. After the failure of Berne Culthwaite to get the whore and the Texas Ranger, Biggs's success in disposing of Luke Dunn seemed unlikely. "Samuel, get word out that I'll still honor my deal with Biggs. Be sure it gets to him." He knew these sorts of things had a way of reaching the right people.

Meanwhile, Thorpe had enough on his mind dealing with the letter he'd received from the French government. Stopping his trade was serious business.

THREE
SOUTH OF THE RIO GRANDE

RIO GRANDE CITY was a bustling trade hub of the lower Nueces Strip. Founded back in 1848, it was little wonder that it attracted all manner of folks. Legitimate and illegitimate businesses flourished on both sides of the river. Not far away were the Ringgold Barracks—more recently designated as a fort—that housed the 1st US Infantry. Like Uvalde with nearby Fort Inge, Rio Grande City benefited economically from the proximity of the military. The land on both sides of the river offered an unobstructed view for miles and made for easy crossings. Cotton and cattle moved across on a regular basis. Outlawing—especially moving stolen beeves—was common, and little wonder that Rio Grande City was a significant contributor to the image of the "Wild West."

Juan Alvarez had endured service as a "volunteer" in Santa Anna's army during the Texas revolt and then served as a sergeant stationed in Monterrey during the Mexican American War. In peacetime, he'd hired out as a *vaquero* to some *gringo* ranches in Texas and made a few dollars as a drover taking cattle to the Kansas railheads. All had gone fairly well until the Texas Rangers came in 1855. As he described it, *"ese hijo de puta Callahan robó mi familia."* Texas Ranger Captain Callahan had destroyed Alvarez's family during his wild foray into Mexico chasing the cattle-thieving Lipan Apache out of Texas. Alvarez held a huge grudge, and simple revenge wasn't enough. He was of a mind to wrestle the entire Nueces Strip from Texas.

From 1856 to 1858, the Nueces Strip was relatively defenseless so far as law enforcement. The military had mostly pulled out to confront Indians far to the north and west. The Texas Rangers hadn't been reauthorized, so towns relied mostly on local sheriffs. While some were good lawmen, many were in the pay of criminal interests. Residents and merchants could never be quite sure.

Alvarez was intent on biding his time. He realized that, with the legislators in Austin not funding the Texas Rangers, there was no one force to fight. He figured that, if he could gather a few dozen worthy fighters filled with patriotism for Mexico, the time might be ripe to sweep north and carve out a chunk of the Nueces Strip for Mexico and in particular for himself. The Treaty of Guadalupe Hidalgo that ceded the Strip to the US still stuck in most Mexicans' craw. In any case, Rio Grande City with its easy river crossing, reduced military at Fort Ringgold, and absence of law enforcement save for the local sheriff, made for a convenient staging point for any forays into Texas.

The biggest challenge was funding his endeavors. Droving cattle certainly wasn't going to make him wealthy, but rustling them might. He had pulled in a core company of about a dozen *soldados*, literally men who'd fought with him during the Mexican American War. Like Alvarez, most held some sort of grudge against the *gringos*. Many were simply frustrated and angry with Santa Anna's failures and his willingness to give up the Strip to the *Yanquis*. Roughly half of the company had driven cattle with Alvarez, so he needed to train the remaining men to be most effective at rustling. More important, he had the necessary contacts to gain top dollar for the sale of stolen cattle in the markets at Veracruz. As Mexico's largest port, it was fertile ground for pulling the necessary resources together.

Alvarez had to be politically sensitive to the ongoing *Guerra de Reforma*, or War of Reform, during the reign of the Second Federal Republic of Mexico. The political collaboration with the French was especially distressing, as many Mexicans also recalled with no love the machinations of the French Emperor Napoleon. In any case, Alvarez strove to stay clear of Benito Juarez, the diminutive but powerful revolutionary who had established a government in Veracruz in defiance of political opponents in Mexico City. Were Juarez to learn of Alvarez's intentions on the Nueces Strip, the outcome could be far more than he bargained for. He knew he'd have to assemble a force greater than a mere dozen. Of course, as his force grew, the more likely it would be noticed by the likes of Benito Juarez. For the moment, he was comfortably ensconced across the river near Camargo in Tamaulipas State just out of reach of any military camps or forts.

"¡*Soldados!*" He chose to call his men soldiers to get them used to thinking like the military units they would become. He called himself *El Coronel* for the same reason. He planned each rustling foray as a military campaign. "*Acérquense, ahora.*" Alvarez called his men to gather around.

He called his two closest advisers *capitán*. "*Capitán González y Capitán Villa liderará esta misión.*" Alvarez was determined to have his captains shoulder more responsibil-

ity, so they would lead the next rustling mission. Soon
enough, they'd be responsible for companies of *soldados*.
The men huddled over a crude map of the region that identified several large ranches.

Alvarez calculated that he'd need a disciplined army
built around a core of at least fifty men. The general sparse-
ness of human life on most of the Nueces Strip lent itself to
conquest with a small force. He relied on recruiting from
among disenfranchised Mexicans on the Strip. He'd need to
have tight disciplinary control on his core *soldados* to offset
the relative lack of training in military regimen of the
followers they'd recruit in their campaign of conquest. He
wasn't so naïve as to think that Juarez wouldn't take notice,
but he chose not to risk his plans by alerting the revolutionary leader in advance. Juarez had an ego that could
pose a serious problem to Alvarez's tactical and strategic
rear. It remained to be seen whether that ego would be an
asset or liability. With Santa Anna in exile, Juarez was seen
as having a clear path to the Mexican presidency. The
actions of Alvarez could help or hinder that outcome,
depending on any relationship between the two men.

When he struck, Alvarez recognized that he would need
to conquer the Strip quickly. It was problematic that he'd
have to hold the territory against those who would wrestle
it from him. While Juarez was likely a threat from the south,
the US Army would surely retaliate along with the Texas
Rangers. It wouldn't take long for the politicians in Austin
to authorize a couple of companies.

The Texas Rangers were a special concern, as they
weren't under the sorts of military code restrictions as the
US Army. He'd heard that James Callahan had been killed,
but knew that other capable Ranger leaders would step up.
Callahan had run the Apache out of Texas and in the
process fought south of the Rio Grande against both

Apache and Mexican troops. Alvarez had avoided those engagements. He'd had a personal encounter with Texas Ranger Rip Ford back in 1846, and he'd lately heard about some Ranger named Dunn who'd been establishing a reputation on the Nueces Strip for bringing lawbreakers to justice, including the infamous hider Carlos Perez. Given that Alvarez's ambitions rose well above merely skinning cattle and selling hides like Perez, he figured to eventually grab Dunn's attention. Rustling was a hanging offense.

The construction on the hill at Heaven's Gate had begun to evolve into something resembling a house. They'd been right about it helping Luke's recovery from his wound, as he'd grown stronger by the day. The days were lengthening as spring drew near.

In the early evenings, after working on the house and cleaning up the stable, he'd go out with Elisa and the twins to practice his marksmanship. They'd set wooden targets, and Luke would blast them to smithereens. Occasionally, he'd hold Peter and John while Elisa practiced her shooting skills. Luke found it amusing that the twins didn't cry out at the gunfire, but actually smiled and even laughed a bit.

Elisa supervised the men's work on the house, ensuring that the niceties she'd dreamed of were included. There were three bedrooms along with a large area that combined as kitchen, dining area, and parlor. A gallery stretched across the front and extended on each side to offer a panorama of the surrounding countryside. Luke even built an outhouse that was conveniently located a mere dozen or so steps from a private entrance to their bedroom. And it was a two-holer.

It was a surprise when Colonel Kinney stopped by one

day. The founder of Corpus Christi was on his way to conduct a bit of business in Austin. He rode up to the new house and doffed his hat. "Captain Dunn, y'all have built a right impressive home." He took a lot of inner pride that his dream of Nuecestown growing was being realized with Luke and Elisa. He didn't wait for a response. "Y'all mind if I set a spell?" He proceeded to dismount and walk to the gallery to greet Luke and Elisa.

Kinney smiled at Elisa and the boys as he extended his hand to Luke.

She hustled the twins inside. They weren't quite ready to walk just yet, so required close attention when outside.

"Good to see you, Colonel." Luke extended his hand and hoisted Kinney up on the gallery. "Next part of this project will be a step." He smiled friendly-like. "Care for some coffee?"

Elisa reemerged from the house and thrust a steaming cup of coffee into Kinney's hand before he could respond. Coffee, after all, was endemic to Texas. He sat on the makeshift bench Luke offered up. "Figured I'd stop by on my way to the capital. I understand that Horatio Thorpe was none too happy with y'all eliminating his man Culthwaite."

Elisa perked up. "They going to arrest Thorpe?"

Kinney looked down thoughtfully. "Not likely…at least not yet. He's got plenty of money and the power that goes with wealth. We need a solid case against the man." He knew that Thorpe managed to keep just enough separation between himself and his illicit endeavors to avoid arrest. "I think they're going after him about paying his taxes."

"Where's the justice?" Elisa felt anger welling up inside. She looked at Luke. "Where is the true justice, Lucas? Colonel Kinney?"

Kinney shrugged apologetically. "He'll eventually make

a fatal misstep. I understand he wants to get you real bad, Luke. Remains to be seen just how badly. He also wants that red-haired woman that y'all helped set up with a seamstress business in Corpus. Apparently, he has some history with her from her days whoring in Laredo."

Luke shook his head. He worried that the reformed prostitute Scarlett Rose would never live down her past. "Anything else special brewing, Colonel?"

"I've heard rumors of some highly organized rustling going on down near Rio Grande City. Some Mexican malcontent named Juan Alvarez is beginning to cause havoc. He's got something like a couple of dozen men. I suspect he may have bigger plans than rustling cattle."

Luke raised his eyebrows and glanced at Elisa. "Sounds like something more than one Texas Ranger would be up to handling, Colonel. Gotta figure it might take two or three of us." He smiled at his obvious exaggeration. "Dare I ask if there's more to worry about?"

"Not sure you'll be anxious to hear this one. That fellow Roy Biggs is still on the loose. I hear tell he's got a gang of four men. The sons of bit...pardon, Mrs. Dunn, they massacred a small Comanche village up on the Pedernales."

Reflexively, Elisa's eyes grew wide and concern swept across her face. Her hand went to the beaded amulet, the gift from Three Toes, that hung around her neck. "Do they know which Comanche?"

Luke shared her concern. He knew that Three Toes had gifted her with the amulet as both protection and out of his respect for he and Elisa. Three Toes had earned a special place of respect and friendship in their hearts. He looked intently at Kinney.

"Don't know. Sorry. The savages are all the same to a lot of folks."

Luke shook his head. "Kind of ignorant, Colonel. But I understand why."

Elisa couldn't handle the possibility that Three Toes might have been killed. "I have some chores over at the cabin, Colonel. It was good to see you." She excused herself, gathered the twins, and headed off to the soon-to-be-vacated cabin. She didn't know whether to grieve for the possible loss of Three Toes, but was determined to pray that he had survived. She saw him as an example of the potential for coexistence on the frontier. No matter Three Toes's still-savage ways, she recognized the heart deep within the man. She reached the cabin and then dropped to her knees and prayed.

Luke's gaze followed Elisa for a moment, then he turned to Kinney. "I expect the house will be finished soon enough, Colonel. I'm figuring to hire a full-time *vaquero* to help here." Luke was of a mind to hire a *vaquero* with a family that would live in the soon-to-be-vacated cabin. "Please stop by on your way back from your business in Austin." The implication was that Luke would be ready...albeit reluctantly...for duty if needed.

"Much obliged for the coffee, Luke. I deeply appreciate y'all establishing roots here in Nuecestown." Kinney quaffed the last bit of coffee and eased himself down from the gallery. Folks like Luke and Elisa brought Kinney's dream of Corpus Christi as a bustling major trade hub ever closer to reality. "You keep an eye out for that Biggs fellow."

★

The ranch near the Rio Grande was suddenly a cacophony of shouting, dust, and baying cattle as Gonzalez and Villa herded in about forty rustled cattle. Alvarez was pleased and concerned. The herd was small enough that the less-experienced men could manage them but large enough to grab unwanted attention. The last thing he needed was attention from the US military down river at Fort Ringgold.

"¡*Felicidades, soldados! ¡Buen trabajo!*" Keeping their spirits up while awaiting the opportunity to undertake his plans for the Nueces Strip was important. He'd deal later with Gonzalez and Villa about rustling less ambitiously.

"*Gracias, jefe.*" They were grateful that their efforts were appreciated.

"*¿Algún problema en el Río Grande?*" Clearing the river without any resistance from the locals was important. "*¿Cualquier vaqueros?*"

"*No, jefe. No vaqueros y no soldados.*"

Not being followed closely enough to engage any cowboys or soldiers was a good thing, but it had been almost too easy. Uneventful forays were going to happen less often once their enterprise was fully discovered. With the existing herd of roughly a hundred head, it was time to drive the cattle down to Veracruz. There, his challenge would be not drawing too much attention. It wouldn't do to have Benito Juarez poking into his business. "*Es hora de ir a Veracruz, soldados.*" He turned to his captains. "*Capitán González, conducirás ganado a Veracruz.*"

In short order, Gonzalez began choosing the drovers who'd drive the cattle to market in Veracruz.

"*¿Mayor, qué hay de mi?*" Villa tried to hide his feelings of being slighted. He and Gonzalez vied for Alvarez's favor.

"*Ah, Capitán Villa, hablaremos de estrategia.*" Alvarez was assuring Villa of his importance by offering to involve him in developing strategy.

With Alvarez's assurance, Villa's psyche was significantly uplifted.

"*¿Negocio precio, jefe?*" Gonzalez had never negotiated the sale of cattle before.

Alvarez nodded, smiled reassuringly, and waved him off. Plans were coming together, and a key part was developing trusted leaders he could rely on. Next time, he'd switch the two captain's roles.

FOUR
BAD BLOOD

SAMUEL KNOCKED SOFTLY on the polished mahogany doors to his master's office. "Master, sir. You have a visitor." His voice was an almost secretive whisper.

Thorpe looked up from his desk. Beads of perspiration competed for space on his forehead. It was a deathly hot and muggy Austin day. He'd even shed his jacket, revealing the spreading dark wet spots under the arms of his shirt. Only some amply-applied fragrant perfumes saved him from being utterly unapproachable odor-wise. "Visitor? Is this some secret, Samuel?"

Samuel offered a timid smile, bowed gracefully, and stepped aside.

"*Bon après-midi père.*" Gascon Thorpe strode into the office, flaunting his French a bit. He gave an arrogant sort of nod of recognition to his father and proceeded to take a seat in the plush leather chair alongside his father's large ornate desk. "Have you become the Duke of Texas yet?"

"Get your ass out of my chair and stand until I invite you to sit!" Thorpe cast a heavy glare on his son. "Don't you sashay in here all dolled up in fancy duds and sass me, boy." His gaze followed Gascon to the center of the office. The young man had wasted no time obeying. He knew better than to challenge his father once he got angry. "You're supposed to be in France." Thorpe could only pray that his two younger children, a son and daughter, didn't follow in Gascon's vain and overbearing footsteps.

"Yes, Father...yes, I am."

It was only now that Thorpe began to appreciate how the boy had grown. He was only eighteen but scraped the sky at a couple of inches better than six feet tall and had broad, well-muscled shoulders. He stared at the man-child standing before him. He noted the empty holster at Gascon's side. At least, Samuel had relieved him of his revolver. "Why are you here?"

"You aren't overjoyed to see me, Father?"

"Why did you leave France? What have you been doing?" Thorpe tried to hold back his anger. He'd paid a substantial sum for his son to go to France and absorb some European culture. He waited for an answer, not some sarcastic retort.

"There were some difficulties, Father. I...er...I had to leave rather quickly." Gascon now stood awkwardly, head hung like a dog about to be chewed out by its master.

Thorpe shook his head. "What happened?" He was already beginning to understand why the French Ministry of Trade had revoked his deal to trade cotton for finished goods. The air smelled of something unseemly that his son was likely involved with.

"Um...I had an...an *altercation*." He used the French pronunciation.

"You killed someone." It was a statement. They'd been down this road once before.

"It was a fair fight, Father."

Thorpe sighed resignedly. "Anyone important?"

"A duel." Gascon shifted his weight from one foot to the other. "I seduced the man's wife."

"Sit down, dammit!" Tinges of redness crept up under Thorpe's collar. "Who did you kill?"

"The son of General de Vallette." Gascon took a seat in a chair alongside an ornate French settee in a small alcove at one side of the office.

Thorpe was inwardly pleased. De Vallette was a veritable pain in the butt as concerned Thorpe's business interests. However, the man was brother to the Minister of Trade. Pushing hard against the armrests, Thorpe levered his ample girth up from his chair and eased himself onto the large settee next to Gascon. Any duel was already history, and now de Vallette would likely become a greater problem. Thorpe's son's anger would need to be addressed. Perhaps he could leverage Gascon's propensity for gunplay and illicit sex to his advantage concerning the matters of the Laredo whore and the Texas Ranger down in Corpus Christi. The boy was nothing if not confident of his own abilities, not uncommon in young men who thought of themselves as immortal and possessing outsized libidos. The diabolical wheels of intrigue were beginning to speed up in Thorpe's ever-scheming brain. As to Gascon, the fruit never falls far from the tree. Bad blood was bad blood by any measure. "Pistols?"

Gascon's chest swelled just a bit. "Yes. Shot to the heart at twenty paces."

"And the wife?"

"I had her one more time after the duel." He smiled at the recollection. "I had to leave in a hurry." Gascon was warming to his story and sensed that his father's vicarious interest as enhanced by Gascon's sexual exploits was deepening.

Thorpe solemnly pulled a folded piece of paper from his pocket and handed it to Gascon. "Read this."

Gascon gasped reflexively as he saw the letterhead. It seemed that French vengeance was swift. He read silently and handed it back to his father.

"I'll take care of the de Vallette problem," Thorpe said. Of course, he would. It wasn't the first time he'd had to clean up after one of his children. In accordance with a sort of unwritten code, he knew that Gascon now owed his father. "I have something for you to take care of for me. I think you'll rather like the work." Not having heard from Roy Biggs, Thorpe figured he couldn't count on him completing what he'd hired him to do. He'd have to deal with that matter at another time.

Gascon perked up at the idea of doing something he'd enjoy. "What do you want me to do, Father?"

"There's this woman. I knew her from a brief…shall we say tryst…in Laredo." He mouthed the words slowly for maximum impact. He had Gascon's full attention. "Her name is Scarlett Rose, and she lives in Corpus Christi with her young child. She's escaped my grasp twice."

"You would have me fetch her for you."

Thorpe shook his head. "No, no, no. She's your reward for the other part of the work." He rubbed his fat hands together with delight. "I need you to dispose of a certain Texas Ranger that's been a curse on my very existence."

"Texas Ranger?" Gascon recalled hearing about the exploits of Texas Rangers. To have eluded his father's wrath meant that this particular Ranger was someone not to be trifled with.

Thorpe could see Gascon's expression change from relishing the task to creeping doubt. He needed to boost the boy's confidence. "Heart shot at twenty paces?"

"Yes, Father."

"That's damned good, Gascon. This particular Texas Ranger has built quite a reputation on the Nueces Strip. He rode with Captain Callahan against the Apache and has single-handedly brought some semblance of law to the region. Name's Luke Dunn. I'm thinking you might best him."

"You say the whore will be mine?"

"Oh, yes. You'll like her. She's a fetching little red-haired pistol of a wench. Best I ever bedded."

Gascon's expression began to show renewed confidence. He'd killed a couple of men already despite his youth. They'd been bested in fair fights. A broad grin spread across his face. What would be one more? "Okay. I'll do it."

Thorpe smiled and then suppressed a groan, as he pushed off from the settee and slowly stood upright. He walked with pained knees over to the sideboard and opened a drawer. He motioned Gascon to join him. "You might find this handy." He slipped a brand-new Colt 1851 Navy revolver into his son's holster.

Gascon grasped the gun and admiringly examined its blue steel frame and the brass-colored cylinder.

"Samuel will give you some ammo." Thorpe had an aversion to men with loaded guns in his presence, even his own son. "He'll give you some money and equipment for your adventure." He smiled and even gave a perfunctory and uncharacteristic hug. It was almost as though he didn't expect to see Gascon again.

As Gascon walked from his father's office, Thorpe motioned Samuel to come in. "Samuel, give the boy some ammunition." He paused. "Have you heard anything on that other matter?" He wondered whether he could still rely on Roy Biggs. At least now he had doubled his chances of getting the Texas Ranger.

Roy Biggs and his gang rode slowly into Corpus Christi. The city was unfamiliar to them. They'd taken a route that skirted Nuecestown, as he wasn't ready to risk an encounter with Captain Dunn. They attracted very little attention as they rode up the main street and came to a halt in front of the Longhorn Saloon. Biggs dismounted and hailed a well-dressed passerby. "Excuse me, sir. Where might some tired travelers find a place to spend the night?"

The man paused and looked Biggs over from hat to boots. "There's a hotel up the street a bit." He turned and started on his way, but then paused, his suspicions aroused. "You have particular business in Corpus Christi?"

At this point, Biggs noticed the lawman badge pinned on the man's vest as partially hidden by his coat. He needed a plausible response. "Actually, we'll be heading to San Diego. The boys here are looking for work as drovers and the season is near."

"Like I said, the hotel is up the street a bit." He scanned the armament the men carried. It was much even for prospective drovers. "I'm Sheriff Bill Meaney. If you have any problems, do come see me." Meaney already figured he'd keep an eye on this quintet. "There's a livery near the hotel."

Biggs felt relief that he hadn't been recognized. They'd need to keep a low profile in Corpus Christi. "Say, Sheriff, one more thing. I've heard great things about a Texas Ranger hereabouts. I admire such accomplishments. Would you know where he lives?"

Meaney found the question interesting. A heavily armed man with four companions asking where they could find Luke Dunn caused just a bit of concern. "He lives on a ranch up the road apiece toward Nuecestown, but he usually comes into Corpus on Thursdays for business."

"Much obliged, Sheriff. We'll be moseying along to that hotel."

"I didn't catch your name, sir."

"Oh...Smith. George...Smith."

Meaney watched Biggs ease on down the street. They were walking their horses now. Something didn't measure up. The man's name sounded phony, like he had to think it over before giving it to the sheriff. Meaney headed over to the sheriff's office. He went inside and over to the gun rack from which he grabbed a rifle. He absentmindedly glanced at the wanted posters on the bulletin board. "Damn!" he whispered. "Roy Biggs." He made up his mind to take a ride out to Heaven's Gate and warn Luke.

Biggs, meanwhile, felt as though he'd dodged a figurative bullet, at least for the moment. He sensed the sheriff's hackles go up just a tad when he inquired about Luke Dunn.

Bert sidled up alongside Biggs as they walked. "That was pretty damned bold, Roy." They called him by his more-familiar first name now that they knew he had a price on his head.

"George, Bert. Call me George." It'd be his luck that the sheriff had already identified him.

"Afternoon, Luke."

Luke hadn't heard Meaney's approach and reflexively glanced over at the new just-out-of-reach rifle leaning against the gallery post. Relieved, he turned to welcome his guest. "Welcome, Bill. Can I offer you a coffee?"

"A bit of water would be just fine, Luke. Mind if I set a spell?"

Luke poured water from a nearby jug and handed it to Meaney. "What brings you out here, Bill? I must believe that it's more than to admire my carpentry."

Meaney sat on the edge of the gallery. "Earlier today in Corpus, I ran into someone who might be of interest to you, Luke. The colonel said I should be on the lookout for a fellow named Roy Biggs. Well, he seems to have shown up in town."

"Can you arrest him?"

"There's a problem."

Visibly concerned, Luke sat down next to Meaney. "Problem?"

Meaney took a long drink of water. "He's got four men with him. They're armed to the teeth, Luke, and clearly looking for trouble. He was bold enough to ask where he could find you. Damn, but that Biggs fellow looks to be pure evil."

That confirmed what Luke had been told. "Did you tell him?"

"Yes, but I let him know that you came into town on Thursdays for business."

Luke nodded and stroked his mustache as he pondered Meaney's news. "So he's primed to set a trap for me in town. Good thinking, Bill. We can likely even the odds and deal with him on our terms." He paused thoughtfully. "I expect I can recruit Dan down at the stable and Preacher Rucker. Do you have anyone that can join us down in Corpus?"

"The colonel let me hire a deputy. I ought to be able to deputize another man or two."

"This Roy Biggs is as evil as they come, Bill. Hard to

believe he escaped our attack on his hacienda up north of Laredo last year. He'd already disposed of some state witnesses, but no one knows who hired him. With the help of a couple of dozen soldiers and my Comanche friend, we tracked him down, destroyed his gang, and pretty much tore his hacienda apart. Heck, Bill, he's so evil, he even killed his own wife." Luke let that all sink in. "He was wounded but managed to escape through a dang tunnel."

Meaney shook his head thoughtfully. "I heard that soldiers on patrol caught up with him a few weeks back, half-frozen to death alongside the Sabinal River. They thawed him out, stuck him in the Uvalde jail for safekeeping, and continued their patrol. They figured Sheriff Warren could hold him until they came back from patrol. The four men with him now managed to overcome the sheriff and spring Biggs's sorry ass. I heard they traveled north, massacred some Comanche up near the Pedernales River, and then rode to Fort Mason to collect their bounty."

"The colonel told me about the massacre." Luke looked a bit saddened. "I'm hopeful my friend Chief Three Toes wasn't one of those killed."

"You friends with a Comanche?"

"Long story. It's about mutual respect." Luke got up from the gallery, stretched, and turned his mind back to Biggs. "Tomorrow is Wednesday, so we have a little time, Bill. Let's see what sort of resources we have. We can meet at the big motte up near Nueces Bay and lay out our plan." He looked appreciatively at Meaney. "Bill...I'm thankful we have the opportunity to face Biggs in Corpus and not here at Heaven's Gate. Your quick thinking has given us an opportunity to bring that evil excuse for a human to justice without endangering my family. After all, it's me he wants."

"I hear Biggs is plenty smart as evil ones go, Luke.

They're likely to hang out at the saloon tonight. I'll see what the barkeep might learn of their plans."

"He's not all that smart, Bill. He tipped his hand to you." Luke caught himself. "But maybe that was intentional. Wonder why he'd do that?"

FIVE
GUNPLAY IN CORPUS CHRISTI

GASCON SAUNTERED down to the stable and chose one of his father's best horses for the trip to Corpus Christi. The sorrel stallion was big as horses go and suited Gascon's tall frame. He eschewed the mule and chose a black gelding for his pack horse.

Samuel had already directed the stable hands to be sure the master's son was well outfitted. It wouldn't do for him to be under-equipped or underfed. He tried to avoid looking like some fresh-from-the-city dandy. The French influence simply had to go. Gascon would stand out like a sore thumb if he wore continental duds.

Horatio Thorpe actually walked down from the house to the stable to see his son off. As Gascon stood beside the horse, he sidled up beside his son. "Gascon, take this." He opened a cloth to reveal a Bowie knife. "You might find this handy in close quarters."

Gascon looked quizzically. He found it hard to imagine this corpulent man ever using such a weapon, much less a gun. Perhaps it was a sad measure of their relationship that Gascon knew little of his father's past. No man carved a plantation from the lowlands of East Texas without being able to defend himself. "Er…thanks."

"Do well, son. Enjoy that little red-haired whore. Don't underestimate the Texas Ranger. It won't be like a duel. He's not going to stand like a target in front of you like the Frenchman did."

Gascon mounted the sorrel, tipped his hat to his father, took the lead of the packhorse, and headed out.

★★

"You tell me, Rip. Thorpe doesn't need the money. Why would he risk so much running a gang stealing from the Indian agencies?" Kinney looked quizzically at Rip Ford.

"It's not about money, Henry."

"What then? Power? Sex?"

"You're on the right track," Ford told him. "We just need to pin the crimes on him. He's slippery for a big man. We sure gotta get him on more than not paying taxes."

"I hear his son caused a lot of trouble for him in France. The fruit doesn't fall far from the tree." Kinney rubbed his chin thoughtfully. "Maybe we can draw him down to Corpus. I've been wanting to grab more cotton business for the port."

"What do you have in mind to lure him?" He had Rip's attention.

"We could appeal to his greed, of course," Kinney said. "But I hear tell that his son was seen heading south pretty heavily outfitted. He's up to something for his old man, but he's taking his sweet time and enjoying the sights along the way. The brothels and saloons of San Antonio better be ready. He's his father's son. But back to luring Horatio Thorpe to Corpus Christi. Now, if young Thorpe were to meet with trouble in Corpus, it might draw the father to us to bail out his son, plus help satisfy his lust for wealth. Don't think he'd make a trip just for the son."

"Wish they had that newfangled telegraph running to Corpus Christi. If you travel at a fast pace, you might get there ahead of the boy."

"I'll leave this afternoon. Meanwhile, let's plant some more rumors of Mexican unrest to motivate the legislature to fund the Texas Rangers. Lord knows, the Nueces Strip is a haven for desperados, and there aren't enough Luke Dunns out there."

"Wilson, how you doing this afternoon?" Sheriff Meaney placed his foot on the brass bar rail and eased his coat back over his holstered revolver to reveal the badge pinned to his chest. This signaled that he was there on official business.

The barkeep wasn't surprised by Meaney stopping by, though he was early. "Can I help you, Sheriff?" He rightly figured that the sheriff was in need of something. He didn't offer a drink, as Meaney didn't imbibe liquor.

"Five men rode into Corpus this afternoon. I think they may be up to no good."

"And you'd like me to keep my ears open?"

"That's about the size of it, Wilson. Be much obliged."

"Will it be obvious who they are?"

"Don't think you'll have a problem. They're from west of here, up near Uvalde. The leader has a face you can't miss. High cheekbones, small chin, squinty eyes…looks sort of like a rattler. He likely even has a forked tongue. He matches the description of an outlaw named Roy Biggs."

"I'll let you know what I hear, Sheriff."

They'd been hanging around the hotel for about an hour, and the men were growing restless. "Let's get ourselves to that saloon up the street, Roy."

"Patience. Be patient. We'll wait 'til near dark. We don't want to be noticed any more than we already have."

Bert, Ty, and the other two were still flush with a touch of blood lust despite the more than two weeks since massacring the Comanche camp. "We didn't come all this way to lie around some flea-bag hotel, Roy."

"Who's running this job, Bert?" Biggs was beginning to worry about his ability to control the four men. He sensed that they'd as soon turn him in for the price on his head and forget about the Texas Ranger. Money and their fear of him were his only protection.

"Tell us again what we'll do after we kill the Ranger?"

"If you don't shut your mouth, we might never get the chance. The walls have ears, Bert."

"I don't see no ears."

"Dumb as a cow pie," thought Biggs. "The walls are thin...people might hear about what we're up to." He scanned the faces of the others. "Don't y'all get liquored up tonight and start talking about it. There'll be big money for getting this job done." Biggs realized that he'd need to get away from these useful idiots as soon as the Dunn job was finished. He assumed he still had a deal with Thorpe to kill the Texas Ranger. Revenge played into his perspective, but the money was important to keep the loyalty of this group of ne'er-do-wells.

Bert lay back on the settee and let out a loud impatient sigh. He had begun to consider the quick reward to be had in turning in Biggs versus the risk of pursuing some Texas Ranger.

A half-hour passed. Biggs casually strode over, pulled back the curtain, and looked out the window. He slowly scanned the street which was pretty much empty. "Okay, let's ease over to that saloon. Remember to keep your lips sealed about our plans."

Bert checked to be sure his revolver was loaded.

"Bert! No gunplay." Biggs was having increasing doubts about controlling Bert and the others. He turned to the rest of them. "Don't walk together. That'll arouse suspicion."

They ignored him, lazily making their way up the street to the saloon, laughing and carrying on as they went. They had that bounty money in their pockets and had plans for whiskey and women.

Biggs could only shake his head and follow at a distance.

"Evening, Mr. Smith." Sheriff Meaney stepped from the shadows.

Startled at first, the normally calm Biggs was initially speechless. He'd even momentarily forgotten the name he'd given himself. "Er...Sheriff. Good evening."

"We've got a right peaceful city here, Mr. Smith. Please be sure y'all keep it that way." He turned and headed to the sheriff's office. "Have a nice evening."

"He knows who I am," Biggs whispered to himself. He could sense that he'd been discovered. He should never have asked where Dunn lived. He'd been bold...and stupid.

Biggs walked through the doors of the saloon. He looked over at his gang, clustered around a table. Bert already had a woman in his lap and had one hand up her skirt. A cigar stuck out prominently from between his lips. Biggs nodded in his direction. The others were equally distracted with plenty of whiskey.

Biggs walked over to the bar and leaned against it. He hailed the barkeep. "Whiskey, barkeep."

"Sure, pardner." Wilson poured the man a drink. "Where y'all from, if you don't mind my asking?"

"West of here. We heard great things about Corpus Christi and decided to visit. We'll be headed back out in a day or so toward San Diego, as we're looking to do some droving." Biggs stuck to his lame cover story.

Wilson smiled. "Well, have a welcome-to-Corpus drink on me, mister." He poured a second. "You say you were from out west. Whereabouts?"

Biggs smiled. The barkeep was asking too many questions. He downed the second drink.

"Hey, Roy!" Bert motioned him to join their table.

Wilson smiled and poured a third drink. "Looks like your friends are calling." He made a mental note of Bert having called him Roy.

Biggs walked over to the table. The men were already drunk. "Damnit, Bert. You know better than to call my name." If he didn't need them, he'd have settled the matter right then and there. His hand moved teasingly across the grip of the revolver in his holster.

Bert saw the hand movement and got the message.

"I'm going to get some air," Biggs said. "See you back at the hotel."

"You don't want some of Rosita here?" He lifted her skirt to show a little more of the woman's thigh.

"Don't bring her back to the hotel." Biggs's firm voice let it be known that this was not a choice. He needed to get a peaceful night's sleep to clear his head and figure how best to ambush the Texas Ranger. The third drink was already muddling his thinking.

"Guess it's goin' to be your place, Rosita." Bert belched, wiped drool from his beard, and buried his face in her ample breasts. He pulled back, let her slip from his lap and, as he got up, wobbled for two steps before crumpling to the floor in his drunken stupor.

Ty and the others looked at each other, shrugged, and let

Rosita take them to her room. Off they went, drinking and laughing, as they left Bert lying on the floor in the sawdust and spilled booze.

The barkeep nodded to a couple of men he employed to ensure a touch of decorum in the saloon. They dragged the nearly passed-out Bert to a chair off in a corner. Once he was sure his companions were engaged with the resident whore, Wilson pulled up a chair next to Bert.

"You okay, cowboy?"

Bert opened his eyes at about half-mast. "Need a couple minutes," he offered groggily.

"So, where y'all really from, friend?"

Bert belched again. "Uvalde."

"Why did you come here?" The barkeep was never surprised at how liquor tended to loosen tongues. It was like a truth serum, as inhibitions were set free.

"Whupped a bunch of Comanche up north."

"But why are you in Corpus Christi?"

"Biggs's idea."

"Biggs? A big idea? What big idea?" Wilson pressed.

"No-no-no. Biggs. Roy Biggs. It was his idea." He raised his head and squinted at Wilson. "Promise you won't tell a soul?"

"Cross my heart." Inside, it was all the barkeep could do to contain himself. This was too easy. Sheriff Meaney would be pleased.

"We gonna kill us a Texas Ranger...a famous one." Bert was on the verge of fully passing out.

Wilson ventured a final question. "Where you figure to get him?"

"Don't know." And Bert passed out.

★★

Three Toes had made peace with the Great Spirit concerning the loss of his family. He was focused on traveling to Nuecestown, eluding US Army patrols and other Indians while staying clear of farms and ranches. Once he had to evade a gang of marauding Mexican bandits. He'd chosen to travel light, so carried only what he could carry on himself and his pony. Gone were his days of enjoying a herd of a hundred or more horses worthy of a Comanche chief. Gone were his days of keeping three wives happy. Or so it seemed.

He lived from the land as he traveled. Game was still plentiful, and he had plenty of arrows, so he never feared going hungry. The chief still carried the Colt revolver in his waistband. Twice he came upon the aftermath of an Army patrol campsite and enjoyed the food they'd left behind. Once he had to chase off some coyotes—nasty critters but quite fearful of aggressive humans.

As he drew ever nearer to Nuecestown and his friend Luke Dunn, he was saddened by the extent of settlement. Land was clearly partitioned. People limited themselves to what they owned. He couldn't grasp this idea of owning land. The White man's ways were disturbing to him. Even his friend Luke was a landowner. He also felt sad that Luke only had one wife.

Sheriff Meaney stood beside his horse at the big motte on the south shore of Nueces Bay. He checked that his revolver was loaded and kept an eye on the horizon. The sun had set, and the darkness of the night moved in.

"Psst. Bill."

Meaney was startled by the voice. Luke Dunn had snuck up to within five or six feet before making a sound. "Damn,

Luke. You want to scare me to death? You coulda been shot." He knew better.

Luke laughed. "Lots of luck, Bill."

"Elisa know you're up to no good?"

Luke gave him an "of course" look. "You learn anything about our friends in Corpus?"

"The barkeep confirmed that the leader is Roy Biggs and they're aiming to ride out to your Heaven's Gate Ranch and kill you and likely your family."

Luke shook his head. "Any ideas on where to take them on? I got Dan and Pastor Rucker to volunteer to help us."

"Well, I don't think it'd be a great idea to let them attack the ranch. You don't want your family hurt. And we don't want to take them on inside the Corpus Christi city limits, as innocent folks might be hurt. So I'm thinking we lure them up the road and set an ambush about a half mile out of Corpus."

"You talking about that road that goes by my cousin's place?"

"Yeah. There's a knoll overlooking the road and a little tree cover. I've recruited another man. Along with my deputy, we'll outnumber them and have the advantage of the higher ground." He knew that high ground was a relative term in these parts, as the landscape was mostly flat.

"And what if we aren't able to lure them out?" Luke asked. "What if they get suspicious and go around us?"

"You have another idea, Luke?" Meaney cocked his head.

"You know I'm partial to doing the unexpected, Bill."

Meaney anxiously awaited Luke's proposition.

"They're all staying in the hotel, right?" It was a rhetorical question. "They know I'm coming into town on Thursday, right?" Another rhetorical question.

The sheriff sensed what was coming. Luke continued, "I

think we should take them tonight, Bill. We surround the hotel, and you and I go in and arrest Biggs. They'll be half-asleep and not up to much of a defense if any."

"Tonight?"

"Why not? I'm confident it'll minimize any gunplay. Bet it won't take but a couple of minutes, and you'll be slapping manacles on Biggs's wrists. It'll be safer for the citizens of Corpus Christi, too." Luke strove to judge Meaney's reaction.

At that, Horace Rucker and Dan emerged from the shadows. "We're ready to head to Corpus, Captain."

Meaney shrugged. It appeared that the decision had been made. "We can pick up my deputy on the way into town." He was amazed at Luke's thinking. Little wonder the Texas Ranger had earned such an impressive reputation in South Texas.

"Bill, it still won't be easy. You're going to have to be ready to shoot the man in an instant if he resists. He's a killer—some say the devil incarnate. I've heard that he's killed something like thirty people. I saw him kill his own wife."

"I'm with you, Luke. Let's get this done." Meaney checked his own weapons. "We ready?"

Luke pinned on his Texas Ranger badge and the four of them mounted up and began the short ride into Corpus. Luke carried both of his Colt 1851 Navy revolvers and his newly acquired rifle. This would be close quarters, so the revolvers would be the weapons of choice.

"You take the bed, Bert. I don't mind sleeping in the easy chair." The other three men had already sacked out in the adjoining room.

"You gonna get any sleep, Roy? Big day tomorrow."

"Just go to sleep, Bert. I'll explain our plan in the morning." He took a deep breath and slid his hat down over his eyes. Soon enough, he was snoring. One hand lay on his lap, the other hung at his side. His gun belt was on the table with his revolvers.

Bert struggled to get to sleep as Roy's snorting and snuffling seemed loud enough to wake the dead.

Biggs waited until he heard Bert stop tossing and turning and had finally fallen asleep. Evil as he was, he had a sort of sixth sense that something was amiss. He eased from the chair and sat on a bench beside the door. He pretended to snore.

Roy Biggs's snoring seemed like a bonus camouflage for Luke. He and Meaney positioned the men outside the hotel. One was beside a hitching rail across the street, a second took a position on the roof of a building opposite the hotel with a view directly into Biggs's room, a third covered the rear stairway, and their fourth man positioned at the door to the room occupied by Biggs's men. It was now left to Luke and Meaney to engage Biggs. They removed their spurs to ensure their stealthy approach.

By now, it was a couple of hours after midnight. Luke and Meaney looked at each other. Luke nodded. His well-placed kick broke the door in, and the two men stood tall over Roy Biggs's chair. "Don't move, Biggs. You're under arrest!"

A shot rang out, and Meaney spun from a bullet ricocheting off his gun belt. Luke fired in the direction of the sound. There was a groan and the telltale thud of a body hitting the floor in the darkened room. A spreading pool of blood shimmered in the moonlight under Bert. They hadn't seen Biggs slip out the door behind them.

Luke poked at the form in the chair. Turned out that the

hat-covered bedding stuffed into old clothes. "Where the hell is Biggs?" The man was nowhere to be seen.

There was a ruckus in the adjoining room. A door opened, and a shot was fired. Then a blast from a shotgun brought silence. Two men lay wounded, and the third stood with hands held high. "Get up, you sons of bitches!" Pastor Rucker stood with his shotgun pointed at the trio. "Out into the hall, now!" He silently asked God's forgiveness, as he prodded the men toward Luke and the sheriff.

Shots rang out in the street followed by the sound of a horse at full gallop. Meaney ran to the window. "Damn, there he goes."

"Where's he head..." It struck Luke that Biggs was heading west toward Heaven's Gate. "Come on, he's headed to my ranch." He sprang into action.

"We'll be along right shortly, Luke." Meaney and Rucker manacled the three men.

Luke dashed from the hotel, corralling Dan and the others. Soon enough, they were mounted and giving chase after Roy Biggs.

Meaney took no truck with any delay, not even worrying about the wounded men. "Get your butts moving, dammit!"

"I'm bleeding," one of the men whined. A second stoically limped on his wounded leg.

"Tend to yourself." Once the sheriff had the men jailed, he and Rucker followed after Luke.

Roy Biggs had a general idea as to the location of Dunn's ranch. As he proceeded up the road toward Nuecestown, he had to slow down and keep his eyes peeled for the arched gateway he was told marked the ranch entrance. This gave

Luke, Dan, and the deputy a chance to close the gap and reduce the distance advantage Biggs had.

Upon spotting the Heaven's Gate entrance, Biggs turned up the ranch road, spurred his horse to a gallop, and quickly had the cabin in sight. He was intent on the element of surprise, but was so focused on the cabin that he initially failed to note the house up on the hill.

Elisa had just finished feeding the twins. Every now and then she peeked out the window to watch for Luke. She saw smoke pouring from the chimney of the cabin that served as their former home. Now, it housed Jaime and Julia Sanchez. Jaime was turning out to be a true asset, as his skills as a *vaquero* were quite superior. Julia occasionally helped Elisa with chores ranging from making butter to tanning hides to sewing.

Elisa thought she heard a horse in the distance and ran to the window. Seeing that it was a stranger bearing down on the cabin, she instinctively grabbed the heavy Sharps rifle from above the fireplace mantle. She slipped a round into the breech and dashed out onto the gallery. She knew the Sharps had a serious recoil and braced herself against the front of the house.

Biggs had just about reached the cabin and was already dismounting with revolvers in hand. He'd barely cleared saddle leather, when an ear-shattering blast and wood splintering near his head brought him to a full halt. Elisa's shot had nearly cut the gallery roof truss in two.

As the sound reverberated inside the cabin, Jaime and Julia sprang into action. Jaime grabbed his rifle and Julia wielded an iron skillet. Jaime stepped onto the gallery, caught Biggs's shadowy form in his peripheral vision, and began to aim the rifle. He was a split second too late as Biggs's bullets hit him twice.

Elisa had a second round chambered in the Sharps,

braced herself harder against the wall, aimed the big gun as best she could, and fired. Biggs's horse fell, mortally wounded.

By this time, Elisa had fully drawn Biggs's attention. Jaime was writhing in pain and Julia dared not step from the house to help him. Biggs turned toward the house and began to walk. Both guns were at the ready. He began to think he might have some perverted fun with this seemingly vulnerable little woman with the outsized rifle. He fired a shot in Elisa's direction, the ill-aimed slug ricocheting from a gallery post.

Elisa strove to remain calm as she loaded a third round into the Sharps. She knew that if she even only wounded him, it'd likely stop him. What a Sharps slug had done to Luke months ago remained fresh on her mind in the heat of this moment. It had torn him up badly enough to nearly kill him. Her shoulder already hurt from her first two shots. She was desperate to stop this threat. She fired again with Biggs a mere twenty yards from the house. The bullet tore through Biggs's left arm above the wrist, sending one of his guns flying and leaving his hand dangling uselessly with a couple of shattered bones and tendons barely keeping it attached to his arm.

Biggs recoiled and cringed momentarily with the excruciating pain and stared at the profusely bleeding wound. He stopped, and it was as though a shroud of total evil swept over him. Through his pain, his dark expression couldn't have been more diabolical. He raised his right arm and aimed carefully at Elisa, who had ducked behind a gallery post that offered only partial cover.

The heavy iron skillet crashed full force on Biggs's head just as he pulled the trigger. He was so concentrated on Elisa that he hadn't heard Julia creeping up behind him. His shot went wildly high into the night as he crumpled to the ground unconscious.

Luke and the others finally arrived. He dismounted, ran past Biggs, and embraced Elisa. "Thank God, you're all right." He saw the bruise already forming on her shoulder from the force of the Sharps recoil. Still holding her, he looked over the area. The sun had just peeked above the horizon. Dan and the deputy were seeing to Jaime's wounds, and Julia stood ready to clobber Biggs again if necessary. Luke parted from Elisa, kissed her gently, and walked over to where Biggs lay. He almost reluctantly put a tourniquet on Biggs's arm. Better to save him for a hanging. "Julia, you've done well. Now go tend to your husband."

Luke's eyes took in the dead horse, the damaged cabin gallery post, and Biggs's now useless arm. He looked back at his brave wife and the Sharps now laying innocently on the gallery floor. "Lisa Dunn, you are an amazing woman." But he already knew that. He'd seen a Sharps recoil knock men down, yet she'd fired it not once but three times.

Sheriff Meaney arrived and placed manacles on Biggs's ankles, as the man's left wrist was virtually gone. Dan fetched the buckboard from the barn, and they loaded Biggs, along with Jaime, onto it for the trip to see Doc in Nuecestown. Meaney also figured it'd be better to have Biggs in the Nuecestown jail rather than with the others in Corpus Christi.

"Captain Dunn, it appears that your wife and *Señora* Sanchez here have done your job." Meaney's smile brought relief to the tension of all that had just transpired.

"Go ahead with Bill into Nuecestown, Lucas. I'll be fine here." Elisa wanted to be certain that Biggs was safely ensconced in the Nuecestown jail. With that, she grew momentarily pale and collapsed in a heap on the gallery. Luke rushed to her side.

"I'm sorry, Lucas." She shook off the faintness. "Go, go with the others." A child's cry from inside the house was a sort of clarion call to get back to some semblance of normalcy. "I've got everything here under control, love. Go with them." Indeed, she was the true pioneer woman, tougher than her circumstances and able to handle most any challenge as attested by the ever-darkening bruise on her shoulder.

The big sorrel walked easily under Gascon's saddle as they traveled the road from Austin to San Antonio. But for the newness of his outfit, he was ready for pretty much anything he might encounter. Samuel had fixed him up with enough grub to last until he reached San Antonio. There, one of his father's people would resupply him for the remaining journey to Corpus Christi. All told, he'd be riding for a couple of weeks, though he already foresaw delays to grab some relief from the saddle and sample some feminine wiles. At that, he found himself occasionally dismounting and walking the horses.

It didn't take long for the buckboard to cover the five miles to Nuecestown and pull up in a cloud of dust in front of Doc Andrews's place.

Arriving first, Luke dismounted and banged hard on the front door to wake Doc. It was still early in the day, and Doc generally enjoyed sleeping in. "Doc! Doc! We've got some folk needing your attention."

Meaney and the others began to unload Biggs and Jaime Sanchez from the buckboard. Jaime was in decent shape, despite his wounds—however, Biggs had grown deathly pale from pain and loss of blood. Biggs's paleness had the perverse effect of making him appear even more evil.

Doc cracked open the door and peered out. "Oh, my, bring 'em in, boys. I'll make some room." Since putting his battle with booze behind him, thanks mostly to Pastor Rucker's influence, Doc had been taking far better care of himself. The sight of Biggs's half-amputated hand didn't affect him so much as what he'd been through ten years earlier as an Army surgeon during the Mexican American War.

"Jaime here works for me, Doc. The other man will be recuperating in Sheriff Meaney's jail so he can meet his judgment day."

Doc quickly examined the men's wounds. "This here Mexican...Jaime, you say? His wounds are superficial, Luke. If a couple of y'all would be kind enough to clean them up, I'll deal with him after I amputate this other man's hand. No way I'm gonna be able to save it." He saw Biggs offer an angrily resentful reaction to the news despite his stupor, and it sent a chill up his spine. He fully sensed the evilness of the man. Doc turned to Luke. "What the hell hit him?"

"Elisa shot him with the Sharps, and Jaime's wife clobbered him with an iron skillet."

"No way! You've got an amazing wife, Luke Dunn. And I guess Jaime over there didn't do so bad himself."

Biggs began to arouse a little. His eyes looked slowly around the room, and his gaze settled on Doc. "You cut off my hand, I'll kill you, sawbones," he hissed. The words emerged in a seething tone from somewhere deep within Biggs.

Doc backed away for a moment. "Seems you're gonna

die whether I do or don't, mister." He pulled a saw from his kit. "Bill, Luke, I need you to hold him down."

As the saw touched his arm, Biggs mercifully passed out.

"Tough one, eh, boys?" Doc went to work dressing Biggs's stump. Soon enough, he let Biggs be carted across the street to the Nuecestown jail. "He's gonna be thirsty and hungry when he comes to, boys. Shame Bernice finally learned how to cook that pot roast." It was a standing joke in the town, as Bernice, who owned a boarding house with her friend Agatha, had been famous for her over-cooked pot roasts. Doc figured there would be a degree of justice if the prisoner had to deal with that old roast recipe.

Luke laughed. "Maybe we can place a special request." That eased the tension in the room. Luke turned to Jaime. "We got his wounds cleaned up for you, Doc. If you'd be kind enough to bandage my *vaquero* here, we'll be on our way."

Doc shrugged and did his doctorly duty. He obviously harbored some bit of prejudice against Mexicans, but he couldn't refuse Luke's request. It was his experiences in the Mexican American War field hospital that had driven him to drink in the first place. Now, he'd pushed aside the bottle and renewed his commitment, striving to heal the wounds of those caught in the midst of man's violence to man.

SIX
FACEOFF IN CAMARGO

BENITO JUAREZ definitely didn't like what he was being told. He had enough of a challenge navigating near civil war in Mexico than to have to deal with some upstart pretender out of the no-account town of Camargo.

"Jefe, vendieron cien cabezas de ganado." The man half-cowered in fear at having to bring bad news. *"Ellos eran de Alvarez."*

Juarez's brows furrowed. A hundred head of Juan Alvarez's stolen cattle sold right there in Veracruz. The port was to become Juarez's temporary headquarters city, owing to the revenues it generated from customs fees. Alvarez's sale of even so modest a herd was a major affront, but a still greater distraction. Making matters worse, he was still hiding from the revolutionary General Zuloaga.

Juarez had been fortunate to be freed by the outgoing President Comonfort. His situation was tenuous, despite his alliance with the rebel Manual Zamora, barely friendly relations with the red-bearded Rio Grande troublemaker Juan Cortina, and protection of General Ignacio de la Llave. These men formed a boiling stew of revolution in

Mexico from which Juarez would eventually emerge as president.

Alvarez counted on the geographic distance between Camargo and Veracruz and his selling just enough cattle to be profitable, while not inciting Juarez to take action against him. He appreciated Juarez's delicate political situation, and it gave him confidence toward pursuing his mission. If and when he was successful in conquering the Nueces Strip, he'd surely have Juarez's full attention. Meanwhile, he'd walk the fine line of not overly riling up the man.

"Mantengaun ojo en Álvarez." Juarez ordered that an eye be kept on Alvarez. He didn't want some loose cannon, possibly revolutionary upstart, ruining his plans for becoming president of Mexico. *"Envía un agente para obtener información sobre sus planes."* Juarez figured it was better to be safe now than sorry later, so ordered that one of his agents travel to Camargo to learn what Alvarez was up to. He needed to head off this possible upstart before he could become a serious problem.

Luke swung the wagon around, dropped Jaime off at the cabin, and assured Julia that her husband was going to heal just as good as new. He drove the rig over to the barn and let the mules loose in the corral before heading up to the house.

"Too close, Lisa." Luke had just walked through the doorway. He could see the bruise that covered her right shoulder from the butt of the Sharps and its recoil. "We're blessed that Colonel Kinney warned us." He drew her close to him.

Elisa hugged her man, being careful to protect her shoulder. "I'm happy you're safe, Lucas. Praise the Lord."

She broke away and held him at arm's length. "I've got some news, love."

Luke strove to read her eyes. "Are you...we?"

"Yes, indeed. All the more reason to stay safe, Lucas."

Luke nodded agreement and looked over at the twins sleeping peacefully. "So, Peter and John are to have a brother or sister." He pulled Elisa to him, and they kissed a deep love kiss. His hand caressed her face and stroked her hair.

"Later, Lucas Dunn." She gently pulled away. "Tell me about Nuecestown and how Jaime is doing."

"That Biggs fellow that the colonel warned us of is in the jail. He was none too happy about losing his hand. He's so full of hate. He'd kill us all if he had half a chance. Hopefully, we can get him tried and hung soon. Everyone will be safer for it." Luke sat on the edge of their bed, watching Elisa nurse the twins. "As to Jaime, his wounds weren't serious. He'll be back in the saddle in no time at all. Oh, and I thanked Julia for her mighty swing with that iron skillet. She likely saved the day."

"I don't think I could have fired that rifle again, Lucas."

"Likely Bill's going to need some help with taking care of four prisoners and with three of them being wounded. We had a great strategy to surprise them in their hotel room, but that Roy Biggs fellow was one jump ahead of us. We were lucky, Lisa." Luke poured himself and Elisa some coffee. "So I'll likely go into Corpus tomorrow. If these are the men that attacked that Comanche camp, maybe I can find out whether Three Toes is safe."

The sound of hoofbeats got their attention, and Luke peeked out the front window. "It's Pastor Rucker. Wonder what he's up to?" Luke went out on the gallery to welcome him while Elisa put the boys down for their nap. "What's up, Horace?"

With nary a word, Rucker dismounted and hitched his horse. He stepped up on the gallery. "I came to apologize, Luke." He handed him a piece of paper.

"What's this?"

"This fell from Berne Culthwaite's pocket back when we were disposing of his body a while back."

"It looks like an order to kill me, Horace. Damn. Whose initials are these? Who is HT?"

"I'm thinking they belong to Horatio Thorpe. He has the wealth and power to hire killers like Culthwaite and Biggs, and I know that my commanding officer back then, General Truax, met with Thorpe on occasion."

"Where does Thorpe get his wealth?"

By this time, Elisa had joined them on the gallery and overheard Rucker. "My Daddy knew of him. He owns a huge plantation...I think it's called Magnolia...and has more than a thousand slaves. They say he's one of the richest folks in Texas."

Luke glanced into the envelope. "This is a good-sized envelope for a little note, Horace. Was there anything else?"

"It had some banknotes with it that have been used to help build the church in Nuecestown."

Luke smiled. "Sounds worthy, Horace."

"Thanks, Luke. Doc and I rather hoped you'd see it that way."

"I'll let Sheriff Meaney know about the note. With Culthwaite's failure, I wouldn't be surprised if this man Thorpe might try again."

"I'm thinking that Scarlett Rose ought to be on guard, Luke. General Truax never named this Thorpe fellow, but the man apparently had an obsession with Scarlett. Guess he's right nasty when he can't have something he wants."

"You ever seen the man?"

"No, but I hear he's well-dressed for a rather large man."

"You mean he's fat?" Luke asked.

"Let's just say horses aren't too fond of him." With that, Rucker relaxed and gave a bit of a chuckle.

"Name's Gascon...Gascon Thorpe. I'd like a room for the night." Gascon had finally arrived in San Antonio and expected that his name would carry weight with the hotel staff. He knew his father had lodged here previously, and Gascon would accept no less than the first-rate service he was certain his father had enjoyed here.

The desk clerk eyeballed him from boots to hat and pegged him as a wet-behind-the-ears cowboy wannabe. He stared through the glasses perched on his Romanesque nose. "Are you related to Mr. Horatio Thorpe?" His snootiness was reserved for Texas white trash. Despite the elder Thorpe's wealth, he'd made no friends here with his treatment of the staff.

"Yes. Is that a problem?" Gascon could be just as haughty.

The clerk sighed resignedly. After all, money was money. "No, sir. We're pleased to have you. Do you care for a room or a suite?"

"A room is fine. Where might I find some dinner?"

"Dinner is served in the dining room at six." He pointed to a side room off the lobby. "Or you may enjoy one of our fine nearby San Antonio establishments."

"Is there any place I can get a drink?"

The clerk was impatient. "Across the street, sir, is a saloon. It stays open quite late."

"I think I'll go there before dining. Please have my

bags taken to my room and stable my horses." Gascon placed a gold coin on the counter. He knew how to ensure service.

"Yes, sir, Mr. Thorpe. We will take care of all of your needs."

Gascon had dealt with these hotel-type people before. He turned, headed out of the hotel, and strode across the dusty street to the saloon. He double-checked that the chambers were loaded in his Colt Navy before entering through the double-swinging saloon doors. He stood for a moment to take it all in. He suavely slipped one of his father's Cuban cigars from his pocket and lit up. The smoke quickly intermingled with the haze hanging over the crowd. In fact, the place was surprisingly crowded for a mid-week evening. Given his height, fashionable dress, and confident demeanor, he was immediately noticed by every woman in the place. They were, first and foremost, attracted to money like moths to a flame. From Gascon's perspective, he hadn't enjoyed the company of a woman since his final night in France. There was the prostitute in New York City, but he didn't figure to count that as she didn't satisfy his tastes.

He'd barely made it to the bar when a very pretty young woman sidled up beside him. "You passing through, cowboy?"

Gascon paused and tapped on the bar. "Whiskey here, barkeep." He looked down at the woman and smiled engagingly. "Make it two." He grabbed the two drinks.

She led him to an empty table off to one side and pulled two chairs close together. "Where you from?"

"No matter. I'm no cowboy, miss. I am from East Texas and grow cotton. And, yes, I'm passing through."

"Business somewhere?"

"What's your name, miss?"

"You can call me Francette." She leaned forward to reveal her ample bosom.

"*Est-ce que tu parles français?*" He saw her expression go blank. Clearly, she spoke no French. "Sorry, I spent time in France, so assumed with your name..." Despite her obvious profession, he found himself aroused by her blue eyes set off dramatically with long dark curly hair. "You can call me Jim. Is there someplace private we might get to know each other better?"

She drew his hand to the inner softness of her thigh and then pulled it away. "Upstairs." She took his hand and led him to the staircase.

In a small town close to the border like Camargo, Juan Alvarez quickly took notice of the overdressed stranger. One didn't see many folks ever wearing suits, even on Sunday mornings. There was no question in his mind that he had to find out who the man was and where he was from. He watched as the man walked his horse up the main street and stopped at the cantina. The man looked left and right before hitching his mount and entering.

Alvarez couldn't hold back. He checked that his revolver was loaded and strode to the cantina. He checked out the horse. It bore a brand he'd never seen, and the tack was of high quality. Strangely enough, the saddle blanket featured a military insignia that he also was unfamiliar with. He shrugged and boldly entered the cantina. He felt reasonably safe, since the owner was his cousin.

The stranger nodded as Alvarez entered.

He had a feeling the stranger knew him. "*Disculpe Señor, ¿puedo unirme a usted?*" It was a bold move to invite himself to sit with the man, but he sought to control the situation.

"Por favor. Toma asiento." The stranger motioned him to take a seat.

Pablo, the cantina owner, placed a bowl of chili before the stranger. *"¿Tú también, Juan?"*

Alvarez wished he hadn't been called by his name, but Pablo was clueless. *"Si, tendré chile, Pablo."* He felt confident in any case that this wouldn't be his last meal.

"¿Habla usted Inglés, Señor Álvarez?"

"Un poco...si. ¿Por qué?"

"Habla Pablo Inglés."

"No."

"Good. I don't want anyone to know what I will tell you." The stranger hesitated.

"¿Qué es eso?" Alvarez caught himself. "I mean, what must you tell me?" He was sizing up the man before him. The stranger exuded raw power that was accentuated by his dark beard and mustache. Still, he didn't feel especially threatened...yet.

"I am from Veracruz." The stranger let that sink in. "It's a great place to sell longhorns." He saw the recognition in Alvarez's eyes. "Oh, and you can call me *Señor* Santana."

"What about my longhorns?" Alvarez was beginning to feel just a little uncomfortable.

"We counted three different brands. Two were from ranches in Texas."

Now Alvarez wondered whom the "we" was?

"We are concerned that you might attract too much attention from the United States and be a distraction to us in Veracruz." Santana leaned back in his chair to reveal a pearl-handled silver revolver in his holster. It wasn't exactly a threat.

Not to be outdone...or outgunned...Alvarez let his set of old but powerful Walker Colts catch Santana's eyes. "My business is my business, not someone in Veracruz."

It quickly became clear to Santana that this wasn't going to be so easy. He inwardly cursed what he saw as the small-town thinking of people like Alvarez. "Juan, my friend, this is far bigger than you."

"You are going to stop me?" Alvarez asked.

Santana lowered his face but kept his eyes on Alvarez with a glowering look. "You have been warned. Be careful." He stood and tossed a couple of pesos on the table. *"Via con Dios, Juan."*

SEVEN
JUSTICE PERVERTED

THE SUNRISE SHOWED promise of a beautiful day, and Gascon sat straight in the saddle, having validated his masculinity with the little whore in San Antonio. He calculated that he was just a three- or four-day ride from San Patricio, where he could enjoy another night of purchased passion. The prospect kept the journey from being overly boring. His curiosity over the red-haired whore that his father was obsessed with occasionally entered his daydreams. He rightly figured that this Luke Dunn fellow must be pretty important to his father for him to give up on the whore he coveted. She must be exceptional.

He stopped from time to time to rest. He occasionally took advantage by practicing his marksmanship. He was confident in his prowess with the revolver and only practiced with it a couple of times to familiarize himself with the feel of it in his hand. Most of his practice was devoted to his Colt Model 1839 carbine, as he figured he wouldn't want to get within pistol range of the Texas Ranger.

Like most of those who built their killer reputations during this era, Gascon much preferred ambush or back-shooting. The duel with de Vallette was as close as he or most any gunfighter might dare to confront in face-to-face gunplay. They were not noted for bravery. The dime-novel image of face-downs on the muddy streets of some no-account western towns was total fiction. Gascon rightly figured that no one in his right mind would expose himself to that sort of vulnerability. Of course, he wasn't a gunfighter—at least, not yet.

★★

Elisa's pregnancy had rekindled Luke's conflict over ranching full time versus bringing justice to the Nueces Strip as a Texas Ranger. The former was far and away more attractive, but his sense of duty to the citizens of the Strip competed with it. Now, when he left the house on Ranger duties, he'd increasingly faced fears of possibly meeting some dark fate. Even the seemingly innocuous prospect of transporting a seriously wounded Roy Biggs to Corpus Christi to stand trial posed concern. "Lisa, Sheriff Bill will be stopping by with the wagon. Appears that Biggs is in no condition to sit on a horse. I'm going to saddle up Big Horse and ride as escort." Big Horse was the name Luke had conferred on the big gray stallion that had served him well since shortly after his arrival in Corpus Christi. With his tall frame, a big strong horse was essential to carrying out effective law enforcement duties. He didn't need some smaller nag collapsing out from under him.

"Will you be home tonight, Lucas?" She intuitively knew he'd likely need to spend the night, so the question was more rhetorical.

"I'll try, but it's unlikely. The colonel's out of town, so I expect I'll stay at his place." He drew her close. "There's a new judge in Corpus, and I hear he's what they call a hanging judge." Luke half-grinned at the justice of the situation. The man had wounded him and threatened his wife. Only the business end of a rope...a hangman's noose... would equate to justice. And justice it would be, as Biggs was thoroughly beyond redemption. Yet there'd never be true justice for the people Biggs had murdered. "Might be a right speedy trial."

Elisa shared Luke's feelings. Evils needed to be eradicated. "We can hope, Lucas." She paused in thought, absentmindedly stroking the amulet hanging from her neck. "Try to learn of Three Toes's fate. I pray he wasn't among the massacre victims."

"I know, sweetheart. I'll see what I can find out." Luke half-expected Three Toes to suddenly emerge from one of the live oak mottes near their house. "I'll make it a priority, Lisa."

Elisa gave him a sack with some victuals, knowing that her man would miss her cooking for a couple of days. Soon enough, Meaney and the wagon carrying Biggs broke the relative silence of the morning and pulled up in front of the house.

Luke kissed Elisa and headed out the door. "Just be a minute, Bill. I've got to saddle up."

It didn't take long before Luke was in the saddle, and he and the wagon disappeared from sight down the road to Corpus Christi.

Alvarez had been none too pleased with the visit from *Señor* Santana, Benito Juarez's man. He resolved to redouble his recruiting efforts. Rustling was working as a fundraising strategy and as a sort of cover for his grander scheme of conquest. However, he needed more money sooner than later. The bank in Rio Grande City stood as a temptation. He could rob the bank, and he was confident that no one would risk chasing him back into Mexico. There was a small contingent of Mexican federal troops stationed outside Camargo that served as a deterrent.

Robbing a bank was risky, but time was of the essence. With Juarez watching from afar, his hand was being forced. He called his captains in for a meeting. "*Capitán González y Capitán Villa, necesitamos recaudar más dinero y acelerar nuestro reclutamiento.*" Loosely speaking, raise money and recruit faster. "*Crujir el ganado es demasiado lento.*" They knew the rustling was not raising money fast enough. Gonzalez and Villa were not quite prepared for what came next. "*¡Debemos robar un banco!*" They rightly saw this as high risk, though expected that the eventual invasion of the Nueces Strip would be even higher risk.

"*¿Rio Grande City, El Coronel?*"

"*No, está muy cerca.*" Too close? If not across the river in Rio Grande City, then where?

"*¿Donde?*"

Alvarez made full eye contact with each of his captains and turned deadly serious. "Edinberg." A bank in nearby Edinberg was bold indeed. In fact, it was downright crazy. Alvarez sensed doubt from the two. "*Nadie lo esperará.*" Certainly, it would be unexpected. "*En tres días.*" The colonel wasn't wasting any time.

"The court will come to order. All rise for Judge Nelson."

The judge in his ample black robes strode confidently into the smoke-filled courtroom and sat at the large ornate mahogany desk that dominated one end of the room. Word had it that the desk had been a captain's desk, salvaged from a shipwreck off the coast of Corpus Christi. The gavel in the judge's hand by contrast looked as though it had seen better days, but he rapped it gently enough on the desk to bring everyone to attention while testing its durability.

The prosecutor and the accused with his attorney sat about fifteen feet distant behind a couple of oak tables. The gallery behind them was all atwitter with bets as to how fast the judge would convict and sentence Biggs. Luke sat quietly off to one side next to Sheriff Meaney.

Biggs sat with his partially amputated arm in a sling. Strangely enough, he did not look like a man about to face the hangman. He could even be described as inordinately confident, much to the consternation of the court officers and the crowd. He stared intently at the judge to the point that his honor seemed to squirm uncomfortably just a bit.

Judge Nelson tapped the gavel. "What are the charges against this man?"

The prosecutor read the list of charges, mostly describing various murders, though there were a limited number of witnesses. It was what they termed an open-and-shut case. Conviction on any one charge was punishable by hanging.

Judge Nelson nodded upon the prosecutor's completion of reading the charges. So far, so good for the citizens of Texas. "How does the defendant plead?"

Biggs smiled deviously. He leaned forward as his assigned attorney began to speak. "Your Honor, my client pleads..."

"Not guilty, Your Honor." A voice boomed from the rear of the room.

Biggs's attorney, in fact everyone in the courtroom, looked incredulous.

It was at that moment that Luke saw Judge Nelson suppress a smile, quickly hiding it behind his hand.

A man in a dark suit and broad-brimmed white hat had suddenly entered the courtroom, carrying a rather large portfolio. "If the court pleases, I am Colin Jones, Mr. Biggs's attorney." He walked through the silence and shooed the court-appointed attorney away. "Mr. Biggs pleads not guilty, Your Honor." With great drama, he laid several documents on the table.

The prosecutor was nearly apoplectic. "This is out of order, Your Honor."

The judge stood and leaned forward. "Silence, counselor, or I'll hold you in contempt." He sat back and stared intently at Jones for a moment. "Do you have evidence to present on your client's behalf, Mr. Jones?"

"If I may approach the bench, Your Honor?"

Judge Nelson nodded.

Jones grabbed two documents and strode to the bench. He handed the documents to the judge, who briefly scanned them. Jones took the documents and returned to his seat.

"I'll see the defense and prosecution in my chambers. Court is recessed for fifteen minutes." He banged the gavel just hard enough to shatter the handle.

By this time, the prosecutor was both angry and confused. He followed Jones and the judge into a back room that served as the judge's chambers. It smelled more like a privy.

Luke looked quizzically at Meaney and then over at Biggs, who sat with his legs manacled to the table. "What's this all about, Bill?"

"Guess we're going to find out, Luke." The judge, attorney, and prosecutor emerged much sooner than expected.

"The court will come to order."

Judge Nelson cleared his throat. The prosecutor sat fully red-faced with frustration. Biggs and Jones smiled politely.

"It is the judgment of the court that the accused, Roy Biggs, is guilty of the crimes of which he has been accused."

Everyone waited in anticipation of the punishment.

"Roy Biggs is hereby sentenced to time served and is now a free man."

A roar of protest went up in the room. Luke and Meaney stood in their astonishment.

Biggs's ankle manacles were unlocked. He looked around the room with a broad smile, and then he was escorted out the back door in the company of his attorney to a waiting stagecoach. The judge quickly exited the courthouse.

Luke and Meaney strode forward and grabbed the prosecutor by the arm. Luke was livid, spitting mad. "Texas justice, my ass." He was ready to tear the prosecutor apart. "John, what the hell was that about?"

The prosecutor was thoroughly disgusted. "The man owns the judge. He not only holds deeds to nearly all the judge's properties, but someone is holding the man's family hostage. It's ugly, men, damned ugly."

Luke wasn't certain what to do next. Two questions lingered: who was Colin Jones and who was he working for? "Bill, you ever heard of this Jones fellow?"

"Not from these parts, Luke. Must be Thorpe's man. Let's check on those men we have in the jail." Meaney was concerned that they might be sprung by Jones as well. He moved toward the door, but Luke lagged behind for a moment.

"John, you know what Rip Ford would do?" The implication was, of course, to take preemptive action against Biggs.

"Luke, I didn't hear that." The prosecutor was none too happy with Luke's solution, even if he wasn't serious.

"I'll take that as a no, John." Still angry, Luke turned and followed Meaney out the door, all the while muttering cuss words under his breath.

"Never seen you quite like this, Luke." They'd reached the jail, and Meaney unlocked the front door. The prisoners were lounging in the two cells. The wounded men had been patched up by a local sawbones, so had dressings on their wounds.

"Bill, please be kind enough to get the short man out of the cell, the one who isn't wounded."

Meaney hesitated but unlocked the cell door. He put manacles on the man's wrists. "Sit over there." He pointed to a chair in the middle of the room. The man sat, and Meaney secured him to the chair.

The wounded prisoners watched with trepidation. Luke stood within inches of the man. "I understand your name is Ty."

The man nodded nervously.

"Y'all massacred Comanche up on the Pedernales River. I have that right?"

The man nodded again. Meaney simply stood back and watched.

"You're going to have to find a voice, boy. Head nods are disrespectful." Luke leaned into Ty's face. "Do you know who I am?"

"A Texas Ranger?"

"I'm Captain Luke Dunn. I work to keep order on the Nueces Strip. You boys are in my territory. Do I make myself clear?"

"Yessir, Captain Dunn, sir."

This was more like it. Ty had begun to sweat. "When you killed those Comanche, did you kill a chief?"

"I don't know, Captain Dunn."

Luke drew closer, almost touching noses. "You can tell a

chief from women and children, can't you?" Luke looked over at the wounded men in the other cell.

"Do you not know, or are you lying to me?"

"I...I don't know."

"Untie him, Bill. I'll need to take him out back for a moment. You can put one of those men in the chair." He looked at them again.

Meaney had a vague idea of what Luke was trying to do, though he didn't yet understand the importance of the Comanche chief.

Luke pulled Ty out the back door. There was a gunshot and a thud. Luke reentered the jail. He looked at the prisoner in the chair. "So, what do you think? Who did you kill in that massacre?"

The man was sweating profusely. "Honest, Captain Dunn, there were two warriors that we counted. None looked like a chief."

"Put him back in the cell, Bill. I'll fetch the man out back. He ought to be coming to." He smiled at Meaney's look of incredulity.

"Amazing, Luke. You did that quite well."

"Learned it training in Ireland. The British used it on our clan leaders." He didn't reveal that the ploy never worked, due to clan loyalty. He stayed until Meaney had everything secured. "I'm going to head back to the ranch. Guess I've got good news and bad news for my wife. I'm worried about that Biggs fellow. He's got even greater reason to get revenge."

"Don't think he'll be doing much until that arm heals, Luke. After that, who knows?"

"Whiskey, barkeep. One for her, too."

The little tart hung on Gascon's arm. She had quickly realized that he had money and parted ways with the cowboy whose lap she'd been occupying. The cowboy was none too happy, and he turned his ire on Gascon. "Hey, who the hell do you think you are, coming in here and stealing a man's woman?"

Gascon had been clueless as to where the woman had appeared from. She hung on his arm, smiled, and quaffed the whiskey he offered. The cowboy's voice took him by surprise. He looked up, twisted away from the woman's grip, and scanned the room.

The cowboy wasn't hard to miss, as he'd risen from his chair and struck a threatening pose with one hand on the handle of the gun in his belt. He was a rough-and-tumble looking sort with disheveled hair under a much-used broad-brimmed hat. A scar ran its way from his right ear to the corner of his mouth. His clothes had seen a lot of recent travel, likely as not droving cattle to Kansas. He wasn't a big man, but he was mean-looking and drunk. He had figured he was going to have a fine night with the woman that abandoned him for Gascon's company. His masculinity had been challenged in a big way and, in his inebriated condition, he was inclined to defend it.

A hush of anticipation fell over the saloon. From his perspective, Gascon wasn't sure what he might be getting into. The man could have friends among the patrons. He looked down at the ruby-lipped opportunistic whore standing beside him. Avoiding any gunplay was paramount. "Meant no harm, cowboy." He nudged the woman away, if for no other reason than to have a clear line of sight in case the man drew his revolver.

The cowboy took two unsteady steps toward Gascon and toppled forward on his face. As his inebriated, nearly passed-out body hit the floor, his gun exploded in his belt.

The bullet tore through his leg, shattering his femoral artery. He writhed in pain as a pool of blood spread under him. "H-H-Help!" The color was already ebbing from his face.

Most of the saloon clientele was aghast. Two men, apparently acquaintances, dashed forward to turn him over and try to stem the bleeding. It would be far too late.

Gascon stood emotionless at the bar. It certainly wasn't like that relatively civilized duel he had in Paris with seconds in attendance. But it was his good fortune here in San Patricio that fate had intervened, and he thought only of having avoided a confrontation that might have ended badly for him. He looked around, tossed a couple of coins to the barkeep, grabbed the whore, and dragged her out the door. He didn't even steal a glance at the dying cowboy. "You have a place we can go, sweetheart?"

For her part, the whore was briefly conflicted between the horror of what she'd just seen and the cold heartless reaction of the man that was about to bed her. She chose to not lament the past and led Gascon next door. Better a handsome, wealthy, virile young man than a grizzled no-account and now-dead drunk.

EIGHT
A CHIEF'S REVENGE

COLIN JONES HAD, immediately upon the issuing of the verdict, headed to the jail and pressed Sheriff Meaney to fetch Biggs's personal effects and process his release.

Luke had left the courtroom about as angered and frustrated as he'd ever been and headed for home. In a just world, he'd encounter Biggs sooner than later and have cause to render judgment, but...not this day.

It was Meaney as sheriff who had to do the administrative paperwork formally releasing the man. He was none too happy as Biggs's attorney hovered over him until the release papers were in his hand.

"Here you go, Mr. Jones. I advise that your client stay far away from Corpus Christi. There are folks that were none too happy with the verdict, and there's been talk of a vigilance committee. I only have one deputy, so I wouldn't be able to vouch for your client's safety." In his heart, Meaney would have headed one of those vigilance committees himself.

"My client is coming with me to Austin, Sheriff. After that, I cannot assure you that he won't be back."

"Just sayin', Mr. Jones."

The carriage carrying Jones and Biggs moved hurriedly out of Corpus Christi.

Biggs sat quietly enduring the discomfort to his arm from the jostling of the carriage. "I appreciate you being at the trial, Mr. Jones. It's reassuring to know that our boss hasn't forgotten me." Biggs rightly figured that Horatio Thorpe had been behind sending Colin Jones to defend Biggs.

"Mr. Thorpe is anxious to see you, Roy."

Biggs wasn't sure what to make of that. "Any idea what about?"

"Can't say as I do. I expect it concerns incomplete work." Jones's smile was nearly as sinister as Biggs's but with a lawyerly flair. "Actually, we're meeting Mr. Thorpe in San Antonio."

A silence settled over their ride. Even with a brisk pace and change of horses in San Patricio, it would take better than a week to reach San Antonio. The bouncing and jostling of the carriage on the rough road would continually tend to irritate Biggs's still tender freshly amputated arm.

There was an unintended irony in that Gascon Thorpe passed the coach just northwest of Nuecestown on his way south. Jones saw Horatio Thorpe's son ride by, but did not acknowledge him. Gascon would apparently be attempting to do what Berne Culthwaite and Roy Biggs had failed to do. Jones shook his head. He rightly saw it as the father willing to sacrifice the son to his obsessions with Scarlett Rose and Luke Dunn.

Luke had arrived home from Biggs's trial highly discouraged by the tenor of justice meted out in Corpus

Christi. It seemed patently unjust that men would get away with heinous crimes and pay no price for them because of some sort of blackmail they could exercise over the legal system. It seemed that money and sex spoke far too loudly.

He and Elisa had shared several conversations about the sad state of the justice system. They especially worried that a man like Biggs might seek revenge on their family.

"Lisa, it seems more efficient to kill lawbreakers outright than to bring them to trial and risk them being set free."

Elisa fully understood his frustration. She thought about the physical price she'd paid with her shoulder bruised by the recoil of their Sharps rifle. Had it not been for Julia's heavy iron skillet, Biggs might have killed her. Now, Biggs had been set free, and she had never felt so vulnerable. "I understand how you feel, Lucas. There's been no closure. But I know you are the sort of man that always does what is right."

"Maybe I should hang up my badge," he said.

"I'd never tell you to do that, Lucas. You must do what you feel is the right thing. In all our time together, you have always striven to be a protector. It's up to you, love."

A knock at the door got their attention. They'd heard no hoof beats, so whomever it was must have traveled on foot. Luke peered out the front window from behind the curtain. "It's Jaime." Luke opened the door and invited his *vaquero* in. "*Bienvenido, Jaime.*"

"*Señor* Luke, I have news." He was just a little out of sorts as he hadn't fully recovered from his wounds received in the fight with Roy Biggs. He held his hat in his hand. "One of my cousins told me that there are some dangerous things happening on the Rio Grande. It's as you say, no blarney."

While Luke often spoke Spanish with Jaime out of respect and at times efficiency out on the range, he was appreciative of Jaime's excellent English. Hanging around Luke, he'd even picked up an Irish word of two. "The Rio Grande? What's happening, Jaime?"

"My cousin said there's men in Camargo that come across the river and steal cattle that they sell in Veracruz. They are led by a man named Juan Alvarez."

"I've never heard of him. There's lots of cattle rustling, you say? Why is this man important?"

"*Señor* Luke, rumors say he is planning to rob a bank in Texas. He needs money quickly to build an army."

That got Luke's undivided attention. "An army? Why? How quickly?"

"My cousin says Alvarez wants to get rid of the Treaty of Guadalupe Hidalgo."

"You mean steal the Nueces Strip?"

"*Si, es verdad*. And he is hurrying because Benito Juarez feels that Alvarez is a distraction to his own plans for Mexico."

"Yeah, Jaime, I understand that Juarez is squabbling over who runs Mexico. Someone causing problems north of the Rio Grande would be a big concern." Luke appreciated that Jaime was not only a great *vaquero*, but he exhibited raw intelligence. He figured there were likely more folks of Mexican heritage that had Jaime's sort of smarts, but they were repressed by powerful social and political influences.

Jaime smiled. "*Señor* Luke, I tell you this because you are a great Texas Ranger, but only one man."

Luke appreciated Jaime's respect for his prowess as a Ranger. "I wonder whether they know down at Fort Ringgold? They're close enough to at least hear rumors."

"But they cannot cross the river and take care of the problem."

Just then Elisa stepped out and handed Jaime a cup of coffee.

"Gracias, Señora Dunn."

Elisa never held back when she heard men talking. "Couldn't help but hear your conversation. Sounds like someone needs to warn the troops and likely the sheriff at Rio Grande City."

Luke appreciated Elisa's sentiments. "Lisa, the sheriff won't have enough men and the Army may not be able to get there in time. If this Alvarez is in an all-fired hurry to put together an army, we likely won't be able to warn anyone in time to stop any bank robbery."

"He is right, *Señora* Dunn. It would take a week riding a fast horse to get to Rio Grande City. By that time, Alvarez will have already robbed the bank."

Elisa pondered that a bit. For a young woman and mother just turning eighteen, she had rapidly matured. No one would dare question her bravery, as she twice fought and killed Comanche and most recently had taken the measure of Roy Biggs. She had developed a wonderful sense of what motivated people and could weave it into strategies. "We don't have time to tell Rip Ford or other folks up in Austin, either." She thought a bit more, as Luke and Jaime awaited the idea that was obviously coming. "Perhaps someone could get to this Juarez fellow in Veracruz. He'd be anxious to stop Alvarez. It might not stop a bank robbery, but it could slow down his invasion plans."

Luke nodded and turned to Jaime. "Any chance one of your cousins might be able to get to this Juarez fellow? He'd more likely listen to a fellow Mexican than a *Tejano Diablo." Tejanos Diablos* was the name many Mexicans had given Texas Rangers as an expression of resentment and fear. "As Lisa says, I doubt we'll be able to head off a bank robbery, but I could take a ride down to Fort Ringgold and see what I can stir up."

Jaime seemed agreeable. "I can ask my cousin, *Señor*

Luke. He's happy in Texas and wouldn't like to have someone like Alvarez ruining what he's built."

Elisa frowned just a little, wrinkling her nose more in a cute way than an irritated manner. "Might waste your time going to Ringgold, Lucas." The frown turned to a smile. After all, there was plenty to do on the ranch. "Without orders from the military, the Army is unlikely to do anything. They won't even go across the Rio Grande."

Luke thought on that. Likely as not, it would be a wild goose chase and a waste of his time. "I expect you're right, Lisa sweetheart." He sipped the last of his coffee. "Jaime, see whether your cousin is willing. Meanwhile, we have some cattle to go check on." With that, he gave Elisa a kiss and led Jaime off to the stable to saddle up.

Sheriff Bill Meaney smiled as he prepared the convicted men for travel. "You fellas have a long trip ahead. I've heard that the new prison up in Huntsville is right nice, and y'all will learn all you ever wanted to know about processing wool and cotton."

Unlike Roy Biggs, these men had no influence over Judge Nelson. As if to make up for his miscarriage of justice with Biggs, the judge threw the book at Biggs's gang. Their resistance to arrest coupled with springing Biggs from the Uvalde jail earned them a few years in the newly constructed prison facility in Huntsville.

A stagecoach had been brought around with a couple of serviceable nags pulling it. Its windows had been modified with bars over them. It was a rugged-looking contraption with stiff wooden springs and didn't offer the prospect of a very smooth ride. The three felons would be cooped up in it for the two weeks it would take to reach the prison.

The manacled convicts were loaded into the coach and were soon heading out of Corpus Christi. Meaney was glad that he didn't have to accompany the coach to Huntsville, as the state had paid for a driver and outrider. They were a capable enough looking pair, so the sheriff had reasonable confidence that the prisoners would reach their destination.

There was a well-hidden set of eyes watching Colin Jones's carriage. Three Toes had traveled a long way, though journeying alone was a blessing given that it was easy to avoid settlements, Army patrols, bandits, and the like. With but two horses, he had covered the distance from the Pedernales River rather easily. Picking up the trail of Roy Biggs and his thugs wasn't especially difficult. He was a great tracker and equally adept at covering his own trail. He'd even watched the courthouse in Corpus Christi, unbeknownst to any of the citizenry. He had a choice to make as to whether to eliminate Biggs first or go after the gang that had massacred his people.

Three Toes knew a place on the opposite shore near the Nuecestown ferry where he could wait in ambush. The coach carrying the prisoners was far slower than Jones's carriage and would make an inviting target as it slowly crossed the river onboard the ferry. He knew that the coach would be most vulnerable as it disembarked from the ferry on the north landing.

He didn't have long to wait. There was a lot of noise on the south shore of the Nueces River as the coach pulled up. Soon enough, it was loaded onto the ferry. The driver climbed down from the coach and the outrider guard dismounted and joined him on the deck for a smoke as the ferryman pushed off from the dock. The faces of the prisoners were visibly pressed against the bars as they tried to get a view of the river, along with some fresh air. It only took a few minutes for the ferry to reach the north side and tie up to the landing. There was no one waiting for the ride back across, so the coast was clear and the ferryman took his sweet time.

Three Toes wasn't inclined to shoot the driver and outrider, but he had his work cut out for him, given the limited line of sight to the interior of the coach. He didn't have a choice. He judged that the heavily armed outrider was the greatest threat, nocked an arrow, and took aim.

"Glad to get this crossing behind us, Fred..." The man's words were his last, cut short by the arrow through his throat. The driver and the ferryman immediately dove into the river and sought shelter beneath the ferry's hull.

Three Toes mounted one of his ponies and was on the deck of the ferry almost instantaneously. The prisoners were now very much aware of the threat and cowered back from the coach door in horror.

The outrider lay bleeding and dying on the deck, the arrow protruding from his neck. He pulled his Walker Colt with his final breaths, but to no avail as Three Toes's lance swiftly found his chest. The chief turned his attention to the prisoners. "You kill my people."

The prisoners pulled back in abject fear as far away from the threat as possible in the confines of the stagecoach, as Three Toes pulled out his pistol, aimed carefully, and fired three shots through the window. At point-blank range, there was no doubt as to the outcome.

With the door locked, he was deprived of his three gory symbols of triumph. The dead and dying prisoners would keep their hair. He glanced up to see the driver and ferryman swimming madly toward the south shore. He decided to let them flee. Several people had gathered helplessly at the landing on the Nuecestown side. Three Toes calmly dismounted and took the outrider's scalp. He boldly waved his reward at the gathering crowd, leaped onto his pony, and was gone in a swirl of dust. Soon enough, he blended into the landscape and headed north along the river's shore. He hoped to catch up with the carriage carrying Biggs, but it wasn't to be for now.

Lieutenant Belknap had extended his patrol, having learned that Biggs and his thugs were headed to Corpus Christi. He'd heard the shooting off in the direction of Nuecestown. He was only a half mile away, so picked up his pace intending to reach the ferry landing in short order.

Upon rounding a bend in the road, the chief and the soldiers nearly ran headlong into each other. Only the jangling of sabers and braying of pack mules gave any fore-warning to Three Toes that enabled him to stop and avoid collision. He pulled up within a mere ten feet of Belknap.

The soldiers instantly were on alert. A wild-looking Comanche with a freshly cut scalp earned their fullest possible attention. Belknap stayed cool, as he readily recognized the chief.

"At ease, men," he said calmly. He raised his hand with palm facing the Comanche as a sign of peace. "Chief Three Toes, we meet again." He quickly dismounted to show his men they had nothing to fear.

Momentarily surprised at seeing the lieutenant, Three Toes hesitated, but dismounted and somewhat disconcert-edly greeted Belknap. "It has been a long time, my brother." He stepped forward, and they clasped hands.

The men of Belknap's patrol sat their saddles with mouths agape. This was not what they had been led to expect of the feared Comanche savages. The last they'd seen of the chief had been up on the Pedernales River at a massacre site. This man now wore black face paint and bore self-inflicted scars on his arms from his ritual of mourning.

The lieutenant wasn't put off in the least by Three Toes's appearance. "Have you seen Ghost-Who-Rides?" Belknap had not forgotten the name the Comanche had bestowed on Luke Dunn. He saw that the chief was in a hurry and sought to calm the situation.

In his tunnel-vision focus on avenging the massacre of his people, the chief had nearly forgotten that his Texas Ranger friend lived close by. However, he considered that the townsfolk of Nuecestown might not be too pleased to see him right now. It was likely that they'd already pulled the ferry back to the southern shore and were unloading his victims. "I had nearly forgotten, Lieutenant." It was hard to lie.

"We are headed toward the ranch, Chief. You're welcome to join us." Belknap felt no threat from Three Toes, though he was surprised at the chief's body language that indicated a desire to escape. The fresh scalp on Three Toes's lance had not gone unnoticed. He decided to probe a bit. "Did you hear any shooting?"

Given that he was the one doing the shooting, Three Toes was increasingly uncomfortable. "Not a good idea for me to go to Nuecestown with you. Thank you for your offer." Of a sudden, he couldn't wait to put distance between himself and the town. "I must go, Lieutenant. It has been good to see you."

"Wait, Chief. Did you find the men who killed your family?"

It was all the chief could do to contain himself. "I will keep looking." Now mounted, he desperately wanted to ride away.

"Chief, you have taken a scalp. Should I be concerned?" Belknap pretty much knew the answer to the question. His men still silently sat in their saddles with weapons at the ready, curious as to the lieutenant's questioning and simultaneously anxious to kill a Comanche.

Three Toes didn't care for where this was heading. He needed to leave. "Man attack me. I kill him." Even in his halting English, the bluntness of the chief's admission took the lieutenant aback.

Belknap felt the need to stop dallying and hurry on to Nuecestown. His instinct was to arrest the chief. His sergeant wasn't around on this patrol to advise him. If Three Toes resisted, the situation could get ugly very quickly. He glanced at his soldiers. They were waiting to see what he'd do.

Three Toes made the decision for them, as he dug his heels into his pony's flanks and dashed up the road before anyone could react. His pack horse instinctively followed him.

The patrol was ready to give chase. "Stand down, men. I know where to find the Comanche. Let's head to the ferry." With but a few looks back over their shoulders, the patrol dutifully followed the lieutenant at a canter toward Nuecestown.

Belknap and his patrol pulled up on the north side ferry landing to see that the ferry had already been pulled back to the south shore and the wagon driven from it. Several folks were milling about the wagon, including Doc Andrews, who was dutifully pronouncing the deceased as indeed dead. The four bodies had been laid out about ten feet up from the river bank. The women were repulsed by the scalped condition of the outrider, and someone had the good sense to cover the remains with a blanket.

Belknap didn't hesitate as he plunged in and led the

patrol in a swim across the river. They held their weapons above their heads as the horses navigated the current and emerged on the south shore.

He recognized Doc. "Doc, what happened?"

"Dang Comanche is what happened, Lieutenant."

"How many warriors?"

"One, dammit." He shook his head. "Same one whose warriors raided the Corrigan place a couple of years back. I think they call him Three Toes."

Belknap suppressed a knowing smile, having just encountered the chief only moments earlier. He wasn't about to admit having encountered the chief. His soldiers would stay mum. "Do you know the victims?"

"The stagecoach driver says the three manacled men from inside were prisoners being escorted up to Huntsville Prison. Apparently, they'd been involved with a fellow named Roy Biggs, who they sprang from jail. They massacred a bunch of Comanche. The other dead man was a fellow hired as an outrider to guard the coach."

Belknap felt an inner peace that Three Toes had gotten some revenge. "Thanks for the information, Doc. Any word on that Roy Biggs fellow? We've been trying to catch up with them for a couple of weeks."

"You're late, Lieutenant. He was tried in Corpus, released with a slap-on-the-wrist sentence, and is headed north with his attorney on some sort of business. That's 'bout what I know of it. I got it from Captain Dunn, who saw the trial firsthand."

"Sorry about the misfortune here, Doc. I think I'll pay my old friend Luke Dunn a visit as long as I'm down this way." Belknap saluted Doc and headed his men out toward Heaven's Gate Ranch. He could bivouac there before heading back north.

Gascon Thorpe pulled into Nuecestown not long after the ferry incident. He was dead tired from riding nearly all day. Even though he was close to Corpus Christi, he decided to spend the night. Since he'd been riding on the south side of the Nueces River, he had no cause to use the ferry and was unaware of the afternoon's goings on. The town had already settled into an eerie stillness.

He stopped at the livery stable on the north edge of town. "Where might a tired person find lodging in this town?"

The blacksmith, Dan, was happy to direct him to Bernice and Agatha's boarding house. "Right up the way, sir. Just 'round the corner up on the main street. Nice little place. Bernice serves up some decent roast these days, if you're hungry." He began to unsaddle Gascon's horse and relieve the pack horse of its load. "Right nice horses you've got here, mister."

Ignoring Dan's comment, Gascon turned and walked the few yards to the boarding house and checked in.

Bernice was her usual inquisitive self. She glanced at his name on the register. "Welcome to Nuecestown, Mr. Thorpe. Where you from and what you up to?"

Gascon was not used to folks prying into his business. He didn't understand the ways of small-town Texas where folks were naturally curious about strangers passing through. They needed something to talk about. "You can call me Gascon, ma'am. I'm from Eastern Texas though recently from Austin. I'm headed to Corpus Christi on some business."

"Well, you must meet Colonel Kinney, Gascon. He knows most anything that goes on in the city."

"Do you know a lot about Corpus, Bernice?"

"Some."

Gascon quickly realized that Bernice was the town gossip. Nothing got by her inquisitive nose. "Any famous people around that I should know of?"

Bernice lit up. She loved being the font of all knowledge. "Well, aside from the colonel who founded Corpus Christi, there's a famous Texas Ranger living between here and the city."

"A Ranger? Really? Whom might that be?"

"You folks up north ever heard of him? Captain Luke Dunn is famous throughout the Nueces Strip."

"I'll have to look him up. Colonel Kinney, too." He picked up his satchel and started to go to his room when a thought occurred to him. "Anything exciting ever happen in this town?"

Bernice thought it a curious question. "You a writer, Mr. Thorpe? Never mind that. We did have an incident at the ferry today...you know, Colonel Kinney founded Nuecestown so he could build a ferry here...well, some crazy Comanche attacked a coach carrying prisoners and..."

Gascon raised his hand to stop her. "You still have Indian attacks here?" He shook his head in feigned amazement.

"Oh, yes. Comanche attacked the Corrigan place a couple of years back. Only one survivor; a young girl who wound up marrying that Texas Ranger I mentioned."

Bernice was turning out to be a source of mostly useful information. "Is there a sheriff here?" He decided not to show interest in Luke Dunn just yet. He didn't want to tip anyone off as to his intentions. This was a game of deception, after all. Deceit was in play.

"Sheriff Meaney visits occasionally from Corpus. The previous sheriff was killed in a big gunfight. He'd been lover to a woman who had escaped prostitution in Laredo. They even had a child."

Bernice was on a roll, but Gascon's ears perked up with the mention of a whore from Laredo. "Does the woman from Laredo still live here?"

Bernice didn't think twice as Gascon's questions became more pointed. "Oh, she's settled down in Corpus as a seamstress. You ever need clothing repaired, she's the one to go to."

He didn't want to seem as though he was prying, though he was sure Bernice had more information to offer. "Well, Bernice, I'm quite tired. I'd be interested in some dinner, and then I'll be turning in. I do have a shirt in need of repair, so I'll ask directions to that seamstress in the morning when I head out." Gascon saw the opportunity to see whether the Laredo whore his father was gifting him was all he said she'd be. He would have plenty of time to double back from the city and take care of the Texas Ranger.

NINE

BANK ROBBERY

ALVAREZ HAD ALREADY DECIDED the bank at Edinberg would be too obvious a target for his robbery plans. Edinburg was isolated from any Army presence. He figured no one would expect the bank at Rio Grande City to be robbed under the noses of the nearby troops at Fort Ringgold. He'd ruled out simply robbing the stage carrying the payroll, as he was convinced that the bank would yield more treasure in addition to the payroll. Call it greed, but Alvarez sought to make the most of this opportunity. He brought his two captains together to discuss strategy.

"*¿Capitán Villa, cuándo llega la nómina del ejército?*" Alvarez needed reassurance as to when the Army payroll would arrive at the bank in Rio Grande City.

Villa had easily blended into the citizens of the town, secured their trust, asked a few questions, and learned the payroll schedule. He stayed in town to observe the payroll delivery. He answered with confidence. "*El Coronel, la nómina se entrega el jueves.*"

That made sense to Alvarez. The payroll delivered to the bank on Thursday to make a payroll to the troops on Friday.

"Muy bien. Así que, robamos el Banco el jueves por la tarde." They would rob the bank on Thursday afternoon, giving them plenty of time to retreat across the Rio Grande without fear of being followed. He was confident that the US Army would never pursue them into Mexico. *"¿Capitán Villa, tienes un mapa?"*

"Si, El Coronel." Villa handed him a map folded to a small enough size to have been easily hidden on his person.

Alvarez carefully studied Villa's sketch. The captain was no artist, but he was detail-oriented. The approach to the bank offered no obstacles and escape should be swift. Now he wondered as to the inside layout of the bank. *"¿Qué aspecto tiene el interior del Banco?"*

Now it was Captain Gonzalez's turn to shine. *"El Coronel, aquí está el diseño."* Gonzalez had made multiple trips to the bank, even setting up an account enabling him to get a view of the vault. He was bust-a-button proud of himself.

As with the map, Alvarez made a point of studying the diagram carefully. *"Mantienen la bóveda abierta?"* It was important to know whether they kept the vault open or closed.

Gonzalez was ready. *"El Coronel, está abierto a las dos en punto durante una hora cuando la nómina llega."* That would make the robbery a tightly scheduled undertaking. With the vault open for an hour at two o'clock, timing was critically important.

Alvarez spent the next hour laying out his strategy, including number and placement of men, who would enter the bank, how the money would be gathered, the guarding of their escape, and a rendezvous once back across the Rio Grande. Finally, he folded and pocketed the map and bank diagram and dismissed his captains.

It was Tuesday, so they only had one day to prepare the men. The short timeframe meant it was less likely that any word of the robbery would get out. He was worried that Juarez might have a man spying on him. Santana, the man Juarez sent to threaten him, had him more worried than he'd imagined. It certainly loomed as a great concern. Alvarez found himself looking over his back, wondering at what sort of deceit might be lurking in the shadows.

Three Toes had followed the carriage carrying Roy Biggs and his attorney Colin Jones for nearly two days. After his brush with Lieutenant Belknap and his patrol down near Nuecestown, the chief moved stealthily. He had quickly realized that Belknap wasn't following him, so that fact enabled him to focus on the carriage. He knew intuitively that he needed to catch up with Biggs before they reached San Antonio. As it was, they were drawing close to San Patricio.

He was down to only three cartridges for his revolver, and he needed more arrows as well. He'd have to get close enough to use his lance and knife. In a way, Three Toes regretted having wasted bullets on the three men in the coach—however, time had been of the essence. He feared that someone on the Nuecestown side of the river might find their courage, dig up a rifle, and start shooting at him. Regardless, hindsight hardly mattered at this point.

He'd observed several travelers on the road, so he had to seek an opportunity where Biggs would be isolated. He didn't know that his prey had lost an arm that was still very much on the mend. That was likely just as well, as that might prompt him to be overly confident. As the sun found its way toward the horizon, he saw the carriage pull over beside a live oak motte near the Nueces River. This seemed to present a great opportunity. There was no moonlight to speak of, thanks to thick cloud cover. Three Toes found his own shelter about three hundred yards or so downstream from the coach. He was around a bend in the river, so well hidden from the carriage. The chief began his approach on foot using the tall grasses as cover.

As he got to within a hundred yards of the carriage, he found the driver just feet before him and quite distracted as he answered nature's call. The unarmed man was humming as he went about his business. Three Toes moved ever so silently, like a butterfly on air. His knife found its way into the driver's back. The man grunted, but not so loud as could be heard by Biggs and Jones.

Now, the chief could turn his attention to his quarry. He slowly made his way toward the carriage where Biggs and Jones were already enjoying a small campfire. He was upwind, so had to be especially cautious. Smells and sounds seem to amplify in the darkness of the night air.

Roy Biggs hadn't survived so many years in the gold fields, gambling halls, and escapades on the trails of the southwest not to have developed a sort of sixth sense about danger. As he talked with Jones, he reached into his belt and pulled out his Colt.

"What the hell are you doing, Biggs?"

"Shush, dammit. I thought I heard something." He lowered his voice to a whisper. "Something's out there. What happened to our driver? I don't see him."

Jones drew his own pistol.

Three Toes saw Biggs go on his guard. He nocked an arrow and took aim.

Biggs and Jones ducked behind the carriage before the chief could release the arrow. A deadly game of cat and mouse had begun. Who was the hunter now? Biggs's eyes strained to see in the darkness. Nothing.

Three Toes decided the odds were against him. He'd

have to wait for another chance. Disappointed, he snuck back to his horses.

Biggs, his Colt held in front at the ready, moved out toward where he thought the sound had come from. His arm throbbed, likely due to the anxiety of the moment. His senses were on high alert. He tripped over something...the driver's body. Proof positive that someone had been out here stalking them. He grabbed the body by the shirt collar and began to drag it toward the carriage. He felt a dampness. As he approached the dim light of the campfire, he realized that the dampness was blood. Three Toes had scalped the driver. He paused. "Mr. Jones, we have a problem."

The attorney looked at the lifeless body of the driver, and then also saw the head minus its scalp. "We'd better get ourselves to San Antonio...and fast!"

In his inner self, as evil as it was, Biggs sensed that this Indian knew him and was on a mission of revenge. This was more than about counting coup and taking scalps. Indeed, they must hasten to get to the protection afforded by San Antonio.

As dawn broke, twenty-four men saddled up at Alvarez's ranchero. They looked to be all business with rifles and pistols aplenty. Villa and Gonzalez had the men well-disciplined and had divided into four patrols with assigned duties to each. It was to be run like a military operation and, in that sense, was a sort of practice for Alvarez's future plans. Each man wore a white shirt with a red bandanna and a Mexican sombrero, so there was a certain uniformity among them.

They moved out in columns of twos. There were two

pack animals with each of Alvarez's captains. They carried nothing but large empty buckets now, but those would ultimately bear the anticipated bounty of their endeavors.

Alvarez personally led the venture. It was important that the men see him in an at-risk position. It would be key to earning their respect and loyalty.

They didn't leave Camargo unobserved, as one of Santana's men had been sent to keep a keen eye on them. He wouldn't stop them, but the information he'd furnish to Benito Juarez would likely be enough to get the would-be Mexican president to take action against Alvarez.

Alvarez's *soldados* arrived outside Rio Grande City at about one-thirty and waited for the stage with its payroll to arrive. The advance party, comprised of a half-dozen men, moved into the town and began to take up their positions without arousing attention. The second advance party began assuming positions along the escape route from the bank. His *soldados* had a half-hour to wait if the stage was on schedule. When you're waiting, time takes on an endless quality, and the men quickly grew anxious.

"*¡El Coronel, aquí viene!*" The warning broke the tension and brought all the *soldados* to high alert. The stage rumbled by so close that Alvarez could have reached out and touched it. In mere moments, it stopped in front of the bank. Now they'd wait a few minutes while unloading began, a process that began with ensuring the coast was clear. Once the chest with the payroll was carried in, four men moved in as if from nowhere and put the guards at gunpoint. Then, "*¡Vamonos!*" Alvarez went first, spurring his mount to a gallop. The men followed and took to their roles.

Alvarez dismounted a few feet from the stage. With both pistols drawn, he led four men into the bank while six other *soldados* disarmed and then held the stage driver and guard at gunpoint. Once inside, Alvarez quickly established control. "¡*Todos levanten sus manos!*" Hands shot into the air. Everyone fully understood him. He smiled as he saw the vault door standing open. A bank employee moved to push it shut, but Alvarez was on to that. "¡Alto!" He warned the man to stop and a second later filled the room with the sound of a bullet from each pistol. The air was now filled with gun smoke, and the robbery had taken its first victim. The robbers moved quickly to disarm the patrons.

Four *soldados* entered with baskets and proceeded to empty the newest contents of the vault into them. They left some of the "old" money so as to not totally rile the townspeople against them. Alvarez and the others inside the bank kept their weapons pointed at the tellers and patrons. Hands were still held high. The men with the now full baskets emerged and secured them to the packhorses. Alvarez and the others slowly backed out of the bank and leaped onto their horses. The entire robbery had taken less than five minutes. "¡*Ahora, vámonos soldados!*"

A patron came running from the bank brandishing a pistol. One of Alvarez's sentries guarding the escape shot him down in his tracks.

All of Alvarez's men were now on horseback and racing to the Rio Grande. It wasn't far, and they were soon splashing across with all manner of whooping and hollering that belied any military bearing. They weren't soldiers just yet.

Once across the river, Alvarez brought his *soldados* to a halt. He looked back across the river from whence they'd come. No one had been brave or foolhardy enough to follow them. They could relax. "*Bien hecho, hombres. Vamos al rancho.*" The colonel found himself well pleased with his men's work, and they headed for Camargo and the security of his ranch. They had carried the heist off like a military operation—so smoothly that it had minimal collateral damage. Now all that remained was to tally their reward.

Three Toes realized he'd lost the element of surprise and with it his chance for fulfilling his quest to finish Biggs. He decided that his prey could wait. Patience would be the chief's greatest ally.

Lieutenant Belknap had planted the seed of finding his friend Ghost-Who-Rides. If he could find his way to Luke's ranch, he could visit his friends and even replenish his ammunition and arrows. Settled on that course of action, he determined to enjoy a relaxing night of rest alongside the Nueces River.

TEN

SHOWDOWN AT NUECES BAY

SCARLETT WAS UP EARLY. She had some sewing work to deliver, but first made certain that her little daughter Margaret was fed. She'd drop her off with Luke's cousin there in Corpus Christi for a couple of hours. Luke's cousin's husband was a local smithy, and Scarlett was pleased to offer the family her seamstress services in exchange for living quarters.

Scarlett Rose was by now far removed from her days of poor choices in men that led her down the path to prostitution. Her days whoring in Laredo had been both curse and blessing, as she'd hooked up with a notorious outlaw that eventually led her to connect with Luke Dunn. Luke had been her nemesis, protector and, finally, her redemption. With her flowing red hair, she still had the external beauty that had made her a favorite among the men of Laredo and had others dying over want of her. She'd become pregnant by a now deceased lawman and given birth to a daughter that was the focus of her life in Corpus Christi. Now, she'd reached a certain internal beauty, a peacefulness in her soul.

She was resolved that little Margaret would never endure the misfortunes life had thrown at her. Margaret would never be anyone's whore.

As she prepared to leave with Margaret, there was a knock at the door. She was momentarily disconcerted by the unexpected visitor. "Yes, who is it?"

"Gascon Thorpe. Bernice back in Nuecestown said you could help me with some mending."

Scarlett's memory flashed back to her wild journey across Texas to Nuecestown. Her desperado lover had been killed there and the sheriff had raped and impregnated her in her cell in the town jail, but she'd eventually been befriended by Luke and Elisa Dunn and taken in by Bernice and Agatha. She felt that she could open her door to someone being recommended by Bernice. She lifted the latch, swung the door open, and found herself looking up at a handsome young man carrying a handful of clothes.

"Bernice said you were a seamstress, ma'am. I need some shirts and a pair of trousers mended."

The man appeared to be well-dressed and, despite his youth, Scarlett had little doubt he could pay for her services. "Come in for a moment." She quickly looked through the clothing. The repairs were minor. "I have an appointment to tend to, so if you could come back later this afternoon, I could likely have these ready for you."

Gascon watched as she turned away to place the clothing on a nearby table. He couldn't help but admire what he saw as her assets. His father had certainly been justified in being obsessed with this woman. She was a beauty and was very likely the memorable lay he'd remembered. He averted his gaze before she could catch his eyes devouring her. "That suits me just fine, ma'am. I'll be staying at the hotel just up the street and have other business to take care of." If he had his way, he thought, he'd be sampling these promised fruits of his mission before going after the Texas Ranger.

He really had no idea who he was dealing with. Here was a woman that had become quite capable of defending herself against unwanted advances, even having castrated a Mexican bandit rapist with a well-aimed bullet. In his blissful ignorance, he calculated that he might lure her to dinner at the hotel.

"Guess I'll head into Corpus tomorrow, Lisa. I understand the colonel is back from Austin." Luke usually headed into the city on Thursdays to conduct any business ranging from banking to selling livestock. He was learning the cattle speculation business along with one of his cousins and hoped to parlay that into significantly expanding their ranching interests. The only piece of experience in the cattle business that he hadn't yet done was drive cattle to market. His usually unscheduled and occasional time-consuming Texas Ranger duties had preempted that in the past. Now he was giving the idea of a drive to Kansas territory some serious thought.

"You still aiming to be a drover for a couple of months, Lucas?" In a way, she felt that a trail drive was a bit safer than some assignment from Rip Ford or Colonel Kinney to chase down some lawbreaker. She also appreciated that Sheriff Meaney had a deputy and hadn't found the need to ask Luke for help on local law enforcement matters.

"I'm curious as to whether they've heard up in Austin about that Mexican fella Alvarez. Sure would be helpful if they'd get that darned telegraph line run south so we could find out about things sooner." He didn't yet envision himself chasing after Alvarez and held out hope that Jaime's cousin might have reached Benito Juarez down in Veracruz.

Elisa knew that Luke was going to do what he felt he had to do. She was concerned about Roy Biggs and understood how that weighed on her husband's mind. She never left the house without her own Colt Navy revolver. With her pregnancy, she had begun to feel just a bit vulnerable. She certainly wasn't ready to fire that Sharps rifle again. "You know," she told him, "I'll be just fine while you're in Corpus, Lucas. Besides, Jaime and Julia are here."

It was reassuring to have a hired hand around. Luke determined to head out in the morning. He looked over at his not-quite-toddler sons Peter and John playing with a ball of yarn on the parlor floor. "Boys, play nice...your mama and I have some business to tend to." They likely didn't understand a word he said. He stroked his mustache and smiled lovingly at Elisa.

"Just what business do you have in mind, Lucas Dunn?" She winked and led the way to the bedroom. There was something about the prospect of his being away even for a day that made her want to be as physically close as possible to this handsome man she married.

Scarlett rather expected the knock on the door. She'd easily completed the man's mending. As she'd sewn, she considered that most men likely as not wouldn't have made such minor repairs. But she didn't suspect any ulterior motive. She opened the door. "Mr. Thorpe, welcome. I've got your mending ready."

"Thank you, Miss Scarlett. How much do I owe you?"

"Twasn't much of an effort. Five cents should cover it."

As Gascon fished a gold dollar Indian-head coin from his pocket and placed it in her hand, he strove to catch her strikingly green eyes. "I'm sorry, but I have no pennies. Please accept this."

"Oh, I couldn't, Mr. Thorpe. That's far too much."

"Please accept it. Perhaps you'd join me for dinner and tell me about Corpus Christi?"

Scarlett found herself tempted. She hadn't actually talked at any length with a man in quite a while. In her past profession, there hadn't been much of any talking. "If my friends can watch over my daughter, I'd be pleased to join you, Mr. Thorpe."

"Please...call me Gascon."

Shades of Scarlett's long-ago past attractions to seemingly well-heeled, well-traveled men crept into her mind. Was she about to make the same mistake and with a man a couple of years her junior? She smiled nervously at him. Intuitively, she sensed this would be a mistake.

"I'm sorry. I've been forward. I didn't mean to make you feel uncomfortable." He was his father's son to the bone. "I'll be having dinner at the hotel at six o'clock. If you decide to join me, you'll be most welcome." He bowed slightly in a continental manner and left.

Scarlett was torn. She wished Elisa or Luke were close at hand to ask for advice. She hadn't been attracted to a man in such a very long time. Dare she yield to her desire to be physically close to someone, to yield to raw animal passions? Could she do it just this one time? Perhaps...just dinner?

The Nueces Strip landscape around Corpus Christi had changed in the few months since Three Toes had last visited. There were more settlers. It was much more challenging to travel undetected. Were word to leak out that a Comanche was roaming the region, he'd be hard pressed to avoid being hunted down.

He still had his two ponies, which made stealthy travel even more difficult. He stuck to the grasslands far off the new roads that had been carved from the Strip. He traveled mostly at night, using the occasional live oak motte to hide near during the day. With the onset of warmer weather, it was just as well to avoid the oppressive South Texas heat and humidity.

The chief had managed to cover the distance from north of San Patricio rather quickly. He expected that he'd have Nuecestown in view by the next day. He was confident in Luke's and Elisa's protection from folks who had in mind that the only good Indian was a dead Indian. Traveling alone meant being on high alert for lurking threats. A lone Comanche...even a chief...could be an easy target for most any itinerant Indian hater with a rifle and a grudge.

Gascon glanced up from his table. There she was, passing through the doorway to the dining room. She looked beautiful in a deep blue dress that set off her fiery-red hair and those captivating green eyes.

The *maître d'* escorted Scarlett to Gascon's table. He arose from his chair. "Miss Scarlett, it is indeed a pleasure that you have decided to join me." He laid on a thick southern plantation accent with a nasally hint of French.

Scarlett curtsied and took the seat he proffered to her, sitting opposite him. She wanted to say that she shouldn't be there at this time and place and with him. "I'm pleased to join you, Mr. Thorpe...er...Gascon."

They spent the next hour savoring dinner, enjoying some French wine Gascon had brought with him, and discussing the merits of life in Corpus Christi. It was likely too much wine.

Scarlett felt the warmth of the wine coursing through her body. "Gascon, I feel...I think...it's time for me...I really must go home." She felt as though she was losing control, and another sip of wine would be her undoing.

Gascon sensed her discomfort. He was like an animal sensing the weakness of its prey. It was reflexive with him, part of his nature. His father's habits hadn't been lost on him. "Would you care to rest a bit in my room?"

She knew she shouldn't. The wine hadn't fully diminished her faculties. "I...I think I should go home."

Gascon felt that another glass of wine would be enough. He grasped the bottle and topped off her glass before she could stop him. "A final toast, then I'll escort you home."

Scarlett took a symbolic sip. "Er...it's not far. No need to escort me." She moved to rise, but nearly lost her balance.

Gascon moved quickly. "Let me help you." He grabbed her arm and led her from the dining room and toward his room.

"No, Gascon," she offered meekly. "This won't do at all." She strove to pull away.

Gascon tightened his grip on her arm. He was now the beast moving in for the kill. "Not to worry. You'll be all right."

Fear can have a way of sobering folks, and Scarlett was recovering her senses. Another glass of wine surely would have been her undoing, but thankfully she'd refrained.

Gascon had her to the door to his room and was pulling her inside. It was taking greater effort on his part as she began to seriously resist. One arm was now around her waist, while the other grasped a breast. "Come on, Scarlett. I won't hurt you." Her perfume and closeness were driving him to a sexual frenzy.

As he strove to squeeze them through the door, she drew close enough that she found the handle of his revolver. She simultaneously pushed Gascon and drew the weapon. "No! Back away." She leveled the Colt at him and cocked the trigger.

"No, no." Gascon reached his hands out in self-defense as he backed away. "You wouldn't hurt me." He was tempted to grab the gun, but the sound surely would have stirred unwanted attention.

"You wouldn't be the first I've shot, Mr. Thorpe. Back away." She didn't waver. She'd become stone sober. "Stay here. I'll leave your pistol in the alley." With that, she backed away and half-ran, half-stumbled out of the hotel.

Anger spread its tentacles throughout Gascon's psyche. He thought for a moment about giving chase but realized, even in his frustrated temper, the folly of that action. He breathed deeply to calm down. The momentary feel of her breast under his grasping hand had aroused him. And, upon reflection, he rather admired Scarlett's feistiness. Little wonder that she'd defied capture by the men his father had sent. Now, he'd have to work to regain her trust. As if a dark diabolical cloud suddenly floated through his mind, he considered that Scarlett's daughter might be a way to get to the woman.

Gascon resolved to head out early toward where the Texas Ranger's ranch was supposed to be. He determined that he needed to get that task done before he could rightly sample his reward. The Ranger was only a man, and Gascon felt confident he'd be the measure of most any in Texas. He didn't give a second thought toward counting, having already been on the losing end of a scuffle with a woman.

Between his father and a couple of talkative men in the hotel bar, he had a pretty good idea what Luke Dunn looked like. Big men with red mustaches were not common.

Luke had headed out toward Corpus Christi at first light. He knew the day was going to be a scorcher, so the cool of the morning was best for traveling. Big Horse, his gray stallion, was especially frisky, as though he appreciated his owner's consideration of the weather.

Luke stuck to the road Colonel Kinney had built, so fully expected to encounter fellow travelers. Likely, they'd be folks he knew. He wasn't prepared for whom he came upon after about an hour of riding. "Scarlett Rose, where are you headed so all-fired early?"

She brought the wagon to a halt. "Luke, I'm so glad to meet up with you."

Luke smiled at her and little Margaret, who was curled up in a blanket on the seat beside her. "Something going on I should know about?"

"There was this man."

She had Luke's rapt attention. Elisa had told him about Scarlett's poor choices in men. "A man? Did he give you trouble?"

"I did some mending for him. He said Bernice sent him. He persuaded me to join him for dinner. After some wine… oh, Luke…I should have known better."

"Did he hurt you?" Luke asked, concern in his voice.

"He tried to drag me to his hotel room, but I was able to grab his gun and fend him off."

"Wasn't any shooting, was there?" Luke knew of what she had done to the Mexican bandit Carlos Perez.

"No, Luke. No shooting. I escaped and threw his gun in the alley."

"Do you know his name or anything about him?" This was a natural question of someone of Scarlett's past profession.

"He said his name was Gascon Thorpe," she told him. "He comes from big Texas money, Luke. I'm scared he'll be coming after me. I thought I might hide with y'all for a couple of days, and you could see what he's up to."

Of course, Luke had no idea that *he* was actually Gascon's primary target. He sat straight in the saddle for a moment, thinking out the best way to handle this situation. As he gazed out across the Nueces Bay, he saw the brief glint of something reflecting the early rays of the sun. It was pretty far off. "Scarlett, you go on to Heaven's Gate. I'll see what I can find out about this Thorpe fellow in Corpus."

"Luke, before you go, do you mind answering a question for me?" Her expression of concern became one of earnest curiosity.

Luke pulled up on Big Horse's reins, bringing him to an abrupt stop. "Sure, Scarlett. What's your question?"

"Why do you do this? Why do you put yourself at risk?"

Luke stroked his mustache for a moment. Part of him was anxious to head to Corpus Christi, but Scarlett had posed a question that was clearly important to her. In reflection, it was important to Luke. "As a young lad, back in Ireland..." He paused thoughtfully, trying not to make his answer too complicated. "My dad believed that God gave us instructions on living our lives. He used to quote Romans about how everything done in the past was aimed at teaching us, so that we might endure and be encouraged, so we'd have hope. Scarlett, I expect you might say I'm a

Texas Ranger to offer the justice that enables folks to hope."
He started to turn back away but paused. "And maybe to
sustain my own hope."

Scarlett cocked her head and sat quietly for the minute it
took to grasp Luke's words. His words were far deeper
than she was used to hearing. "I think I understand." She
spoke to the horses, and the wagon lurched forward.

Luke sat a moment as though contemplating the words
he'd just shared with Scarlett. Indeed, it was about delivering justice to enable folks to safely hang on to hope.
After watching her resume the drive toward Nuecestown,
Luke turned the big stallion back toward Corpus. He once
again caught the flash off in the distance. He couldn't
know at the time that Gascon had the luxury of a spyglass.
The glint Luke had seen was the sun reflected off of its
barrel.

Gascon had identified Luke and decided to take care of
business then and there. He dismounted and drew his rifle
from its scabbard. For the moment, he was fairly well
hidden behind a motte of live oak. He was a pretty fair
marksman, but this would be a tough shot at distance.

Luke brought Big Horse to a slow trot as he continued
his journey. He heard a whine as something whizzed past.
Then, almost instantaneously, he heard a rifle report. He
grabbed his Colt rifle, dove from his saddle, and gave Big
Horse a slap on his rear flank to get him out of any line of
fire.

Gascon was cursing himself. How could he possibly
have missed?

Meanwhile, Luke lay low. He had a rough idea as to the
direction of the sound. A horse's neigh came from the same
direction. There were no hoof beats, so whoever was out
there hadn't left. Luke stayed low and began to stalk his
attacker. He doffed his hat and cautiously peeked above the

tall grass. Once again, he saw a flash reflected from something.

Gascon didn't realize that the spyglass was giving away his location. Now he felt certain he'd seen something move off in the grass. He knew the Texas Ranger was on foot, as he'd seen him dismount and heard the horse run off. Now it was two men blindly stalking one another in the tall grass of the Nueces Strip.

It was too much for the teen. His father hadn't sent him to Corpus Christi to be killed. After all, he was supposed to be the hunter, not the hunted. He mounted up. To his regret, the horse decided to turn two circles before Gascon could set his direction.

Luke stood and took careful aim. He turned out to be a far better marksman than Gascon.

Gascon's horse reared. Seriously wounded, the young man was dumped into a clump of cactus. Rolling off the cactus, he sat upright, looking down at the blood seeping from his chest. He began to have some difficulty breathing, a resultant combination of the wound and the fall. He felt a shadow sweep across him.

"Who are you?" Luke had quickly retrieved Big Horse and now sat high in the saddle looking down at Gascon. He assessed the wounded man's condition. He kept one of his Colt Navy revolvers aimed at Gascon and dismounted.

The morning sun caught Gascon full in the face as he looked up, squinting at Luke. One hand covered his chest wound—the other tried to shield his eyes. "I...my... Gascon...Gascon Thorpe." He managed to get the words out between pain spasms. He was growing ever paler.

Luke figured this was the man who'd made trouble for Scarlett. Luke mentally calculated the distance between where they were on the shores of Nueces Bay to Nueces-town versus Corpus Christi. His natural inclination was to finish off Gascon, to put him out of his misery. But that violated both his oath and his sense of Christian morality. What was justice for attempted murder? He needed to get his attacker help so long as he was alive. His ranch was closer still, but he didn't want to put Scarlett through dealing with this Gascon Thorpe fellow. "You're going to have to ride. We have to get you to the doctor in Nueces-town." Luke mounted up and left for a few moments as he retrieved Gascon's horse.

When he returned to Gascon, it appeared the lad had passed out. Luke dismounted and examined Gascon intently from a few feet away. So far as he could tell, Gascon was barely breathing, if at all. His bullet had apparently delivered a mortal wound. "Mr. Thorpe?" There was no response. He was inclined to be cautious, drew one of his revolvers from his waistband, and nudged the wounded man's boot.

Gascon's hand, filled with the pistol his father had gifted him, came up of a sudden.

Luke was faster. Much faster. His was the only shot fired.

Gascon lay still.

Given the situation, Luke decided to take the body to Corpus Christi and let Sheriff Meaney deal with it. There was surely a next of kin. He recalled Scarlett saying the man had traveled from Austin and apparently came from a wealthy influential family. Luke figured this was likely Horatio Thorpe's son.

Had the father hired the son to do his dirty work? He shook his head with the realization that this man had squandered his life. He was so young, likely no more than eighteen. Luke hoisted the man over the back of the horse and tied him to the saddle. He noticed the spyglass and made a mental note to get one for himself. He was thankful that the sun's glint on the spyglass had alerted him and that Gascon's shot had missed. He'd reflect later on his seeming to increasingly be a target of ambushers. Such was apparently the all-too-common fate of successful lawmen on the untamed frontier. The Nueces Strip was no exception.

At least Scarlett would be able to return safely to Corpus Christi.

ELEVEN
CAMARGO EXACTION

SIX HEAVILY ARMED RIDERS, led by Santana, pulled up at the gate to Alvarez's ranch. Under their sombreros, they displayed an impressive array of weaponry, including Colt Model 1855 revolving carbines that effectively served as force multipliers against single-shot rifles. Their crossed bandoliers afforded them plenty of extra ammunition and coupled with Colt Model 1851 revolvers and long knives, they were a fearsome lot indeed. Little wonder that Santana felt confident riding into a ranch with better than fifty *soldados*-in-training.

They rode up to the main ranch house. He stared menacingly at the front door. "*¡Juan Álvarez, venga ahora!*"

For his part, Alvarez had been forewarned by his sentries. He considered facing Santana unarmed but, at the last moment, he strapped on his holster and grabbed a rifle. Smiling broadly, he strode out his front door with an almost belligerent swagger. "*Señor Santana, bienvenido a mi casa.*"

Santana was fully unappreciative of Alvarez's pomposity. "*¿Estás bromeando?*" This was no joking matter to Santana.

It had been roughly ten days since the bank robbery in Rio Grande City. Alvarez rather expected someone from Juarez's people to show up. *"Lo sentimos, Señor Santana. ¿Cómo puedo ayudarte?"* The apology and more conciliatory tone were quite definitely an order, especially given that he had now fully grasped the demeanor and armament of the force arrayed before him. *"Vamos a tener paz."* A call for peace was very much in order.

"Señor Benito Juárez ha oído de su pillaje. Exige una parte." It was quite simple. Juarez demanded a piece of Alvarez's action, and Santana was there to see that he got it. *"Requiere un diez por ciento."* Juarez was demanding ten percent of Alvarez's takings, a rather substantial amount, given that no one in Veracruz had lifted a finger to help in the robbery.

"¿Entiendes que tu demanda es imposible?" By now, Alvarez was feeling confident in negotiating. A couple of dozen of his *soldados* had gathered in a formation surrounding Santana. He could tell Santana that his demand was an impossible one. He recognized as well that he could not afford to raise the ire of Juarez. He could ill afford having Juarez's troops harassing his rear while he tried to invade the Nueces Strip. Meanwhile, neither he nor Santana were interested in a bloodbath here on the ranch.

By now, Villa and Gonzalez had armed themselves and joined him. *"¿Señor Santana, te importaría entrar y discutir esto?"* Alvarez made a sweeping gesture toward the door, as he invited his visitor inside to discuss Juarez's proposition. *"Sin embargo, no hay armas, ¿de acuerdo?"* It wouldn't do to be armed during any such negotiation. Alvarez could ill afford anyone being trigger-happy.

The two men left their guns and knives outside and faced down in Alvarez's parlor. Alvarez knew he had to satisfy Juarez, and he figured that Santana had offered up a higher amount as a starting tactic for negotiation. After a few moments of meaningful deliberation, an agreement was reached to share five percent. Moreover, it was agreed that this was to be a standard fee or stipend for any of Alvarez's subsequent fundraising enterprises.

It was well that negotiations and small talk had not lasted much past a half an hour, as Santana's men and Alvarez's *soldados* were beginning to joke and carry on. Neither leader especially appreciated any breakdown in discipline. Santana had accomplished his mission, negotiating the exaction of a sufficiently hefty consideration from Alvarez. He hoped it would be the gift that kept on giving, a sort of residual source of income to help fund Benito Juarez's ascent to power in Mexico. Santana and Alvarez shook hands amicably as a signal of non-aggression as they strapped on their respective weaponry. The irony couldn't be lost on anyone privy to their negotiation. For Alvarez's part, he planned at least one more bank robbery, but had to wait until the sheriff in Rio Grande City and troops at Fort Ringgold got back into their routines and let their guards down.

A deer presented a lot more meat than Three Toes could hope to devour at a sitting, but it was easy prey. He nocked an arrow, took careful aim, and let it fly. The single arrow brought the deer to its knees. It fell on its side soon enough. The chief was on it quickly, taking prime cuts of meat and leaving the rest for the scavengers of the Nueces Strip. He stored the venison in a sack he carried for that purpose and hoped he'd find time to dry the meat. For now, he was hungry. He built a fire, cooled strips of the venison on a spit, and soon sated his appetite.

Non-human predators were quite plentiful on the

Nueces Strip. Bear, fox, coyote, and wolf freely roamed the vast grasslands. With plentiful deer, sheep, antelope, javelina, and the like, the predators were well-fed. Perhaps the most feared in the psyche of settlers of the frontier was the mountain lion. It was an ubiquitous creature ranging across the entire Texas landscape.

A mountain lion on the hunt was a creature of innate stealth and seemingly infinite patience. There was a beauty to a hunting mountain lion, so long as you were not its intended next meal. Their easily camouflaging coloration and lithe muscular form coupled with tremendous leaping ability made them formidable hunters. Males weighing upward of one hundred eighty pounds and eight feet long nose to tail gave them a significant advantage over most any prey. They preferred to avoid humans, as deer, sheep, and smaller mammals were more their dietary staples. An injured mountain lion or a female protecting her young might be inclined to pursue human quarry.

The sun was nearing the horizon and heralded some relief from the heat of the day. The mountain lion had rested much of the day, but now thirst and hunger had roused him to seek a meal. His left front paw was still painful enough from the antelope's horn that he was unable to put his full weight on it. But he was hungry...very hungry. He'd already exhausted his kills of the past few days, before the mishap with the antelope. Now, with his finely tuned sense of smell, he'd found a new prey...one he was unaccustomed to. He could hear horses snorting, too. With his wounded paw, he wasn't up to tackling a horse just now. He needed prey more his size and possibly less dangerous.

He crept invisibly through the tall grass. He was down-wind, so hadn't yet been noticed by the horses he'd heard.

His quarry was sleeping in the shade of the only motte of trees for a mile or more around. Slowly, ever so slowly, he stalked his prey. Normally, he could cover twenty feet or more with his leap. He'd managed to get even closer. He watched, sizing up his target. The horses still hadn't detected him.

The big cat leaped. The horses reared and let out a neigh that sounded more like a scream. A single bound put the mountain lion on top of Three Toes, and he opened his jaws wide in an effort to sink his fangs into the back of the chief's neck. If he could sever the spine, the cat's prey would be helpless and die instantly. Fangs tore into muscle and scraped bone. Three Toes strove to get out from under the big cat. His arrows, lance, and pistol were useless at the moment. Only his arms initially served as defense as he strove to push the beast away while grabbing for his knife. By now, he'd managed to twist his body such that he was face to face with the lion in a sort of death grip. The heavy weight of the cat pressed him into the ground. Its now-bloodied yellowed fangs and hot breath were mere inches from the chief's face. Three Toes shoved his left arm defensively into the jaws and, with his free arm, he began to plunge the knife into the mountain lion's neck and ribs again and again. Finally, after what seemed like forever but was only moments, the lion began to weaken and, thankfully for the chief, breathed his last.

Three Toes wriggled painfully out from beneath the heavy lifeless cat. His left forearm was mangled and at least one of the bones appeared to be broken. He could feel open wounds on his shoulders and the back of his neck. He hurt all over.

The chief managed to stand and steady his ponies. He was as resourceful and tough as any Comanche, but his wounds bordered on grave. Needing a splint, he strapped his broken arm to the pipe he carried in his bag, pressing the wrapping tightly toward staunching the bleeding. He estimated that he was a day's ride from Nuecestown and Luke's ranch.

He marveled at his fortune—that the mountain lion hadn't killed him with its initial attack. It had likely been attracted by the aroma of the venison. Perhaps the Great Spirit was still looking over the Comanche chief and giving him powerful medicine. He looked down at the lion. Despite the pain from his arm and other wounds, he found some inner strength, seized the opportunity before him, and proceeded to skin the big cat. It would make a worthy gift for Luke and Elisa.

He secured the lion's skin on his pack pony and mounted his other horse. The ponies balked initially at the scent of the mountain lion, but Three Toes would have none of that. Worse was the jostling of the pony's motion that made riding painful, but it was faster than walking. He urgently needed to get to Luke's place. Plus, he had to stay sufficiently awake to keep the ponies headed in the right direction. He couldn't afford to pass out and fervently hoped he wouldn't encounter anyone along the way.

Luke deposited Gascon Thorpe's body with Sheriff Meaney. The necessary report was written, explaining the circumstances.

"Jeez, Luke, what'd you waste a second bullet for? You could've put your fist through the hole in this guy's back."

"Should have told him. He tried to shoot me with his dying breath." Luke looked grimly at Gascon Thorpe's body propped against the tree behind the jail. "Looks as though he came from money, Bill. I heard of a wealthy plantation owner named Horatio Thorpe who holes up in Austin to influence the politicians. Given the name and quality of his clothes, I expect he could be the man's son."

"I've heard that Horatio Thorpe is as nasty as they come, Luke."

"I learned that he was nasty enough to pay that cutthroat Berne Culthwaite to try to kill me...which he nearly did. Shoot, Bill, I wouldn't be surprised if Roy Biggs was on Thorpe's payroll." He looked again at Gascon's body. "Hard to believe a man to be so evil that he'd pay his own son to come after me. Still, they haven't been able to pin anything on him. Or won't."

Meaney flashed an "ah-ha" expression. "It occurs to me that we could lure the man down here to Corpus Christi. We might persuade Colonel Kinney to send a note asking him to come fetch his son's body."

"All this business is getting pretty close to home, Bill. We've had two attacks on me at my home and a third 'tween here and the ranch. I can't keep putting Elisa and the boys at such risk."

"Maybe getting Thorpe will bring it to an end, Luke." He knew it was a forlorn hope at best.

"I'll leave it to you to get the colonel to contact Thorpe. If you don't mind, I think I'll mosey back to the ranch and settle the ladies down. Scarlett was rightly frightened of this young Thorpe fellow." Luke looked forward to getting back home to Heaven's Gate and Elisa's waiting arms.

High-powered attorney Colin Jones, in the unaccustomed role of carriage driver, delivered the still-ailing Roy Biggs to

Horatio Thorpe's hotel room in San Antonio. It'd been a dangerous trip to say the least, and Jones was none too appreciative.

It was late afternoon when he knocked on Thorpe's door. "Mr. Thorpe!"

Thorpe had been sipping a drink while enjoying an occasional cooling breeze that swept across his luxury suite. He missed not having Samuel with him on this trip. "Who's there?" he called. He didn't feature expending the energy to get up from his chair to answer the door.

"Colin Jones, Mr. Thorpe. I've got Roy Biggs with me."

"Are you armed?"

Jones remembered that a cardinal rule in dealing with Thorpe was to never be in his presence with a weapon. He placed his revolver and Biggs's gun and knife on the floor next to the door. "Sorry, sir. We're unarmed now."

Thorpe slowly walked over to the door, glanced through a peephole and, upon his satisfaction that they were unarmed and looked to be who they said they were, opened the heavy mahogany door.

Jones and Biggs strode past Thorpe.

"What the hell happened to you, Biggs?" Thorpe demanded.

"Damned Texas Ranger's wife blew my arm off."

Thorpe shook his head. "What'd she use, a cannon?"

"Sharps. Then this Mexican bitch snuck up behind me and knocked me out with an iron skillet."

Jones was quiet. He rightly figured that Thorpe was none too happy with Roy Biggs. Finally, he interjected softly, "Trial went smoothly, Mr. Thorpe."

"Obviously," sneered Thorpe. "Any trouble getting here? I'm not happy about having to leave Austin." In the back of his mind, he had counted on Gascon and his backup plan to kill Luke Dunn and get that damned whore.

Biggs was finding his tongue. "We were attacked on the road. Might have been an Injun. He killed our driver." His face flushed a light shade of crimson. "I need to go finish off that Ranger, Mr. Thorpe. It's personal."

"With any luck, the job's already been taken care of. I sent my son as backup." Thorpe lit a cigar and blew the smoke at Biggs. "You owe me some money, Mr. Biggs. You didn't finish your work."

Biggs thought about how he'd already lost his hacienda, his wife and children, plus his arm. "I think we're even, Mr. Thorpe." He felt the foul taste of evil thoughts creep into his mind. He asked himself why not get the gun and dispose of Thorpe and Jones right there?

"I said you owe me, Mr. Biggs." Had he known that Biggs's failure had also led to the loss of his son, Thorpe likely would have killed the man right then and there. "If my son sends word that he's killed the Texas Ranger and captured that Laredo whore bitch, I'll decide then what you must do to pay off your debt. If he succeeds, I might even set you free of what you owe."

Thorpe turned to Jones. The attorney had done what was asked, so Thorpe had no issues with him. "You can head back to Austin, Colin. I'm going to stay here for a couple of days and see if Gascon makes it up here to San Antonio." He handed Jones a thick envelope full of cash. This was definitely an off-the-books transaction. "I think this settles us." He nodded toward the door to indicate that Jones should leave.

Once Jones had departed, Thorpe could turn his full attention back to Biggs. "I guess you've paid a heavy price indeed for failing me, Biggs. But I expect before long you'll hardly notice that you've lost the arm." Thorpe's callousness laid a chill on the meeting. "I got you a room up the street. You should take the time to rest." He sipped his drink and indicated to Biggs that he should go. "If I need you, I'll send a messenger. Don't leave San Antonio."

Biggs opened the door and saw his pistol still lying on the floor outside Thorpe's room. He was of half a mind to shoot the corpulent son of a bitch, except the bullets had been removed and it'd have been a hassle reloading the Colt. He felt Thorpe's smile on him as he holstered the empty gun and stuffed the bullets into his pocket.

It was evening, when Three Toes slowly rode up to the cabin at Heaven's Gate. He'd managed not to encounter anyone on his travels. He was about a hundred yards or so from the cabin when he noticed the big house on the hill. Luke had been busy since the chief had last been to the ranch. Even an addition had been built to the barn.

He looked around. He was in the right place. The graves of Elisa's mother, father, and brothers were still up by the live oak motte, and he could see where Luke had respectfully laid out and covered the remains of his warriors killed in the two attacks on the ranch. His wounds hurt too much to dwell on the loss of those brave warriors.

He could see into the window of the cabin and didn't recognize the folks inside. Slowly he turned his pony and walked him up toward the house.

"*¿Hey, quién eres tú?*"

Three Toes glanced behind him.

Jaime was aiming his rifle at the chief. He fired, and the bullet whizzed by Three Toes's head.

The chief fell from his horse as though he'd been hit. Actually, hitting the ground caused him tremendous pain. He was lucid enough to grab his knife. He'd defend himself to the death if necessary.

Luke came dashing from the house at the sound of gunfire. His hands were both filled with his Colts, as he was ready for whatever was happening. Even in the dim early evening light, he immediately recognized Three Toes. "Jaime! Jaime! Stop!" He ran toward the chief. "He's a friend!"

Luke was at the Comanche's side. "Jaime, he's hurt. Help me get him to the house." He pried the knife from the chief's hand.

Jaime didn't understand that there was such a thing as a friendly Comanche, but he nevertheless helped Luke carry the chief.

"Ghost...Ghost-Who-Rides..."

"Save your breath, Chief." Luke and Jaime got Three Toes inside and laid him on a blanket near the fireplace. "Jaime, ride real quick like to Nuecestown and fetch Doc. Tell him to hurry." He saw the inquisitive look on the *vaquero's* face. "It's okay. Now go!"

By this time, Elisa had heard the commotion, ran to the parlor, and seen Three Toes lying on the floor. "Lucas, clear the table. Doc's going to want him on the table. I'll heat some water." By now, both she and Luke had a chance to assess the bite marks. "What got him, Lucas? He's been bitten and clawed terribly."

"Only thing I can figure is a big cat, Lisa. Likely one of those mountain lions. They usually leave humans alone, so this one must have been ailing."

Elisa got on her knees and prayed. She prayed to God, but also stroked the amulet Three Toes had given her as though it might have some extra power.

Three Toes had passed out, so Luke did his best at trying to start cleaning up the wounds. The chief's arm was clearly broken, not badly, but broken enough. "It's amazing that he made it here, darling. He's a man with a strong will to live."

"What was the shot I heard?"

"Jaime. He saw an Indian and reacted as might be expected. He didn't know about Three Toes being a friend. Thank God he missed."

"Hopefully Doc gets here soon. He doesn't look good, Lucas."

"You watch over him, I'm going to put his ponies in the barn." Luke walked outside and grabbed the halter of the pony Three Toes had been riding. The pack horse followed. Upon lighting a lantern in the barn, Luke noticed the blood on the blanket and then the mountain lion skin tied to the pack horse. It was indeed a big cat. Luke was amazed that his friend, as badly injured as he was, had managed to skin the beast. Luke removed all the chief's possessions, curried both ponies as best he could, and left them in a stall. He put the chief's weapons in a corner of the stall, figuring the familiar smell would keep the ponies settled. He hoisted Three Toes's pack and the lion skin over his shoulder and took them up to the house. By the time he was climbing the front steps, Doc and Jaime were riding in.

Jaime was still trying to accommodate why Luke was in such a lather about helping a Comanche. He shared a lot of folks' opinion that the only good Indian was a dead Indian. He stood outside contemplating while Doc and Luke dashed into the house. What if he hadn't missed? Would Luke have forgiven him? Would he have been arrested? Was killing an Indian illegal? His cultural background, his race's history of battling the red man for control of the land, made it just a bit confusing.

Inside, Doc realized that he was about to treat a Comanche. His loyalty to Luke trumped his inclination to let the savage die. "What's this savage to you, Luke?"

"Mutual respect, Doc...plus, he saved my life." His

steely blue eyes penetrated Doc's cultural wall. "Please treat him as you would any man."

"Damned cat made a mess, Luke. He's lost a bit of blood, but I think I can fix him up."

Elisa was doing what she could to help. She heated some water to use in cleaning the wounds. She still carried the image of the Comanche warriors...Three Toes's warriors...that she'd shot and killed when they attacked her family's homestead, but the relationship forged between Three Toes and Luke, the mutual trust and respect, helped her see beyond her trauma. Two years now seemed forever ago. "Lucas, I think he may be with us for a while as he heals. I think he may draw less attention wearing White man's clothes around here instead of his buckskins." She went off to see what she could find for the chief to wear.

Doc was trying to work his medical miracles tending the chief's wounds. Each puncture was cleaned as best as possible and, given the pain, it was likely a blessing that Three Toes had passed out. "You say he skinned the lion, Luke?"

Luke had nonchalantly thrown the Comanche's pack and the mountain lion skin in a corner. "He's a tough man, Doc. Guess he'll have a story to tell."

At that, Three Toes came to for a moment and offered a barely audible whisper. "I tell you story, White man." He forced a smile and passed out again.

"Best let him sleep, Luke. He needs rest. My work here is finished." Doc locked eyes with the Texas Ranger. "I admire you, Luke Dunn. I admire that you can look past this man's nature, a nature that's so contrary to the White man. I expect it's something we all ought to be considering. You're a big man, Luke Dunn. And I'm not referring to your size."

Luke uncharacteristically blushed.

Elisa overheard Doc's comment. "It's what I love in him, Doc."

Doc glanced at Elisa's newly forming tummy bulge. "Apparently so, Elisa Dunn, apparently so."

Jaime was still outside seated on the edge of the gallery when Luke emerged with Doc. "Is the Indian going to stay here, Mr. Dunn?"

"Jaime, you and Julia have nothing to fear. He's a trusted friend."

Jaime shook his head resignedly. "If you say so." He thought a moment. "Where's he going to stay?"

"I don't think the chief cottons to four walls, Jaime. We'll set a shelter of some sort over near the barn."

Jaime enjoyed working for Luke. "You sure, *Señor* Dunn?"

"Have I ever given you cause to not trust me?" Luke asked.

Jaime sighed. It was time to change the subject. "My cousin's friend reached some people in Veracruz. This man Alvarez robbed the bank in Rio Grande City, but Benito Juarez is exacting a price for his distraction. He doesn't want US Federales upsetting his plans for Mexico."

Luke appreciated that Jaime was wise for his years. "Sounds to me like this Juarez fellow won't be able to control Alvarez much longer. I smell trouble." Luke didn't feature the prospect of heading to the southernmost reaches of the Nueces Strip and certainly didn't plan on going without serious manpower to accompany him. He understood the vagaries of politics enough to figure that US troops wouldn't get involved unless there was some sort of invasion. If rustling, bank robbery, and some killings were in play, a few Rangers would likely be up to the task. He also knew that no funding would be forthcoming from the powers that be in Austin until there was even more trouble on the Nueces Strip. "Thanks, Jaime. I expect we can try to get word to Rip Ford up in Austin, but I don't expect anything to happen just yet."

"If I hear more, I'll let you know," Jaime said. "Guess I'll see you tomorrow. We've got some strays at the western end of the ranch." And he headed back to the cabin.

TWELVE
THORPE'S DESSERTS

THE KNOCK at the door was heavy. No mistaking that someone was trying to get the occupant's attention. "Mr. Thorpe! Mr. Thorpe!"

Horatio Thorpe groaned a bit as he lifted his outsized frame from the bed. What the hell time was it, anyway? Who could be knocking so loudly and before noon? He squinted at the sunlight pouring in through a gap in the window curtains. Another bang on the door. "I'm coming, damn it!" He threw a robe over his massive body. At last, he limped to the door. The ride from Austin a couple of days earlier had caught up with his out-of-shape, corpulent, ill-used body. He swung the door open. "Who the hell are you?"

"Just a messenger, Mr. Thorpe. I was told to deliver this directly to you." He handed over an envelope that even had a wax seal.

"Er, thanks. Hang on a moment."

"No need to tip, sir. I've been paid." The messenger turned and left rather hastily.

Thorpe was left standing alone in the doorway with the

envelope in his hand. Another damned official-looking envelope. The last one brought bad news. What of this one? He turned, shut the door behind him, and went over toward the gap in the window curtain to better see the contents of the message. He broke it open, began to read, and reflexively sat heavily on the bed. "Oh my God. No! No!" He read it again.

Mr. Horatio Thorpe, Esquire
Austin, Texas

Dr. Mr. Thorpe,

We regret to inform you of the death
of your son, Gascon Thorpe. You are
requested to report to the sheriff of
Corpus Christi at your earliest
convenience to claim your son's
remains. Said remains will be held
until September 6, after which time
they will be interred.

Respectfully,
Colonel Henry Lawrence Kinney
Corpus Christi, Texas

Thorpe's second reaction was anger. If Culthwaite or Biggs had done their job, Gascon would still be alive. No matter that he had put his son in harm's way. So far as he was concerned, Biggs was now a dead man walking.

There was no way he was traveling alone to Corpus Christi. He had bought-and-paid-for friends in San Antonio. A carriage and armed escort would be easy enough to arrange.

He'd have to send a message to his ailing wife. It wasn't enough that she put up with his philandering ways and rumors of his shady dealings, he was now going to have to tell her that their oldest son was dead. It might even kill her. It was likely that she lived with the hope that Gascon would turn out to be a real man and not follow in his father's footsteps. Of their other son and daughter, their son had moved back east to Philadelphia and their daughter had succumbed to complications in the birth of her bastard child. Thorpe's wife had also already endured the embarrassment of a handful of mulatto children around the plantation, many of whom bore a striking facial resemblance to her husband. Indeed, Gascon's death just might kill her.

Three Toes finally awakened from a two-day slumber. The twins, Peter and John, had made great fun of marveling at the strange-looking man in their parlor. His dark skin and chiseled facial features were so different from other people they'd been introduced to. They wondered why not everyone had white skin and red or blond hair like their father and mother or brown skin and black hair like the folks who lived on their ranch. They understood that they weren't to touch the man, but it was so very tempting. Finally, they could hold back no longer. Laughing, Peter bravely crawled forward and touched Three Toes's hand.

In a flash, Peter's hand was gently imprisoned in the red man's grasp. A look of horror instantly spread across the startled toddler's face. Three Toes slowly sat up and smiled at his prisoner.

With Peter stunned in silence, John took instant action to protect his brother. "Ma! Ma!"

Elisa came dashing in. "Boys, I told you to not bother

our guest." They were growing so very fast, though likely as not didn't understand what she'd said. At the same time, she was pleased that Three Toes had awakened. "Thank God, you're awake…and smiling."

"I am thankful." It wasn't much, but then the chief wasn't a great conversationalist.

"You must be starving, Chief. Let me get you something to eat." She smiled at the twins and went off to fetch some bread and soup that had been warming in anticipation of Three Toes waking up. "Luke should be back soon. He and Jaime went out to corral some wayward longhorns. We look forward to your story."

Ever so slowly, the chief managed to sit up. He could feel his wounds tugging at the stitches Doc had so neatly sewn. "Who?"

"We fetched Doc from Nuecestown. He sewed you together."

Three Toes pointed to the mountain lion skin still laying in the corner with his blanket and bag. "I bring gift for Ghost-Who-Rides and his woman."

It didn't exactly excite Elisa, but she appreciated the Comanche's intent. "We are grateful, Chief."

She urged Peter and John forward. "Chief, these are our boys, Peter and John. Boys, this is our friend, Chief Three Toes."

The chief smiled at the giggling boys. They were just beginning to garble a few words and walk the staggering gait of toddlers. The joyful twins brought back memories of happier days with his own children. He felt a mix of emotions, but maintained his smile. He began to devour the bread and soup Elisa offered. He noticed that she still wore the amulet he had gifted to her. It brought another smile. Friends could assuage pain.

Just then, there was a commotion on the gallery as Luke

stomped the dust from his boots and swept himself with his hat before entering. "Lisa, darling, I'm ho...Chief! You're awake!" He smiled and rushed over to shake his friend's uninjured hand. The twins simultaneously glued themselves to their father's legs.

"It is good to see you, Ghost-Who-Rides."

"It's good to see you smiling. We look forward to hearing your story." Luke stepped back and scanned the chief from head to toe. "It will take several days for you to heal well enough to travel. You can stay here, or I can set up a place beside the barn near the live oak motte."

"The mountain lion skin is my gift to you. The hide needs to be stretched, scraped, and salted. I will be happy to help." Three Toes turned serious for a moment. "What of the man who shot at me?"

Luke smiled. "That was Jaime. He didn't know any better. He's my *vaquero*, the cowboy who helps me with our cattle and our ranch chores. He and his wife Julia live in the cabin. Jaime fetched the doctor who cared for your wounds. We're lucky he missed. He understands now that you're a friend."

Three Toes looked around the room. "Thank you for helping me." He scanned the four walls again. "I agree. It would be better out near motte." It was his inbred call for the freedom of the prairie, of the open skies. He'd be most comfortable in his own shelter under the stars.

"Let's get you settled, and then we can eat and hear your story."

Thorpe cursed the carriage as it swayed and bounced along the rough road to Corpus Christi. It was hot, as the wet blotches under his armpits and the spreading wetness on the front and back of his shirt attested. He carried a bandanna that he used liberally in wiping sweat from his brow. He'd brought extra clothes, and his heavy steamer trunk had already elicited complaints from his hired men.

Thorpe had left Biggs back in San Antonio, as he didn't figure a still-healing, one-armed scoundrel like him would be much help with this task. He determined that he'd deal with Biggs later. As it was, it would be another five days before they arrived in Corpus Christi. He'd likely wind up having to exhume his son's now decomposing corpse. He had struggled unsuccessfully for years to be close to Gascon, and now he found the distance insurmountable. He was effectively estranged from his family and from the world, a world of his own choosing. He had wealth, the wealth of things, of money and property. He had power and knew how to exercise it. But Horatio Thorpe found that he sorely lacked any human closeness in his life. He was a lonely man in an ever more meaningless existence and didn't yet understand his own emptiness and pain. He'd poured himself into ever more obsessions, more using women for his own pleasure, more gluttonous eating, and more outside-the-law activities that falsely fulfilled his sense of power and control. He gauged that were his wife to die, he'd be able to more openly pursue the ladies of Texas. He was morally bereft, a lonely shell of a human being that didn't yet fully grasp the cause of his unhappiness.

With San Patricio and Nuecestown along their travel route, he looked forward to at least two nights of relative comfort. He knew that his prodigious size was a huge contributor to his discomfort and resolved once again to lose weight. Thorpe's girth likely contributed to the low self-image that he was constantly over-compensating for, and he intuitively knew that. Heaven forbid that anyone dared criticize his near-morbid obesity. He feared guns, but

Horatio Thorpe was more likely to die of complications from his excessive weight. Even his stride had begun to resemble a waddle, and his back, knees and ankles were sources of pain.

Given Thorpe's nature, no one would be surprised at the fact that he didn't dwell on his son's death or show any signs of grief. In fact, his thinking began to drift to the possibility of finding Scarlett Rose. He dreamed of the creative ways he might reprise their bedroom antics from a couple of years ago when she was whoring back in Laredo. If by chance he were to encounter her...well, his arm could be twisted to give her a tumble.

His thoughts also drifted to that Texas Ranger Captain Luke Dunn. Dunn was now the bane of his existence. He needed to rid himself of that annoying Ranger if he was going to be truly free to operate. Intuitively, he knew better than to dirty his hands with directly disposing of Dunn. Better to use a hired gun and thereby mitigate any risk. Ironically, he would be spitting distance from Dunn's primary living spaces. If he was up to it and so close, he could do the deed himself. But hand in hand with his unsavory nature was cowardice.

He'd hired four men to accompany him to Corpus Christi. Two of them already had exploits that had run them afoul of the law. The other two...well...their destiny was now tied to Thorpe. The two better-armed of the four rode as outriders, while the others served as driver and guard, respectively. The latter were more like manservants to set camp, cook, drive, and tend to whatever other personal needs suited his whims. For his part, Thorpe's aversion to having armed people near him were cause for concern. He could only hope that the promise of future employment would keep these ne'er-do-wells from even thinking of harming him.

Thorpe's destiny for the present lay ahead on the road to Corpus Christi. It remained to be seen what might befall him. Meanwhile, he dreamed of Luke Dunn's demise and wild bedroom romps with that red-haired Laredo whore.

Three Toes had finished sharing his tale beginning with he and his family abandoning the agency at Camp Cooper and ending with his post-massacre search for Roy Biggs. Peter and John spent the time playing at his feet in childhood oblivion to his story. The boys were growing like weeds in a poorly tended flower garden. Elisa and Luke strove to avoid reacting to the boys' inevitable face-plants on the wood floors. For now, they played. It would be many years before the twins would be able to fully understand how the Comanche's life had impacted their own family for better and worse.

Luke was especially concerned about Three Toes's exploits at the Nuecestown ferry landing. "We better keep you out of sight, my friend. The folks in town won't soon forget you killing those men. Sorry as it might be, they don't especially care for your race to begin with." He knew better than to even intimate that he'd arrest the chief. He smiled. "The sooner we can get you healthy and to a safer place the better."

"I am grateful to you and Elisa. I do need to make arrows and find bullets for the gun."

Elisa gave a cat-swallowed-the-canary grin, nodded knowingly at Luke, and walked over to a trap door that had been built into the floor of the parlor. She lifted the heavy door, reached down, and withdrew a large satchel. "We've been saving these for a long time." She opened the satchel to reveal the quivers filled with arrows from the Comanche warriors that she and Luke had killed a couple of years back when they had attacked the ranch. The memory flashed briefly through her mind but was quickly forgotten given the brighter side of the moment as she saw Three Toes's eyes widen.

Three Toes smiled broadly. "I am grateful." He accepted the quivers and their arrows. Despite the pain from his wounds, his spirits had been lifted. "Maybe arrow here for Biggs?" His involuntary chuckle at the thought was touched with a bit of regret at the opportunity he'd missed just days earlier.

"There's a price, Chief." Elisa had an agenda. "I have been grateful for the peace you shared with your gift of the amulet. Now I have one for you. This is a symbol of the God, the Great Spirit, that watches over all people." She handed the savage Comanche chief a Sterling silver cross hung from a bone-bead necklace.

Luke was as surprised as the chief. "Indeed, my friend, you will have great power surrounding you."

"And love, Lucas...and love." Elisa didn't want the part most important to her left out.

Three Toes hung the gift around his neck. "This good. Love good." He was a long way from becoming anything resembling a Christian, but he'd unwittingly accepted a piece of the faith that many White men held to. He felt at peace in this non-judgmental place. He'd shared what was in his heart about the massacre of his people and his fulfilling, yet hollow seeking of vengeance. He shook his head as though to leap out of a sort of trance brought on by such thoughts of peace. It was all certainly counter to the traditions of the Comanche. "Let us see to my shelter."

Luke and Three Toes walked out the front door. There on the gallery was the mountain lion skin already on a stretching rack, well-scraped and salted. Luke's and the chief's eyes met in mutual acknowledgment. "It is a worthy gift, Chief. We are grateful." While the lion's attack had been pure chance, Luke well understood the effort Three Toes had made in skinning the beast and the chance he'd taken in seeking out the Dunns.

Thorpe had spent two nights camping by the roadside, and there was a measure of relief as the carriage pulled up to the hotel in San Patricio. It promised some level of respite, both in terms of sleeping in a comfortable bed and eating a decent meal. He might even savor one or more of the lovely ladies of the town. After he'd settled in, he gave his hired hands some extra money to do as they wished so long as they were ready to go early. He was ever more anxious to get to Corpus Christi and get this part of his life behind him. By now, his wife had gotten the news of Gascon's death. He'd not as yet received any response, not a surprise given the slowness of communications in southern Texas. He'd already gotten used to having the newfangled telegraph up in Austin and missed it in these untamed parts of Texas.

Against his better nature, such as that was, he found himself drawn to the saloon up the street from the hotel. Given that he'd taken on an obsessive compulsion about guns stemming from his intense fear of being shot, he could smell the gunpowder and even the metallic odor of guns as he entered. Despite the stench of booze, tobacco, and sweat permeating the walls and floors, nothing seemed able to drown out the smells that fed his fear. Everyone in the place had guns except him and the whores. Could be that even those ladies had guns.

With his size, he did draw a bit of attention. He sidled

up to the end of the bar, tapping a dollar gold piece in a puddle of whiskey. It wasn't missed by the barkeep who nearly fell over himself to rush over. "Which of these ladies is the very best, barkeeper?" He laid the coin flat with his hand over it.

The bartender figured he was going to help make one of the ladies a good bit of money that night. "Eve over there, the light-haired woman, would make you a very happy man, sir."

Thorpe nodded. "I'll take your word for it." He lifted his hand and motioned to the barkeep to fetch Eve. He liked what he saw from his vantage point at the bar. He doubted she'd make him forget his red-haired Laredo whore, but he'd give her a try.

The barkeep excused himself, went over to the woman, and whispered in her ear.

The woman in question was entertaining a couple of cowboys at that moment. She looked up, batted her long eyelashes, and smiled winsomely at Thorpe as the barkeep finished delivering his invitation. She sized him up, noting that while he was overweight, his attire was high-end fashion. She made a likely lame erstwhile promise to return to the two cowboys and slinked over to Thorpe.

Thorpe looked down at her and grinned, as she drew close enough that her breasts were lightly pressed against him.

"Is all of you big, mister?" She offered her sexiest smile while her eyes danced with dollar signs and her hand found his crotch.

"Eve, right?" He sized her up at close quarters. Her perfume was just heavy enough to arouse him. "Shall we go to my place?"

They were soon out the door and found their way to his room.

Eve was in for a quick evening. Thorpe was not one to care about pleasuring his whores. She was shown the door after less than a half-hour but was five dollars richer for it. For her, it was back to the two cowboys; for Thorpe, it was sleep and dreams of Scarlett Rose.

Back on the road in the morning, everyone seemed none the worse for wear. At least, there'd been no trouble—especially no gunplay.

A couple of more days, and Thorpe and his hired men would be rolling into Nuecestown.

Sheriff Bill Meaney sat with his feet propped on the desk. His spurs had already worn a groove in the desktop. He'd hung his coat and gun belt on the hook by the door, so the badge on his vest was free to catch the shard of sunlight that shot through the front window of his office. He had taken of late to smoking a pipe, and the combination of pipe and easing back with his feet on the desk offered a relaxation of sorts. He watched the smoke swirl in gentle curls toward the ceiling. He picked up the topmost envelope from the small pile on his desk. He nearly lost his balance as he stretched for it. Disconcerting.

It was an official-looking envelope that had arrived by courier from Austin that morning. With his outsized knife of the Bowie variety, he slit it open and pulled out the folded paper from inside.

He took a draw from his pipe and unfolded the paper. The next instant, his feet were firmly on the floor and he was headed to grab a coat and gun and fetch his horse. An hour later, he was pulling up on his well-lathered mount in front of Luke's house at Heaven's Gate. "Luke! Luke Dunn!"

Elisa appeared first. "Bill? What are you all fired up about?"

"I've gotta talk with Luke."

"He's out on the ranch with Jaime checking for strays."

"Which way?" He'd turned his horse to the ready and awaited her response.

"There's a lot of ranch out there, Bill. If you find him, it'll be by chance. Better you should set a spell. It's nearly noon and he took no food, so I expect him back right soon."

Meaney sighed with a measure of frustration and reluctantly dismounted.

"Set a spell, Bill. I'll fetch you some coffee."

As he sat, Meaney scanned the vicinity of the house and noticed the lean-to up near the live oak motte.

Elisa came back out with a steaming cup of coffee and placed it in his hands.

"What's with the campsite up by the motte, Elisa?" He asked as he savored the coffee.

"We have a friend staying with us briefly. He loves the outdoors so camps rather than stay in our house."

Meaney started deducing what that meant. It was most likely either a frontiersman or an Indian. He figured the latter. "What's an Indian doing here, Elisa?"

This was not the sort of attention she and Luke were asking for. "As I said, Bill, he's a friend."

"Tribe?"

"Comanche...a chief named Three Toes."

Meaney scowled. "Only good Indian is a..."

At that precise moment, the chief walked into view from near the live oak motte as Luke and Jaime rode up.

Meaney had reached for his Colt at the appearance of the Comanche, but backed off as Luke and Jaime rode up so as to block the line of sight between him and Three Toes.

"Bill, what on earth are you thinking?"

"What are y'all doing harboring a Comanche?"

"He's a friend. We saved each other's lives and built a friendship, Bill. It's about mutual respect." Luke decided to take a chance and waved Three Toes to join them.

The chief, fresh scars and all, joined them.

"What's that around his neck?" Meaney asked.

Luke shook his head. "What's it look like, Bill?" He motioned Three Toes closer. "Chief, this is Sheriff Bill Meaney from Corpus Christi. Bill, I'm pleased to introduce my friend, Three Toes. Now shake hands with my friend." It was more command than request.

Meaney guardedly grasped the chief's hand and offered an awkward but friendly smile. Then, of a sudden, he remembered the paper he'd ridden so hard from Corpus Christi to share. He pulled the now well-wrinkled paper from his back pocket and handed it to Luke.

"Dang, Bill." Luke read it and handed it to Elisa. "Seems our friends in Austin have learned about Juan Alvarez's activity in Camargo and are trying to raise money for a couple of Texas Ranger companies."

Elisa didn't quite know what to make of the news. She wasn't anxious to lose her husband to a long-term commitment with a military-style policing action. Then again, and given the political nature of these things, it was not likely to happen until this Alvarez character did something more serious than robbing banks and rustling cattle.

"They might ask you to head up a company, Luke. Likely as not, they were impressed with your work leading the whupping on Roy Biggs and his hacienda." Meaney couldn't imagine a more deserving candidate for the role of leading a company of Texas Rangers.

Luke pondered that for a few seconds. "Don't know, Bill. We'll see what develops."

"By the way, that Horatio Thorpe fella is on his way to

Corpus to claim his son's body. He's likely as not holding a grudge against you, but I hear tell he never does his own dirty work. Wouldn't be surprised if he sent Biggs...or what's left of him...here again."

"I understand that they figure Thorpe to have headed up that operation stealing from the Indian agencies and army forts."

"Prostitution, too, Luke. Seems he's obsessed over Scarlett."

That thought riled Elisa. "If he touches her..."

Luke fully understood. "Guess it'd be an excuse to arrest the man. But...and it's a big but...his habit is to have others do his dirty work. They've never caught him actually doing any lawbreaking, at least not so they could prove it."

Up to now, Three Toes had stood quietly taking in the conversation. "Thorpe is bad medicine. He stole from my people. Biggs killed my people." The chief's intentions became crystal clear.

Meaney looked to Luke. "We can't be having anyone taking the law into their own hands."

Luke stroked his mustache. He gathered that Meaney had no idea that Three Toes had single-handedly disposed of the men at the Nuecestown ferry a few days back. "I'm not the chief's keeper, Bill. Shucks, he could do us all a favor as concerns Biggs."

"Surprised to hear you say that, Luke."

"Justice isn't always delivered the way we'd like, Bill. Three Toes is a free man." The implication was that no one could stand in the way of the Comanche's vengeance. "Still..." Luke turned to the chief. "I'd prefer that Three Toes leave Thorpe to us."

Three Toes nodded. "I will give time. Two moons."

Meaney looked inquisitively at Luke. "Two moons?"

Luke chuckled. "He's giving us two months to bring Thorpe to justice, Bill."

Meaney eyeballed the chief intensely. Despite the wounds from his battle with the mountain lion, Three Toes looked every bit the fierce Comanche warrior. He wouldn't give a plug nickel for Thorpe's life if the chief decided to pursue the man. "Seems fair, Luke. I'm okay with it."

"Three Toes's solution sure would be efficient, Bill, but the law is the law."

The chief shook his head slightly. White man's law could be a bit bewildering. Comanche justice would be swift, far swifter than the White man's ways.

"Luke, I'm going to ride up to Nuecestown and let the folks know that this Thorpe fella will be coming through. He may stop at Bernice's boarding house for the night before heading into Corpus. I've heard that he's a large man, traveling by private stagecoach, and likely will have an escort. It's his escort I'm concerned with."

"You want company?"

"You might want to keep your head down, my friend. No sense stirring the man up any more than necessary. At least, not yet." Meaney was satisfied that he'd convinced Luke to stay put. He noted that Elisa seemed to like the idea. "I'll be on my way, then." Meaney bade farewell, even respectfully acknowledging Three Toes.

Once Meaney was out of sight and Three Toes had returned to his shelter by the barn, Elisa felt she could talk freely. "What if Mr. Ford offers you the opportunity to lead a company of Texas Rangers, Lucas?"

"Let's not fret over that just yet, Lisa." He took both her hands in his and stared deeply into her eyes. Her eyes always seemed to be smiling. Luke figured it was the Irish in her.

THIRTEEN
MANEUVERS AT CAMARGO

BOL RICHARDS WAS SITTING on the front step of the Nuecestown jail as Meaney rode up.

"Bol? That you?" The sheriff cocked his head as though trying to be certain this man was who he thought it was.

"Bill...Bill Meaney. Good to see you," Richards responded with a low gravelly but friendly voice spat from gnarly teeth and a grizzled beard. Richards and Meaney shared a common bond of having fought together in the Texas War for Independence back in 1836. The ensuing twenty plus years had been far kinder to Meaney, as Richards bore the scars of experience gained as trader, trapper, and Indian fighter in the wilds of New Mexico and the Texas western frontier, also known as the Comancheria. He'd nearly made it to Texas in time to help defend the Alamo with his friend Colonel Jim Bowie of Bowie knife fame, but weather and hostile Kiowas had delayed his travels and possibly saved his life. Bowie and more than a hundred Texans lost their lives at the Alamo at the hands of General Santa Anna.

"What brings you here, Bol?"

"I'm not getting any younger, Bill. Thought I might head down to Corpus Christi and see what honest work I might stir up." He caught Meaney's curious look. "Oh…my voice. Had a bit of a knife fight with some Mexicans a few years back in Santa Fe. Lucky to have kept my head."

Meaney recalled that Richards was a man you'd want beside you in any sort of scrap. He knew that Richards was an ardent Texas patriot that had strongly opposed the Republic joining the United States. In fact, it was likely what had motivated him to head west into the wild country.

"I just left a friend of mine who might soon be mustering a Texas Ranger company. If that's of interest, I'd be pleased to introduce you."

"How's he stack up against Hays and Walker?" Jack Hays was one of the toughest and most effective Rangers ever to have led a company and Walker, for whom Samuel Colt named one of his revolvers, had been every bit as capable. They'd cleaned up South Texas of Mexican bandits with a policy of capture and hang. That hadn't set well with many folks in Texas, but it was effective.

"Bigger and meaner, Bol. Understand he fought with Irish rebels against the British before he came to Texas. Rode with Callahan a couple of years back chasing Apache. Solid tracker, great marksman, natural leader, more than a match for any lawbreaker. Gained quite a reputation for bringing justice to the Nueces Strip."

"Must have a weakness," Bol pondered.

"Only if you consider that he's a family man with a growing ranch near here. Doesn't seem to stop him from chasing lawbreakers. Hell, he's been shot serious enough to kill most men, and it hasn't slowed him a lick."

"Damn, Bill. I gotta meet this fella." Richards thought on that a moment. "So you're sheriff around here?" He was impressed with how well-outfitted Meaney was. "Must pay pretty well, Bill."

"Folks respect you more if you dress for the job, Bol." He hadn't meant any disrespect to Richards, who stood in stark contrast before him wearing well-weathered buck-skins and moccasins along with a nondescript broad-brimmed felt hat. "Look, Bol, I need to see a couple folks before I head back to Corpus. Hang on, and we'll go together. I'll introduce you to Captain Dunn on the way."

Richards nodded, and Meaney went on to alert the town to the impending arrival of Horatio Thorpe.

★

His captains had been working out exceptionally well. They were fast learners, and Alvarez needed them to be. He didn't know how much time he'd have before Benito Juarez came to power and decide that Alvarez was a liability to his cause.

"*Soldados, ven aquí.*" Captains Villa and Gonzalez gathered around the old oak table along with a couple of care-fully chosen men who served as adjutants. If anyone fell in a fight, there'd be someone to step into the leader role. Alvarez went on to explain the strategy he planned to use to capture the Nueces Strip. By his latest estimates, he had perhaps two hundred *soldados*. He calculated that he'd double or even triple his force by recruiting sympathizers along his attack route. "*Tomamos Brownsville y luego Corpus Christi.*" Gonzalez's and Villa's eyes lit up at hearing Corpus Christi. That was a big target. Alvarez explained that, with the east coast of the Nueces Strip under his control, he could leave small occupying forces and begin to move westward. The US Army at Fort Ringgold would respond far too late. Alvarez planned to torch Nuecestown and its ferry and then move through San Diego to Laredo where he'd take on troops at Fort McIntosh. The key to a successful campaign depended upon recruiting.

The past two weeks had been spent practicing military-style maneuvers in the pastures outside his ranch at Camargo. He wasn't certain whether Juarez's man Santana was watching or not. At this point, he was far enough along that Juarez couldn't possibly respond quickly enough. Santana's presence didn't matter so long as Alvarez launched his invasion in the next few days.

"No más maniobras. ¡Mañana invadimos!" There'd be no further practice maneuvers. The invasion would be launched the next day. Villa and Gonzalez saluted smartly and went to make final preparations. They had stored supply wagons and a pair of cannons near Matamoros. Thus, they wouldn't initially be bogged down but rather could move rapidly on horseback. It would take six days moving under cover of darkness to reach Matamoros. Once there, they'd remove camouflage from the wagons and canons and immediately cross the Rio Grande into Brownsville. They'd bypass Fort Brown right under the noses of the US Army, leave a small force of three dozen *soldados*, and then sweep north to Corpus Christi.

The sun was casting its initial golden glow as it set on the western prairie. Luke and Elisa sat cuddled on a new bench enjoying the view from the gallery. Luke was officially healed from his wound and awaited orders from Rip Ford.

They were drawn to the sound of horse hooves before

they could actually make out Meaney and a companion on the trail into Heaven's Gate. Luke waved as the two riders pulled up.

"Welcome again, Bill. I assume all is well in Nuecestown?"

Meaney and Richards dismounted, tipping their hats to Elisa. "Luke, this is an old friend of mine. Bol Richards here fought with me at San Jacinto way back twenty some years ago. Bol, this here is Luke Dunn and his wife, Elisa."

"My pleasure, Bol."

Elisa was a bit more welcoming. "We've eaten our evening meal, gentlemen, but I'd be happy to offer you some buttered cornbread."

"That's right tempting, Mrs. Dunn. We'd be much obliged."

As Elisa went inside to fetch the cornbread, Meaney explained Richards's situation and especially his history. "He's about the best man to team with in a fight, Luke."

"Think you might want to be a Ranger if Austin calls us up, Mr. Richards?"

Bol was already taken aback by the imposing figure that Luke presented. He could readily see why men would not be especially inclined to take Luke on in a fight. "You can call me Bol, Captain. I'd take Texas pay but never federal money."

Luke tried not to show concern for Richards's comment. He wasn't generally one to involve himself in politics. "I'm not sure when or if the Rangers will be formed up, Bol. I'm sure Bill here can help you find something to do in Corpus Christi while we wait."

Elisa served up the hot cornbread, which the men devoured ravenously. They were getting ready to depart for Corpus when Jaime came running up about as fast as his legs could carry him. "*Señor Dunn! Señor Dunn!*"

Richards froze and his hand went instinctively to his gun.

Luke as quickly drew his Colt. "Whoa, Bol. This is my *vaquero*, Jaime."

"He's a damned Mexican."

Luke looked at Meaney and then back at Richards. "Damned right he is, and you'd best change your thinking if you hope to Ranger with me, Richards."

Jaime was breathing heavily from his run, but was very much aware of the imminent threat.

"No problem, Jaime. What's so important?"

"Juan Alvarez captured Brownsville and is marching toward Corpus Christi."

Luke's jaw dropped. "The march north likely won't be much of a problem for him. There's no opposition to speak of. Pretty clear he's aiming to wreak havoc on Corpus Christi." It was as obvious to Luke as the mustache on his face. He turned to Jaime. "How many men does he have?"

"It is said he's recruiting along the way. My cousin says he'd got four hundred men. Oh, and he has cannons. Two of them."

Elisa had emerged just long enough to hear Jaime's report. "No Texas Rangers and no soldiers. What do we do?"

"Bill, if Lieutenant Belknap is still encamped up near San Patricio, maybe we can fetch him in time. We dare not let Alvarez get near Corpus. Our defense must be set up well south of the city."

Meaney had mounted and was ready to head to Corpus with Richards. "I'll see how many defenders we can muster, Luke. I doubt we'll gather more than a couple of dozen, and we have no cannon."

"I hear tell there's a man 'o war anchored out in the gulf.

Think they might share a cannon or two?" Luke's logic was that the US military would want to help.

"They've been setting out there for two weeks, Luke. Their guns would be useless to us out there on the Gulf. All I can do is ask."

Luke hastily scribbled a note. "Bill, have a courier carry this to Lieutenant Belknap. Hopefully, he hasn't left San Patricio."

"Will he join us?"

"I expect he's itching for a fight. After our experience with Roy Biggs's hacienda, I'm confident he'll bring his troops to join us. Now, see to the courier and those ship cannons if you will. We've likely only got three or possibly four days to bring this all together."

An increasingly familiar gravelly voice piped up. "I'd be pleased to help, Captain Dunn." Richards was already beginning to respect Luke and his ability to grasp and react effectively to tenuous situations.

Meaney and Richards headed out to Corpus Christi while Luke prepared to head to Nuecestown.

Alvarez had force-marched his men nearly to within fifty miles of Corpus Christi. The men were exhausted. It was at such moments that fateful mistakes were made.

He walked among the men. They were obviously tired and several had been wounded in small skirmishes yet gamely carried on.

"*Los hombres necesitan descanso, Coronel.*" Even Gonzalez and Villa, his trusted captains, were dead tired.

"*Los soldados pueden descansar hasta la mañana.*" The men could rest until morning. The final march toward attack on Corpus Christi would begin at dawn.

Horatio Thorpe saw the courier gallop through Nuecestown on his way north. It struck him that the haste of the rider was in contradiction to the obvious peace and quiet of the town. He was unaware of the wild goings on faced by Nuecestown in the past several months, ranging from Carlos Perez's attack, to Dirk Cavendish's killing, to stopping Berne Culthwaite, and defeating Thaddeus Brown and General Truax. Indeed, the seeming serenity stood in stark contrast to the reality of life on the Nueces Strip. His son's killing simply added another chapter to the story. Just as surely, there would be more chapters added to the Nuecestown legacy.

Bernice had heard Thorpe's coach and opened her door before he could knock. "May I help you?" She was momentarily taken aback by the corpulence of the man standing before her. She quickly sized him up as a wealthy man with a penchant for good food...lots of good food.

"Yes, ma'am, my name is Horatio Thorpe and I'd like a room for the night. I'm on my way to Corpus Christi."

"What of your associates?" Bernice gave the four men standing around the coach a visual once-over.

"Don't fret about them, ma'am. They'll camp outside of town."

Thorpe's answer told her a lot about the man she was putting up for the night, at least as concerned what he thought of people. She quickly had him figured out as an unloved and unloving man. "Well, please do sign the guest register. That'll be a dollar in advance. Dinner is at six and breakfast at sunrise."

Bernice ushered Thorpe to a room. One of his hired men soon followed, lugging in a small steamer trunk loaded with Thorpe's personal travel items. She noted that he liked exerting power over folks, though he hadn't attempted to do so with her. Then again, she'd see what if anything might yet evolve.

"Lieutenant...Lieutenant Belknap!" The courier slowed his well-lathered mount to a canter as he approached Belknap's bivouac outside San Patricio. The lieutenant had just been discussing with the sergeant about pulling back from the Strip and abandoning his hunt for any remaining Comanche. He rightly thought of any hunt for Three Toes as pretty much a fool's errand. At best, it would be like trying to find a needle in a haystack.

"I'm Belknap." He waved down the courier. "You have something for me."

The courier handed him the message from Luke. "Damn," he uttered under his breath, as he read the note.

"Excuse me, Lieutenant?" The sergeant hadn't missed the guttural expletive. He read the note Belknap handed to him.

Protocol demanded that Belknap return to Fort Mason for official orders, but there was no time for that. Insurrections wouldn't wait a month for officialdom to act. "Sergeant, break camp. We are heading to Corpus Christi."

The sergeant smiled. Belknap was becoming his kind of officer. "Yes, sir!"

Belknap turned to the courier. "Rest a while, young man. You're welcome to follow us." He looked at the still-panting horse. "Sergeant, let this man borrow one of our pack horses lest his mount breaks down."

"Pleased to meet you, Mr. Thorpe." Luke had arrived in Nuecestown at dinner time and stopped to visit Bernice as a step toward gathering the town folk for a meeting about the looming threat from the south.

"So you're the Texas Ranger Captain Luke Dunn I've heard so much about." Thorpe had arisen from his seat out of courtesy and found himself eyeball to eyeball with a man he outweighed by at least a hundred and fifty pounds yet he felt that Luke was the bigger man. He was instantly envious of the larger-than-life legend and sworn enemy with whom he was shaking hands. This man had killed... no...murdered his son.

"I'm sorry you are on so sad an errand, Mr. Thorpe. I am deeply saddened for your loss. Would it had turned out otherwise."

Thorpe didn't quite know what to make of Luke. This man was not some bloodthirsty killer lawman proud of having dispatched his son. Thorpe was mostly speechless and sat back down to his meal.

"I'd accomplish the retrieval of your son's body right quickly, Mr. Thorpe. There's an insurrection of Mexicans approaching Corpus Christi, and it's likely to get right nasty in a couple of days."

With that, Luke turned his attention to Bernice and Agatha. "Ladies, I'd appreciate it if you could gather as many folks as possible so I can explain what we're facing in Corpus."

The ladies left to round up whatever town folk they could.

As he turned to leave, Luke redirected himself to Thorpe. "Sorry we couldn't have met under better circumstances, Mr. Thorpe. If you'll excuse me, I'll see to alerting these folks of possible danger." In his mind, he was sizing up Thorpe. What was driving the man? Was it just lust for power? Greed? Avarice? He seemed civil enough, but there were obvious deep character flaws. He showed not the slightest grief, not a hint of emotion over the death of his son...not even in the presence of his son's killer.

Luke did his duty in Nuecestown and headed back to Heaven's Gate. He did recruit a couple of volunteers from the little town, so would feel encouraged when he headed to Corpus Christi in the morning. He prayed that the courier had found Belknap and that the lieutenant was heading to join forces with the good citizens of Corpus Christi.

FOURTEEN
THE STRIP SET AFIRE

JUAN ALVAREZ WAS CONTAINING his temper as best he could. Captains Gonzalez and Villa were having difficulty sustaining the rebellious fervor of the men under their command. Transitioning from rustling cattle to shooting and being shot at hadn't been so easy after all, even on a small scale. Plus, he was worrying as to whether the men holding Brownsville had the discipline to keep order, especially with the possibility of the garrison of troops from Fort Brown counter-attacking. He was relying on the townspeople to rally to his cause.

"¡Debemos apresurarnos a Corpus Christi ahora! ¡Prepara a los soldados para moverse!" They couldn't afford to bask in the easy victories along the march to Corpus Christi, but needed to move out quickly to attack the port city. Corpus was the lynchpin in Alvarez's strategy. There could be no wasted time. He had swelled his ranks to nearly five hundred, though as few as half actually bore firearms. The remainder made do with farm implements and enthusiasm to defeat the gringos and win the Nueces Strip for Mexico.

By this time, he also assumed that a clarion call had

gone out to citizens in the area around Corpus Christi to defend the city. Alvarez would need every man he could muster. Until now, he'd only needed the threat of his cannons, but soon he might actually have to use them.

★★

"Ghost-Who-Rides, do you remember what the man did defending his hacienda? Remember the prairie fire? This is old Comanche way. If wind is right, you can panic enemy and defeat larger force." Three Toes had packed his lodging and supplies and was preparing to depart from Heaven's Gate. With so many people settling in the region, the recent spate of visitors to Heaven's Gate and prospect of a Mexican uprising, it was becoming far too crowded for him to stay.

"You won't stay for the battle?" Luke smiled, though he understood the chief's yearning to reach the comparative freedom of the Comancheria. He appreciated the chief's warfare advice, and he wished Three Toes could stay.

"I am thankful for your help, Ghost-Who-Rides. Your woman is what your people call a blessing. She is strong, Luke Dunn." He fondled the gift of the cross on the bone necklace Elisa had presented to him. "You have strong medicine, my friend."

"I pray that you find your people, Three Toes. You should not have to be alone." Luke got to thinking that his own people would surely welcome him back to the tribe. In a perfect world, he might even have been given a new name, like Lion Slayer. He stepped toward Three Toes and pressed a small leather bag into the chief's hand.

Three Toes peered inside and smiled broadly. Luke had gifted him with the claws from the mountain lion. "It is good gift, Ghost-Who-Rides." Three Toes smiled almost mischievously. "Roy Biggs still awaits my lance." The Comanche chief climbed aboard his pony. "Give my best to lieutenant. He is good man."

As he turned to leave, Elisa stepped out onto the gallery. "Three Toes. You're leaving? Are you not going to say goodbye to me?"

"Saying goodbye makes me sad. I seek to ease that pain." He sighed deeply and put his hand to his chest. "You are both in my heart." With that, he turned his pony and headed out toward the welcome freedom of the open prairie.

★★

"There's no location fully suitable to defend Corpus Christi. It's not as though there's a high ground with a commanding view." Meaney was explaining to Luke and Lieutenant Belknap the challenge they faced. He related how terrain was partly why Sam Houston chose San Jacinto with its marshes and oak groves that gave the Texians a distinct advantage over Santa Anna's forces. The rolling expanse of the Nueces Strip terrain southwest of Corpus Christi offered little tactical advantage. It was going to boil down to a small, but determined group of defenders.

So there they were, a motley group of Luke Dunn, Gordon Belknap, Bill Meaney, Horace Rucker, and Bol Richards, along with a few volunteers set on determining the fate of the Nueces Strip and keeping Texas in one piece.

"Did you convince the captain of that navy ship to spare a couple of cannons?"

Meaney sighed and looked over at Belknap. "The captain is some dandy from Massachusetts who chose to look down his long nose at me and Bol as unwashed trail dirt. I suspect that the good captain never faced a lick of high-stakes battle in his life. Perhaps our fine lieutenant here would have better luck."

"I'll give it a try." Belknap was not surprised at the navy man's reaction. There seemed to always be more competition than cooperation between the military services. But this was an invasion, albeit small, of the United States. "We have a common foe. We really must have that cannon."

Luke agreed but was thinking more aggressively. "If need be, we can commandeer the bloody cannons. I'd hate to have to do that, but will so order if necessary. We don't have time to withhold supplies to his ship, or I'd counsel that action." He stroked his mustache. "Feel free to imply our threat of force to the captain, Lieutenant."

Belknap locked eyes with Luke. He'd experienced what the Texas Ranger captain could accomplish and had no doubt that he'd get those cannons one way or another. He liked the way Luke took action. "Let's get a couple of shallow-draft boats big enough to haul those cannons. We need the ship captain to fully appreciate our intentions." Belknap motioned to his sergeant to exit, so they could prepare to requisition the cannons. "Sergeant, we'll need four men... fully armed. Sheriff, would you be kind enough to get us those boats as quickly as you can?" He nodded to Luke, and the sergeant followed him out the door.

"Sheriff, there's a slight ridge line about fifteen miles to the southwest toward Richard King's ranch. I'm thinking that's where we set our defense."

"Works for me, Luke. I'm gonna see to those boats for the lieutenant while you work the details with Bol and the reverend here."

"One last thing, Bill. Has Horatio Thorpe shown up yet to claim his son's body?"

Meaney smiled. "Cold, Luke. That man is stone cold. Yes, he claimed his son's body early this morning and couldn't get out of Corpus fast enough. Treated that boy's body like a side of beef. Dug it up, wrapped it, and threw it on top of their damned stagecoach. I think he might have hung around but feared the invasion he'd heard about."

Luke wasn't surprised. "I'm sure we haven't heard the last of him, Bill." He turned to the others. "Well, let's go see the ground we're going to defend."

Alvarez skirted wide to the east of Richard King's ranch, as his strategy was to approach Corpus Christi from the south. By now, he figured the city had certainly been alerted and would be defended. It would be the first true test of his *soldados*.

The ground north from Brownsville had been easy to take and hold, as the heavy Mexican heritage population was sympathetic to his cause and offered little or no resistance. Flushed with success and anxious for more victories, the only thing slowing them were the very necessary cannons.

Captains Gonzalez and Villa joined him in his tent. "*¿Podemos confiar en los voluntarios?*" It was a huge question. Half his force was made up of volunteers recruited along his path from Brownsville. Could they be relied upon?

"*Por supuesto, Coronel.*" Gonzalez could always be relied upon to give the answer Alvarez wanted to hear. Of course, they could count on the volunteers. This was about patriotism and reacquiring territory that was rightfully part of Mexico.

Villa nodded agreement, but with reservation. "*Nuestros soldados deben liderar y ganar con la primera carga.*" He opined that they must lead with their core of trained soldiers and win with the initial charge. "*Los voluntarios seguirán.*" His implication was that the volunteers would break and run if there were any sign of a difficult battle.

Alvarez nodded. *"Tienes razón, Capitán."* Villa was quite right. All would rest upon the initial charge.

In the afternoon of the next day, they'd be within striking distance of Corpus Christi.

The captain was alerted to the approaching boats and was quick to stand at the gunnel amidships. "Who the hell is this?" It was mostly a rhetorical question to the sailor standing beside him. The captain was actually a wet-behind-the-ears lieutenant and recent graduate of the Naval Academy in Annapolis. His ship, the John Adams, was a second-class frigate called a corvette and carried modest armament of twenty-four guns. Approaching him were two boats with a US Army officer standing in the lead boat.

"Permission to come aboard, Captain."

What was the captain to do? "What's your business here, sir?"

Belknap saluted. "Lieutenant Gordon Belknap, United States Army from Fort Mason. I wish to come aboard and parlay." He noted that Meaney had been right. The ship's captain had a snooty nose that he looked haughtily down the length of when he spoke. He almost laughed at the absurdity of it.

"Permission granted. First mate, help the lieutenant come aboard."

Belknap climbed on board the ship, accompanied by the sergeant.

The formalities over, Belknap sought to get down to business. Time was of the essence. "Captain, the United States is being invaded by an upstart force of several hundred Mexicans. Brownsville has been captured, and this armed force intends to attack Corpus Christi. Your guns will be useless from this distance." He let this first information sink in. The captain was nodding that he understood the situation. "We would like to borrow two of your cannon to assist in repelling the invaders. Happy to return them after our victory." He could see the captain's expression change and observed his arms cross over his chest. It was a very negative posturing.

"Do you have orders?" the captain demanded.

"Damn, what are they teaching at the academy?" was in Belknap's conscious thinking. "Orders? This is an emergency, Captain."

"I won't release naval weapons without authorization, Lieutenant."

Belknap gave a nearly imperceptible nod to the sergeant, and the ship was quickly boarded by four armed soldiers who promptly surrounded the captain.

"What is the meaning of this, Lieutenant?"

"I believe our meaning is quite obvious, Captain. We are borrowing two of your cannons, with or without your permission. If you have a problem, report me to your superior officers by all means. But I'll have you hung for treason as aiding an invading force."

The captain was simultaneously confused and fearful. The ship crew looked for his command to take action. With a bayonet to his chest, he didn't find himself in a position to order armed action. He let out a deep sigh of resignation. "Take the damned cannons, Lieutenant. But you'd damned well better return the bloody things."

While two men guarded the captain, two cannons and several cannonballs and a supply of black powder were lowered into the boats.

"We are grateful for your gracious offering, Captain.

You are most welcome to come and observe how a small force of patriotic Texans can defeat a much larger force of ill-trained invaders."

The sarcasm wasn't lost on the ship's captain. By now, he was resigned to accepting his fate. "I just may join you, Lieutenant. We have a half-dozen Marines onboard and they're fine marksmen."

"By all means, Captain. We'd welcome you and your men." Belknap chuckled at the irony and was grateful his impromptu borrowing of the cannons had gone well.

Unbeknownst to Alvarez, the troops at Fort Brown had finally responded to the action in Brownsville, took the *soldados* prisoner, and dispersed the volunteers. Now two companies were headed north and would arrive just south of Corpus Christi about the time Alvarez engaged the Corpus Christi defenses. In the eyes of the military, his overconfidence had been almost laughable had it not been for the hate and discontent he'd stirred up.

Down in Veracruz, Benito Juarez was horrified and preparing an apologetic message to Texas and the United States government aimed at distancing himself from the rabble-rousing Alvarez.

"I think we're about as ready as we're going to be, men." Luke had directed Belknap to position the cannons a hundred yards apart and have them loaded with canister. Their effect would be devastating. The Marines guarded the left flank, while Belknap's troopers took the right. Luke, Meaney, Richards, and the other civilian defenders including a handful of Mexicans would hold the center. Off to the left between the defenders and the Gulf of Mexico was a small group under Rucker's leadership. They were a sort of secret weapon. Altogether, the defenders were a ragtag but potentially highly effective force against ill-trained Mexicans.

They heard Alvarez's army approach before they saw them. It was mid-morning and the sun was already casting its scorching rays upon the lines of quick-marching men. The Mexicans were singing, carrying on boastfully, and generally seeming to be in great spirits. It was clear that Alvarez had blundered by not sending any point men to scout for the Corpus Christi defensive line. He was a mere three hundred yards away.

Alvarez was riding in the lead. He crested a rise in the grasses to find the defenders arrayed in full view before him. *"¿Dios mío, qué es esto?"* He signaled Villa and Gonzalez to spread the men to the flanks. The cannons were still well behind in his rear, and there was no time to bring them into action. *"¡Consigue el cañón!"* He called for the cannons, but immediately recognized they'd be defensive weapons at best. His choices were to retreat or charge. *"¡Prepárate para cobrar!"* The choice was made—they'd charge.

Waving his sword, Alvarez urged his captains to rally the *soldados* to charge. He spurred his horse and headed for the Texan lines with his *soldados* following. Four hundred Mexican rebels bore down on about forty defenders.

"Hold your fire!" Luke wanted the canister to have the greatest effect. Patience was hell. Seconds passed. At about fifty yards, Luke gave the command. "Fire!"

The canister devastated Alvarez's lines. Dozens fell— killed instantly, dying, or wounded. His men hesitated. Pistol and rifle fire swept into the wavering ranks. Another round of canister tore into his men. Alvarez, wounded by gunfire, continued to wave his sword as he rode to within mere feet of the defenders. He saw Gonzalez go down. Perhaps half his force had been wiped out. "¡Retroceden! ¡Retírense!" He called to fall back, to retreat.

Alvarez took another bullet as he reached the line where his cannon had finally been set up. Now he faced Luke's secret weapon. The breezes were coming in strong from the gulf. Perfect! Rucker and his men lit the grasses, and the wind blew a hundred-yard swath of smoke and fire at Alvarez's line. His men were now thoroughly confused and insanely frightened. The volunteers began to flee south-ward, barely in front of the flames. A mile or so, and they'd run headlong into the troops from Fort Brown.

Juan Alvarez was not ready to surrender—he and Villa stood fast with a dozen remaining *soldados*. Years of built-up resentment fueled a crazed passion within him. He tried to fire a cannon. It had not been loaded or primed. He went to the second cannon. Same result. His horse was shot from under him by the advancing defenders who by now sensed their victory. "¡Yo muero por México!" He hoped those would be his final words. Waving pistol and sword, he went down in a hail of bullets that mostly missed. Although badly wounded, Alvarez was the only prisoner.

A silence fell over the battlefield as the sound of the final shots trailed off. The fire burned out, as grass fires most often did. Luke stood tall astride Big Horse and surveyed what had been wrought. As if on cue, a tumbleweed rolled across the still-smoldering grass. Corpus Christi, nay, the entire Nueces Strip had been saved from further mayhem.

Belknap drew up beside Luke. "Congratulations, Captain Dunn." He gave the "order arms" salute to Luke, as he raised his saber upward and touched the hilt to just in front of his face. It was the highest tribute he could think of at the moment. Over his shoulder, he could see that the ship's captain had reclaimed his cannons and Marines and was heading back to Corpus Christi. Likely as not, he was not inclined to admit his reluctant contribution to what turned out to be a rapid and quite decisive victory.

"Lieutenant, we whupped 'em good! Thanks for your help." Luke tipped his hat in return to Belknap's order arms salute.

A gravelly voice emanated seemingly from nowhere. "Damn, Captain Luke Dunn. You are one damned good Texas Ranger!"

Luke blushed slightly and stroked his mustache as he watched the tumbleweed disappear from sight. Off in the distance, they could see the approaching Stars and Stripes and the unit standards of the troops from Fort Brown. He looked at the mortally wounded Alvarez in the custody of Sheriff Meaney.

"Bol, thanks for your help. I'll be back to you about Rangering. Lieutenant, I'd much appreciate you helping Sheriff Meaney clean up here before you head back to Fort Mason. You can hand what remains of our prisoner over to the troops marching up from Fort Brown. I understand he's the Juan Alvarez my *vaquero* Jaime was talking about." Luke patted Big Horse's neck. "I'm gonna head up to Nuecestown and Heaven's Gate to let folks know that all's well. Oh, you're welcome to stop by the ranch on your way north."

FIFTEEN
THREE TOES'S QUEST

MORE HILLS, more trees. Three Toes couldn't suppress a smile. The hills and woodlands of the hill country beckoned. It was where his heart lay. Slowly, he made his way skirting danger on a path wide to the west of San Patricio.

Images of Roy Biggs ruminated in the deepest recesses of his subconscious mind. Where was the man with the head of a snake? How and when might they meet? The chief's external wounds were healed, but there were raw wounds inside.

The image he would have struck to someone unfamiliar might be of a solitary, perhaps even lonely, traveler. They couldn't know the twin motivations that drove him nor the sadness that yet festered within his breast.

Twice between San Patricio and San Antonio, he saw small caravans of covered wagons off in the distance. At least once, he saw what appeared to be Kiowa warriors. But Three Toes was intent on not being discovered. He was focused, a man on a mission. His ever-lurking concern was with how to flush Roy Biggs from wherever he was hiding.

★★

Horatio Thorpe had beat a hasty exit from San Antonio. He regretted not having been able to linger to find out more about Luke Dunn and to even find that Laredo whore who'd been the object of his obsessive quest. He cursed the Mexican rebels that had made Corpus Christi temporarily undesirable to him. In his mind, he wasn't going to take the chance that the Nueces Strip might fall back into Mexican control. If it did, he would need to find a way to profit from it. Once he'd finished transporting Gascon's body back to the family cemetery, he'd worry about opportunity in a Nueces Strip conquered by Mexican rebels. If they were unsuccessful, that would be another matter.

For now, he had to get Gascon's body back to the plantation for burial in the family plot. He debated whether to accompany the body, as he was not especially comfortable with having to face his bland ever-patient, ever-tolerant wife. She was likely deeply affected by the loss of her youngest son, and Thorpe hated the idea of facing what would surely be her emotion-driven rantings at him. He was thankful that she'd never know about the task he'd asked Gascon to perform that had gotten him killed. It was his guilt to carry, if he so chose.

There was also the Roy Biggs issue. Dare he give Biggs a second chance at Luke Dunn? The man was now absent one arm. Would it make a difference? Biggs was pure evil, but had his Mephistophelian nature been compromised to the point of not being so useful to Thorpe's mission? He'd have to test the man. In any case, he had managed to save Biggs from the hangman's noose, so the evil son of a bitch owed Thorpe in a huge way.

There was a knock at the door to his suite. He'd sent for Biggs, as he had to deal with the situation before he could head home with Gascon's body. With some discomfort owing to his still recovering from the long carriage ride, Thorpe slowly made his way to the door. "Who's there?"

"Roy. Roy Biggs."

Thorpe cautiously opened the door, scanning Biggs from head to toe as he did so. Biggs had dutifully placed his pistol on the floor next to the door. This was good. "You're a quick learner, Biggs. Come in." He pointed to a chair alongside a large mahogany desk.

"Thanks. Sorry for your loss."

Thorpe proceeded to take the chair opposite. The small expression of condolence to Thorpe over loss of his son was a rarity from a man who'd killed his own wife and essentially fed his children to the wolves.

"How you feeling, Roy?" Thorpe asked, peering at the killer. He saw before him a man that wasn't looking quite so formidable. The snake-like eyes still served as window to the man's soul, but he was physically diminished.

Biggs waved the newly acquired hook that had been attached to where his left hand had been. "You mean am I ready to finish what I started?"

Thorpe nodded.

"I can still ride and shoot and am of a mind to get back at Luke Dunn and his damned wife."

Thorpe carefully observed Biggs's body language, his whole demeanor. Despite the man's words, Thorpe sensed a hint of fearfulness, a loss of just a little confidence. The man earnestly wanted to get his revenge, but he'd been whipped twice by the Texas Ranger. Doubt lingered in Biggs's mind, and Thorpe recognized it. It was understandable, but hardly desirable. He doubted he could fully rely on Biggs. What to do?

"Roy," he said, "I must take care of burying my son back

at the plantation. I need someone I can count on to take care of some business for me in Laredo."

"What about Dunn?"

"That can wait, Roy." He was really saying that Biggs needed to get some rest and do some work that might restore his mental faculties.

"But..."

"You hearing me, Roy? Leave the Texas Ranger alone." He stared intently at Biggs. The man's response reassured him that he was still the embodiment of evil. That having been said, the man's eyes continued to bely him ever so slightly. At the mention of the Texas Ranger, Biggs would almost imperceptibly blink in a disconcerted, reflexive way.

"What do you need me to do, Mr. Thorpe?"

This was better. "I have a storehouse in Laredo. I need to be certain it hasn't been...shall we say...compromised. I've got two reliable men who will accompany you." These two men were the hired guns who had served as guards in accompanying Thorpe to Corpus Christi. Thorpe felt they were reasonably reliable. Left unsaid was that the storehouse contained some of the merchandise that Thaddeus Brown had stolen for Thorpe.

Roy Biggs didn't waste any time setting out from San Antonio with the two companions Thorpe had assigned to him: Cole Hester and Bert Burns. He was anxious to finish this make-work task so he could return to stalking that damnable Texas Ranger whose image still haunted him.

They made great time and soon found themselves nearing San Diego on the Corpus Christi-to-Laredo road that Colonel Kinney had built. The men had begun to get ever-better acquainted.

"What's so special about that Texas Ranger, Roy?" Cole had become intrigued at how Biggs, with more than three dozen killings to his credit, could have failed twice in trying to kill the man.

Biggs might normally have taken Cole's comment as a slight since it implied not so much his failure as his lack of ability. Biggs's hook flashed in the sunlight as he used his arm to wipe a bit of sweat from his brow. The hook added just a slightly more sinister feel to his presence. He decided to let the slight to his abilities pass. "Yeah, he's special. He's a big man...towers over any of us. I think he came from Ireland. Maybe a rebel background. He carries enough weapons for a small army." He had Hester's and Burns's rapt attention. "But that's not what makes him special. It's like he has some spirit, some force around him that gives him an edge. The Ranger's a good tracker. The scary part is that he seems to attract help just when it's needed. I heard that when he ended Bad Bart Strong's string of killing, it was a rattlesnake that did the deed, not a bullet. I also understand that he did shoot and kill Dirk Cavendish. Hell, men like Carlos Perez and Berne Culthwaite have met their demise just getting close to Luke Dunn. I expect I should be grateful I was captured, though the whole thing cost me my arm."

Hester and Burns were listening intently, taking the measure of their companion. "Sounds pretty special, Roy."

"Oh, and the Comanche respect him such that they gave him a name, Ghost-Who-Rides." Biggs looked off into the distance and considered the late afternoon sun. "Let's see if we can make that motte out yonder. It's warm and dry, we've been riding all day, and I'm about ready for some rest."

★★

The Nueces Strip eastern frontier was fast disappearing. Three Toes found himself taking a far wider westward track to avoid ranches and settlements. There were still soldiers and desperados to be concerned with, but he had the advantage of traveling alone. He could be far stealthier.

His solitary situation gave him plenty of time to think. He continued to mull over what might become of his people in the wake of the White man's onslaught. Should he hold to the old traditions? Should he adapt? His hand reflexively rubbed the handle of the Walker Colt in his waistband. In one sense, he'd already begun to adopt the White man's ways. His path took him past a pole stuck in the middle of nowhere. Looking to the north, there were perhaps a half-dozen to be seen from his vantage point. What could the White man be thinking to plant trees with no branches and no roots? Perplexed, he shook his head and moved on.

The daylight was waning, and the chief saw a live oak motte off in the distance. It would be an ideal spot to rest for the night, especially if there was water. He still had dried venison, and Elisa Dunn had taught him the virtues of coffee and given him a small pot. He permitted himself an ironic smile. Coffee had become another of his adaptations of the White man's way. He hoped there'd be no more wayward mountain lions to deal with. As he pointed his pony toward the motte, he noted that the skies were cloudless and the air unusually dry. A good night's rest would surely do wonders for his spirits.

"Rip Ford has asked me to go to Laredo. Seems Thorpe sent a couple of his men there, including our friend Roy Biggs." Luke and Elisa were catching up on the aftermath of the recent attack on Corpus Christi. They'd been blessed to have experienced no casualties, but the Mexicans had been decimated.

Now Elisa was faced with Luke receiving an assignment from Rip Ford. Ford was trying to scrape up the funding to muster out a couple of companies of Texas Rangers, as there was increasing hostility on the Nueces Strip, the US Army was nonresponsive, and it was too much for local sheriffs to handle. "Are you supposed to arrest Biggs?"

"He didn't say, but I think he expects me to do that," Luke said. "The man only has one arm, thanks to your marksmanship, but he'll still be dangerous. I understand he has two of Thorpe's men with him."

Elisa sighed and offered up an unusually wry smile. "Mr. Ford must think a Texas Ranger against three men makes for a fair contest, Lucas." She broke into a little laugh, then got serious again. "What happened to the Mexican that led the attack on Corpus Christi?"

"Politics. Jaime got word from his cousin that they handed Alvarez over to Benito Juarez. I expect Juarez takes none too kindly to any man that would jeopardize his plans for Mexico."

"There's a bit of justice in that, Lucas." She absentmindedly stroked his arm. "You going to head out to Laredo in the morning?"

"First light. I'll stop by in Nuecestown and be sure Dan checks in on you, though Jaime and Julia should be plenty of help."

"Guess you'll be a couple of days or so behind Three Toes. I worry about our friend."

"I hope he returns to his people. Wandering alone doesn't seem to be true to his nature." Luke couldn't help but think on the stark differences among the cultures he'd encountered over his brief life. As a teen in Ireland, he'd witnessed the patriotic uprisings of the clans and the religion-driven oppressions by the British. Here in Texas, the cultural, religious, and political fires constantly flared up and died, whether Mexicans versus Anglos, Indians versus settlers, and preachers versus priests. He'd even begun to see conflict creeping in between cattlemen and farmers and in ranchers versus sheepherders. Coupling powerful forces trying to leverage the economic and social systems for financial and political gain with the winds of change in the air as politicians in Washington took on the issue of slavery, it seemed Luke might never run out of opportunities to deliver justice. Luke gently drew Elisa to him. He could feel her growing belly press against him. His eyes looked deeply into hers. Talk of the state of the world around them was finished for the time being.

Elisa could feel him arousing. She had her real man, and he seemed never to disappoint her. "Back room?" He nodded and kissed her.

Three Toes arrived at the live oak motte and set up his camp. With a small fire to heat his coffee and ease the early evening cool, he enjoyed the dried venison the Dunns had been so kind to give him. He hobbled his ponies, trusting that they never wandered far from him. It seemed as though every star in the heavens was shedding light on the landscape. There was only a half-moon, but it afforded sufficient light to see quite a way off. The chief felt at peace. He'd made his decision to head back north and find his Penateka Comanche people. Perhaps he'd even find another woman. He lay back on his blanket and closed his eyes.

"Slow down, Cole." Biggs had seen the flicker of a

campfire near the live oak motte they had been riding toward. "Someone is at that motte. Dismount, shed your spurs, ready your rifles, and no talking until we see who's there. Watch where you put your feet."

Biggs enjoyed hunting, especially for human prey. He hoped that his companions wouldn't give them away.

They were about fifty yards out when Biggs made out two ponies. He thought he saw feathers attached to the mane of one of the horses, and that might mean they'd happened upon one or more savages. The campfire served as a beacon for Biggs and his men.

Biggs arrived at the campsite first and quickly scanned the scene. Seemed there was only one Indian, a Comanche far as he could figure. The savage was asleep. Then, in the flickering fire, he recognized who he'd happened upon. He got to within arm's length of Three Toes and placed the muzzle of his rifle under the chief's chin. "Wake up, you damned savage," he snarled.

Hester and Burns stood at the ready as Three Toes opened his eyes.

"Don't move, Chief."

Three Toes thought fleetingly about escape, but he knew he'd never make it.

"Turn on your stomach." Biggs knew that Three Toes understood some English. In seconds, the Comanche's hands were bound behind him, and he was sitting up.

Three Toes found himself staring into the most horrifying set of eyes he'd ever imagined.

Biggs's face had turned a dark red, and veins stood out on his forehead and neck. "You're the son of a bitch that threatened my wife." No matter that Biggs had put a 50-caliber Sharps slug through her chest, ostensibly in case she might suffer from Comanche torture. "I thought I'd got you back at your camp on the Pedernales."

Three Toes had suspected it had been Biggs and his band that massacred his family. Now it was confirmed, and he was helpless to do anything about it.

"We have something special for you, Chief." A diabolical grin spread ear to ear across Biggs's face. He scanned the chief's scarred body. "Looks like you tangled with a big cat, Chief." He spewed an evil laugh. "This is gonna be worse...far worse."

Biggs grabbed the necklace Elisa had given Three Toes. "What's a heathen like you doin' with a damned cross? You stealin' skunk!" Biggs threw it down and stomped it into the dirt. "It's been desecrated."

Hester and Burns didn't quite know how to react to all this. They'd seen evil acts before, but this was heading down a route that neither had experienced. "What're you gonna do, Roy?"

"Start digging, men."

Three Toes's eyes widened, though that was the only hint of fear he showed. Biggs wasn't going to simply kill him.

Hester and Burns dug. "How deep, Roy."

"Just keep digging."

At last, they'd finished digging a hole about five feet deep and a couple of feet wide. It'd been tough to dig in the sandy loam soil, as the sides kept caving in.

Biggs proceeded to drive two long stakes deep into the soil about five feet on either side of the hole. "Put the damn Comanche in the hole," he said it with a hate-filled snarl that sent shivers up the spines of Hester and Burns.

They lowered Three Toes into the hole. He didn't resist.

"Tie a rope to each of the damned savage's wrists." Once that was done, he readied for the next step. "Hold tight." Biggs cut the rope that bound Three Toes's wrists together, and they stretched his arms to the stakes. "Tie him to the stakes and then fill the hole."

The chief soon found himself buried up to his armpits.

Biggs sat himself cross-legged in front of Three Toes and stared with all the malicious evil he could muster into the chief's eyes.

Three Toes maintained a passive look, a controlled countenance, almost a trance. He was prepared to endure whatever was meted out.

Biggs slipped his knife from its scabbard. He tested it. It was sharp. He leaned forward and made a dozen vertical cuts on the Comanche's upper chest. He then made similar cuts on Three Toes's cheeks and forehead.

Hester and Burns hadn't seen anything like this before.

Biggs got up to his knees, stretched out, and made cuts along the chief's arms. Blood began to seep into the soil around the body. He turned to the men. "Y'all want a turn?" He made two more parallel cuts on the chief's shoulder, inserted his hook through the two wounds, and yanked hard. It tore Three Toes's flesh and caused excruciating pain.

Cole spoke for them. "I think you have it under control, Roy." He was trying to hold back from throwing up and was grateful his stomach was empty.

Biggs smiled, got up, and walked over to where the chief's ponies were hobbled. He picked up some horse droppings, walked back over to Three Toes, and smeared the excrement all over the exposed body of the Comanche. He forced the chief's mouth open and shoved some inside.

"You're gonna die real slow like, Chief." Biggs had kept the evil grin on his face through the entire process.

By now, Three Toes was grateful that Biggs hadn't thought to scalp him. That was a favored torture of both

Comanche and Apache. As it was, the ants would soon be joining him in his misery.

"We ain't staying here, are we, Roy?"

Biggs pretended to think on it. Part of him did want to watch the chief die a miserable death. He had thought about scalping him, but the blood loss might have hastened his end. He wanted Three Toes to die very slowly. He might even starve before the ants or some scavengers killed him. "No...no, we won't be staying. Let's mount up and get the hell out of here." He figured to ride an hour or so in the starlight, and then bed down.

Three Toes was helpless. The dirt around his chest pressed in and made breathing just a little difficult. He didn't have to wait long for the first ants to appear and have their way with pieces of him. He strained at the straps that bound his wrists, but to no avail.

He saw a few rain clouds gathering. If they reached him, he might get some respite from the ants, though the soil would turn to mud. He didn't look forward to the intense South Texas sun come morning.

At morning light, Luke had already made good headway having passed through Nuecestown, gave Dan a heads up to look in on Elisa and the ranch, let Preacher Rucker know that he was headed to Laredo, and was soon quickly trotting up the road toward San Diego. By his calculation, Biggs was likely a couple of days ahead of him. He hummed an old Irish ballad as he rode. A tumbleweed tumbled aimlessly across his trail.

SIXTEEN
THORPE'S REGARDS

HORATIO THORPE'S carriage rolled unannounced through the ornate gate to his vast plantation and continued up the magnolia-lined roadway to his Georgian-style mansion. It was a classic southern plantation setting. Slave quarters were a half mile or so beyond the big house, and household slaves were now scurrying about as they became aware of his arrival.

Thorpe's wife, a slip of a woman, especially compared to his more-than-ample size, appeared on the veranda. She wore a black dress with matching parasol, and a black veil covered her face.

Thorpe cursed inwardly that she was still alive. He knew she was sick, and he'd rather hoped Gascon's death would push her over the precipice to her grave. Love had long since departed the Thorpe plantation. The carriage rolled to a stop, and the driver leaped down and opened the door. Thorpe eased himself down, being careful to place his foot on the footrest lest he tumble embarrassingly into the gravel drive. He wiped his brow and walked to the veranda. He paused before grasping the handrail, then climbed the steps.

If looks might have killed, the look Thorpe's wife gave him would have finished him. But servants were about, and it wouldn't do to have outward animosity on display. "Hello, Horatio." It was said coldly.

"I've brought Gascon here, Martha. He's lying in back of the carriage."

By this time, the household slaves had brought a casket around. They wasted no time in respectfully laying Gascon's shrouded body inside the box.

"I don't want to see him, Horatio. A grave has been prepared. Just bury him and go." Mrs. Thorpe coughed into a black silk handkerchief. There was blood in her spittle. She wouldn't have many days left in this world.

"I'm sorry, Martha." He wouldn't tell her about Gascon's dalliances in Paris, as it wouldn't matter at this point. He'd been impetuous in his hunt for Luke Dunn, and he wouldn't tell her about that either. "Have you heard from Edward?"

"I told him to stay away." Thorpe's wife discouraged her remaining child from journeying to the plantation, lest he too fall under the perverse influences of his father.

Thorpe bowed ever so slightly to her and silently followed the servants to the family cemetery. A young mulatto girl sang a hymn as they lowered the casket. No question but she had Thorpe's eyes.

With interment over, Thorpe returned to the veranda, but his ailing wife was nowhere to be seen. He shrugged and climbed back into the carriage. He didn't intend to waste time dealing with Martha when he could be getting back to business. Given her condition, he'd likely need to be back soon enough.

Thorpe planned to stop briefly in Austin, and then head to San Antonio to await Roy Biggs.

The air was thick with cigar smoke as Bol Richards found himself trying to find relief from another evening of boredom by drinking whiskey and generally carousing. He wasn't inclined to stand at the bar, had no intentions on any of the local whores, and rather disliked gambling at cards. So he sat alone at a table staring into the whiskey bottle set before him. Every now and then, he'd look up and scan the saloon. No matter his acquaintanceship with Sheriff Bill Meaney or his prospects of joining a company of Texas Rangers if Austin ever managed to find the money to fund them. He was also still wed to the buckskin garb that tended to make him stand out in most any crowd. Richards looked as though he was some hard-case loner mountain man who'd just come in off the fur-trapping lines of western Texas. An ample growth of rough beard stubble amplified that woodsman characterization.

"Mind if I sit here a spell, pilgrim?" The place was crowded, and the man wanted to get off his feet.

There were three empty chairs at Richards's table. He shrugged. "Take a load off, cowboy. Just leave me be." The last thing he wanted was somebody yakking his head off. "And I ain't no pilgrim."

"Thanks. Just trying to be friendly." The man plunked himself down and joined Richards in looking around the room. His silence didn't last three minutes. "Where you from?"

Richards gave him the visual once-over. "You're welcome to sit here, but I don't care to talk."

The cowboy was put off by Richards's less-than-polite response. "Name's Wilson. Yours?"

Richards sighed audibly. "You deaf?" His gravelly voice rather enhanced the impoliteness of his response.

"Just got back from droving a thousand head to Kansas. They be having fighting up there over owning black folk. It's some slavery thing." Wilson wasn't letting up in trying to engage Richards.

"Don't give a tinker's damn about slavery. Texas don't need to be messed up in that slave thing."

The cowboy wouldn't let up. "Texas being part of the Union, it matters."

Richards was done talking. "Texas don't belong in them United States. We killed Mexicans at San Jacinto to set us free. Lost hundreds of good men at the Alamo and Goliad. Now, be done with your talking." Richards wasn't an especially big man, but he was wiry and looked as though he'd be as downright tough to handle as an angry nest of rattlesnakes if pushed too far.

"You threatening me?" The cowboy had drunk just enough booze to be feeling over-confident.

"Name's Bol Richards, and I didn't fight for Texas to have some sorry-ass-for-brains cowboy sass me."

Wilson's hand moved toward the revolver in the holster at his hip, but he never saw Richards's fist coming. He hit the deck like a ton of longhorn just before it was slaughtered.

Richards was on the man like a cat. He kicked the cowboy's gun away, pulled him up from the floor by his collar, and proceeded to pummel his face with punch after punch.

The noise in the saloon grew louder with every punch. They alternately cheered Richards and urged the cowboy to fight back. Soon, another saloon regular stepped in to defend the cowboy, and the melee was on.

Not five minutes had passed when a gunshot brought it all to a halt. Bill Meaney stood at the saloon doorway with his gun still smoking. He nodded thanks to the barkeep who'd called him. "Who started this?" It was a rhetorical question, as he'd already noticed Bol Richards.

Richards was the only one standing among a half-dozen dazed patrons. He dusted himself off and smiled at Meaney. "I still got it in me, Bill."

Meaney sensed a bit too much tension in the crowded saloon. "Damn it, Bol. You're under arrest for disturbing the peace."

"What!" Richards made a move toward the sheriff.

"You remember what happened the last time?" Meaney was one of the few men still alive who'd put a whupping on Richards. "Now let's go. If you come along easy-like, I won't put the manacles on you."

Meaney escorted the grizzled Texan from the saloon, and the crowd went back to whatever they'd been doing before the melee. There were a few murmurs about the tough old man in buckskins. They figured him for older than his forty-five years but no less tough.

As they approached the jail, Meaney stopped. "Damn, Bol. You sure still have the touch. That cowboy never knew what hit him, did he?"

"Hey, I warned him. He was going for that peashooter he was carrying. In any case, no way I was putting up with any disrespect about Texas."

"Well, you can sleep it off in one of my cells. I'll leave the door unlocked. When you've sobered up, you can leave."

"Sounds fair, Bill." Richards struck a more contrite pose.

"You heard anything more about forming up Texas Rangers?"

"Not yet. I think Captain Dunn is following some men headed to Laredo. I think it has to do with a scam to steal from the US Army and the Indian agencies. He'll be gone a couple of weeks." He saw a hopelessly impatient look creep across Richards's face. "Let me talk to Colonel Kinney about finding you something to take advantage of your special skills, Bol."

Richards sat quietly on the cot in the cell. The whiskey and the fight had pretty much taken its toll on him for the evening. "Thanks, Bill," he offered meekly, his gravelly voice trailing off as he laid back and fell asleep.

"Howdy." The man raised his hand and hollered out to hail Luke. He'd spurred his mount forward to more quickly close the gap between himself and the big Texas Ranger he was approaching. "You're a Texas Ranger, ain't you?" He'd come to within ten yards or so of Luke and noticed the badge on his shirt.

"Yes, I'm Captain Dunn. You lookin' for help?"

"Just up the road a piece there's a bunch of vultures circling near a live oak motte. I didn't check out what they were so fired up about, but there's a couple of ponies nearby. From where I was lookin', they seemed like Injun ponies." The traveler's implication was that there was a human that had caught the vultures' interest and it was possibly an Indian. He didn't want to see for himself, lest he get involved in something he wasn't up to.

"Did you ride to the motte?" Luke already knew the answer.

"Nope, but you bein' a lawman...well...you might want

to check it out." He tipped his hat and spurred his mount past Luke. "Have a good day, Ranger."

A few moments later, the live oak motte came into view. Sure enough, vultures were circling overhead. Shortly, he could see the ponies as well. They looked familiar. Curious, Luke picked up his pace and headed for the motte.

He arrived to find something or someone partly buried and a bunch of snarling coyotes that he scared off upon entering the clearing. By the long black hair and dark skin, it was certainly an Indian but Luke had come onto the scene from behind. The victim's arms were tied to stakes and ants were crawling over him. Luke dismounted, drew his knife, and made his way around to see the man's face.

"Three Toes!" Luke dropped to his knees and cut the bindings before dashing over to grab his canteen. The chief was totally oblivious to his presence, as though in a trance. Luke began to dig frantically at the dirt imprisoning his friend. Soon enough, he was able to lift him out and get him to the shade of the live oaks. He poured water down Three Toes's throat, nearly drowning him in the process but reviving him all the same. He was glad he'd arrived in time to chase off the coyotes...and the ants.

"G...G...Ghost...Who...Rides?" The chief was waking up, but in terrible shape. Luke continued to pull ants from his wounds and give him sips of water, as he was seriously dehydrated.

"Who?" Luke placed a blanket over his friend as Three Toes was shaking with chills despite the summer heat.

The Comanche coughed. "Biggs." He was beginning to regain his senses. "Biggs...and...two men."

"Son of a..." Luke couldn't quite squeeze out the curse. "Where they heading?"

"West."

That confirmed that Biggs was going to Laredo.

"How you come here?" Three Toes was amazed that none other than Ghost-Who-Rides had found him.

"On Big Horse." Luke smiled at his own humor. "Rip Ford asked me to follow Biggs to Laredo. A bit ago, I met a traveler on the road who said he'd seen ponies and a bunch of circling buzzards. He'd avoided this place, but I was duty-bound to investigate. I had no idea it would be you, my friend. But I'm happy it was me that found you."

"Again, you have strong medicine, my friend." Three Toes's eyes expressed eternal gratitude.

"Can you stand?" Luke asked.

"Weak...but...can ride." The Comanche seemed to be able to ride no matter what their condition. They were one with their ponies.

Luke gathered what remained of the chief's belongings and helped him mount one of the ponies. Three Toes was weak and in pain from his wounds, but would survive. Luke was amazed at the Comanche's recuperative powers. Between the damage from the mountain lion's teeth and claws and now the wounds from this knife attack by Biggs, he was becoming a gnarled mass of disfiguring scars. He hardly cast an image of noble Indian chief as the scars belied the proud soul of the man inside. Roy Biggs would yet rue the day he crossed this Comanche chief.

Luke was about to mount Big Horse, when Three Toes stopped him. "Wait. There...in dust." He pointed to the bone necklace with its cross half-covered in the dirt near where he'd been buried. The sun's rays glancing from the silvery surface of the cross had caught his eye. It had survived the heel of Biggs's boot.

Luke fetched the necklace and handed it to Three Toes.

The chief smiled with gratitude. "Elisa right. Strong power in this."

Luke nodded in acknowledgment. If only the chief fully

understood where the power came from. All in due time. Perhaps Three Toes would learn to trust what it represented.

"Are we tracking Roy Biggs?"

Luke never ceased to be amazed at his friend's strength. "If you're up to it."

"Yes...but slow for now." He offered a weak but game smile.

"DAMN, Roy, you think that redskin died yet?" Cole asked.

Biggs smiled. "Coulda done more, but I wanted him to suffer a slow death more deserving of his race."

"You'd have done worse?"

"You seen what Comanche do to their captives, Cole?"

"Can't say I have." Cole Hester watched fascinatedly as Biggs got agitated at the thought of Comanche torture. He wondered what made this man tick. "Like what?"

"They cut off captive's eyelids, cut out tongues, slice off noses, castrate and, of course, scalp...all while the victim is alive." Biggs's eyes danced with excitement. Then he thought on Three Toes. "Yeah, I could have done that Indian far worse, but he'd have died too fast."

"How can we be sure he died?"

Biggs laughed aloud. "Hah! He died. Be assured, Cole. Ants...coyotes...vultures...the damned Comanche is dead. Likely vultures are plucking his eyeballs out as we speak."

Bert Burns had been listening silently. "No wonder Mr.

Thorpe likes you, Roy." The implication was that Biggs was Thorpe's sort of people.

"He doesn't like me, Bert. He needs me." He'd settled down from the momentary blood-lust excitement of describing Comanche tortures. "Hey, we'll have some fun in Laredo. They've got some of the best booze and whores on the Nueces Strip." With that, he spurred his mount to pick up their pace a bit.

"*¡Disparale!*" Benito Juarez couldn't have been clearer. Execute him! He ordered Juan Alvarez to be taken out and shot to set an example to anyone else with a mind to upset his plans to be president of Mexico. He was grateful to the US Army for delivering the wretch to him.

Juarez's men didn't waste any time as they marched the critically wounded, heavily bandaged man to the courtyard behind Juarez's residence and sat the blind-folded rebel in a chair before a white stucco wall. He was a sorry sight, too weak to stand. Even the blindfold couldn't hide the bruises from the beating he'd taken. Plus, the defenders of Corpus Christi had put at least four bullets into him, none of them quite enough to kill him right away. Five *soldados* aimed their rifles at him. "*¡Dispara!*" Five shots echoed in near-unison within the small space. Alvarez crumpled from the chair. It was done.

With Alvarez's death, any hope of reversing the Treaty of Guadalupe Hidalgo was ended. The Texans certainly wouldn't let such a threat fester again.

Santana reported the execution to Juarez. "Esta *completa.*"

"*¿Quien derrotó a Álvarez?*" Juarez wondered who had

defeated Alvarez after his initial successes in Brownsville. He'd heard that the rebel had several hundred men.

"*Si. Era un Ranger de Texas con cuarenta hombres y dos cañones.*" Santana had been impressed that the small group of Corpus Christi defenders had so easily routed a larger force. Then again, it brought back dark memories of defeat at San Jacinto two decades previous.

"*Debe ser un buen luchador.*" Juarez was impressed that the Texas Ranger must have been a great fighter.

"*Es el mejor. El capitán Luke Dunn tiene una gran reputación.*" Santana gave Luke due credit, lauding his reputation as a fighter.

"*Debo recordarlo.*" Indeed, Benito Juarez would do well to remember this Texas Ranger's prowess.

"Not much of a town, Roy." Cole wasn't especially impressed with Laredo at first sight.

Biggs laughed, a cackling evil sort of laugh. "It'll grow on you, Cole. Give it a chance." He led them up the main street to the town livery stable. "We'll board our horses here for a couple of days. There's a boarding house up the street."

"What we doing next?"

"You men thirsty? Damn, we've been riding for a week. Except for that redskin, we ain't seen nor spoke to anyone. Tomorrow we do Thorpe's business, today we do our business. Let's get some Laredo whiskey…and women."

"Anything we should know, Roy?" Cole Hester was determined to stay alive in the rough-and-tumble town.

"Watch out for Sheriff Stills. He's a mean son of a bitch who ain't been quite the same since some Mexican named Perez was sprung from his jail. Oh, and don't go talking with any soldiers from Fort McIntosh. The less we see of them just yet, the better." Biggs didn't share his bigger worry, as he was fairly confident that a wanted poster or two about him had made its way to Laredo. Still, he was a bit curious as to whether the reward had been increased.

He led the men to Texas Jack's Saloon. As he strode through the door, there was a momentary pause in the revelry. Most of the clientele knew of Roy Biggs and had some vague idea as to his appearance. Evil was hard to miss. He walked over to a table that immediately cleared as men scrambled to make room for he, Cole, and Bert. Biggs nodded to the barkeep. Soon enough, a bottle and three glasses appeared.

The saloon was hardly atypical. Sawdust mixed with booze and urine littered the floor, and the aromas of sweat, tobacco, and whiskey permeated what little breathable air there was. The clientele talked in hushed whispers while trying to avoid looking at Biggs.

"They scared of you or what, Roy?"

"They'd be right to be just a little scared. I'm thinking that if the sheriff showed up, they wouldn't want to be close to any trouble." Roy smiled reflectively.

"You expect trouble?"

"Not if we can avoid it." He nodded to a couple of ladies that had just entered the back door of the saloon. They didn't hesitate to join the trio. "Wanda, Chloe, these gentlemen are Bert and Cole. Would you be so kind as to make their visit to Laredo enjoyable?" He placed two five-dollar silver coins on the table.

Hester and Burns soon found their laps occupied by this pair of voluptuous Laredo prostitutes. Their perfume bouquet and ample curves of their breasts poking up from tight bodices captured the rapt attention of the men.

"Why don't you boys go and get to know the ladies a little better?" Biggs winked and waved them away.

The barkeeper ambled over. "Carla will be a few minutes, Mr. Biggs."

"No problem." Biggs could be a patient man. He absent-mindedly tapped his hook on the table, finally able to think about his situation. He had no hacienda to return to, as his lands had been forfeited to Texas with his defeat at Twin Creeks. He'd killed his wife. He had no idea what had become of his children. He figured he'd removed the Comanche threat from his life, but he still seethed when he thought of Texas Ranger Captain Luke Dunn and his wife. Damn her and that buffalo gun. On the upside, he still had his fortune from the California gold fields stashed away and might yet get an opportunity to dispose of those damnable Dunns.

"Roy, nice to see you back in Laredo."

Biggs's spirits lifted at the sweet sound of Carla's voice. In the morning, he and his small entourage would be heading out to find Thorpe's barn.

"We ought to be close, my friend." Luke looked over at Three Toes. The chief's wounds were slowly healing, but he looked terrible.

"We camp outside city?"

"Likely for the best." Luke knew quite well that folks in Laredo didn't cotton to Indians in general and Comanche especially. Aside from killing settlers in years past, the Comanche had the temerity to rustle local cattle and then try to sell the beasts back to the very ranchers they'd stolen them from. Unlike the Apache that stole beeves from the Texans, sold them to the Mexicans, and vice versa, the

Comanche lacked such semi-subtlety of thievery for profit. Given the ever-present potential for raids and scalp-taking, the ranchers for the most part reluctantly bought back their cattle. "Let's scout around. Biggs will stay away from Fort McIntosh. He's supposed to be looking for some sort of storage building. Likely, it'll be a barn."

"Ghost-Who-Rides, we should split up and meet back here."

"Biggs likely spent a long night in Laredo. It's mid-morning, so I expect he'll be fixing to set out and find this storage place. I'd feel more comfortable if I go into town and ask the stable boy and the sheriff what they know. Could be they can tell us what direction they left town."

Three Toes nodded affirmatively. "I wait here." He walked his ponies to a grove of trees hidden from the road.

Not wanting to dally further, Luke turned Big Horse and headed into Laredo. He calculated that the stable boy would know the direction Biggs had headed. He'd as soon avoid Sheriff Stills—he didn't care to engage in conversation that might delay his hunt for Biggs. It didn't take long to find the livery stable.

"Howdy, son. I'm Texas Ranger Captain Luke Dunn, and I'd appreciate some information."

The young man appeared to be fifteen or sixteen years old and not the brightest star in the galaxy. He had long hair and wisps of hair on his chin as if trying to grow a beard. That having been said, he was no one's fool in day-to-day practical matters. "What kinda information, Mr. Ranger?"

"Like to know where one of your recent guests might be headed."

"Seen a couple of folks this morning. Anyone special?"

"Likely was three men traveling together. One lost an arm."

"They told me that if I wanted to live another day to not tell anyone which way they headed, Mr. Ranger. Gave me this silver coin."

Luke sighed and thought a moment. "How about you tell me which way they didn't go? That way you've done what they asked."

The stable boy thought on that. It made sense to his simple mind. He raised his finger and pointed. "Well, they didn't go that way or that way." There were only three roads they could have taken, so only the road to the north remained. "Be sure to tell 'em I kept my promise."

"Sure will, son." Luke nodded and shook his head just a bit at the boy's gullibility.

The three men turned from the road and rode up a low-lying hill dotted with shrubs and trees and into a clearing. If you didn't know it was there, you'd have easily passed it by. Before them was a nondescript barn-like structure of modest size. Biggs surveyed the surrounding area. Nothing seemed amiss, and they hadn't been followed, so far as Biggs could tell. "Bert, you ride up to that high ground over there and keep a lookout. You hear or see anything suspicious, let us know." Biggs and Hester dismounted and walked over to the barn.

Biggs produced a key Thorpe had given him. The door was hung from a rail and secured by a lock. It was rusty, but the mechanism turned easily. Biggs fumbled a bit with it due to the hook he now wore, but he managed it. He and Hester put their shoulders to it and slid the door aside. Biggs pulled a piece of paper from his pocket with a list of the inventory on it and handed it to Hester. "You can read, right?"

"I'm not stupid, Roy 'Course I can read."

They stepped inside. It took a few moments for their eyes to adjust to the dim light, as just enough peeked in through vents near the roof to allow them to see the contents.

"Damn, Roy. There are some incredibly fine things here." Hester was taking in the mahogany chairs, desks, and bookcases, the gilt-framed mirrors, ornate settees, fancy lights, and more. He thought it was a waste that it was all sitting in the barn gathering dust.

As Biggs called out the items, Hester checked them off on the inventory list. As they made their way between rows of furnishings, they came upon three large chests. They were locked, but Biggs produced a ring with a key for each. He opened the first, and stood back in amazement. "Damn, Thaddeus Brown was good." The glittering silver and gold jewelry decorated with precious stones lent a little extra light to the area.

"Don't look like it's been touched." Biggs closed and locked the first chest. He proceeded to open and then close and lock the other two. "Nothing's been tampered with. We don't have to check off the contents." He glanced at Hester, who was still shaking his head in amazement at the riches he'd just seen. "Don't even think it, Cole."

"Steal this stuff? Naw, I ain't stupid, Roy." But it had crossed his mind.

"Roy! Roy, we got company!" Bert had rushed down from his lookout perch.

"You see somebody?"

"I heard 'em." About this time, a trio of deer came loping through the clearing. Bert hung his head.

"Next time, be sure. Now get back to your post, Bert. We won't be but another hour or so."

Luke rendezvoused with Three Toes and shared what he'd learned from the stable boy. They skirted wide of Laredo to avoid the attention of folks concerned with Comanche or Indians in general and followed the road to the north as not directed by the stable boy. Recalling Three Toes's technique used in chasing down Bad Bart Strong a while back, they rode in the rough prairie and woods parallel to the road. It was slower going, but not so obvious to anyone looking to spot them.

Luke whispered, "Can't be much farther. Let's walk." They dismounted and proceeded cautiously, about fifty feet apart. Luke carried his Colt rifle and Three Toes was at the ready with an arrow nocked in his bowstring. The horses followed on long leads. It was almost too easy.

Another half mile of walking, and Three Toes stopped, gave a low bird whistle in Luke's direction, and pointed ahead. He could see a roof just peeking above a low hill.

They hobbled the horses and stayed low as they moved toward whatever was under the roof. Finally, they found themselves looking at the backside of a barn surrounded by a bit of a clearing. They heard voices. Luke pointed off to a man on horseback and armed with a rifle on a hill opposite them.

Three Toes saw him as well. He pointed to himself and unsheathed his knife. The chief pulled back from their position and began a wide circle so as to approach the apparent lookout from behind.

Luke waited patiently. He admired the chief's technique.

Three Toes moved slowly, partly out of caution and partly from his still-healing injuries. He got to within about twenty feet of Biggs's sentry. The ground cover was thick but dry. It didn't lend itself to sneaking up on anyone close enough to use a knife. He saw Luke watching. His prey was looking in the opposite direction. He made a bow-and-arrow motion to Luke. With that, he nocked an arrow, aimed, and let fly.

Bert looked down at the arrowhead protruding from his chest. "Roy..." His voice trailed off as he dropped to his knees. He tried to take a breath but choked as he gurgled up blood. His eyes momentarily grew wide as he realized his fate. Then he collapsed on his face.

Inside the barn, Biggs and Hester barely heard Bert's weak cry.

"Roy, Bert's in trouble. That's not how his voice sounds." It was obviously a death cry.

"Damn." Biggs had left his rifle with the horses hitched outside the barn. With his one good arm, he drew his gun. He poked his head out the door.

Luke couldn't see Biggs, but he'd moved to a position where he could see the horses.

Three Toes had circled to the opposite side of the barn from Luke.

"Cole, can you get to the rifles?" Biggs wasn't going to take a chance fumbling with his only good arm.

Hester looked at him incredulously. "I don't have a death wish, Roy. Somebody out there killed Bert for sure." He could see Bert's horse with its empty saddle.

"Roy Biggs, come out unarmed and your hand held high." There was a touch of sardonic humor in Luke's call, as he obviously recognized Biggs's disability. It was cruel but an ever so deserving fate for so foul a human being.

"Damn! I know that voice!" Luke's temerity at referring to Biggs as one-handed wasn't lost on the killer. Images of Elisa and that damned Sharps rifle swept through him. Psychologically, it fueled Biggs's rising anger. He was seething with rage. "Cole, get the damned rifles!"

Hester was frozen with fear.

At that, a warning shot ricocheted off the barn door-frame. "Surrender, Biggs. Both of you." Luke let that sink in. "You ready to die today, Roy Biggs?" The memory of Biggs walking away from Corpus Christi as a free man after a sham trial still festered in his mind. It had totally offended his senses of honor and justice.

The thought of surrender didn't exactly hold any attraction to Biggs, but neither did he figure to waste away in jail awaiting another trial and this time a hanging for certain.

By this time, Three Toes had made his way to the corner of the barn about twenty feet from where Biggs and Cole hid just inside the entrance.

Hester had moved forward, as he'd thought seriously about making a break for it. If he could just duck Luke's bullets, he might get away.

The chief nocked another arrow and took careful aim. Cole Hester found himself groveling in the dirt with an arrow through his neck. He couldn't speak and was slowly choking to death.

Luke waited patiently for Biggs to come into sight. He reassured himself that he would be delivering justice, not vengeance, and this man surely deserved to die. He'd refused to surrender. There was little choice—there was no choice.

Biggs turned to see where the arrow had come from and was horrified at what stood before him with another arrow at the ready. He looked as though he'd seen a ghost. He raised his revolver...too late. A shot rang out from behind him. He fired wildly into the air as he fell. Nueces justice had been served. Moreover, with discovery of the barn, the full extent of Horatio Thorpe's deceitful dealings had just begun to be revealed.

Biggs lay in the dirt bleeding out from Luke's bullet.

Three Toes stood over him as Luke walked up and kneeled beside the dying outlaw. "He...he...should be..."

"Dead? You underestimated his strong medicine, Biggs." Luke fully appreciated the irony as this personification of evil was drawing his final breaths.

Biggs was growing paler and experiencing ever-greater agony by the moment. "My...children?" Despite his fading strength, he partially drew an envelope from his breast pocket. It featured a bullet hole, but was intact. He feigned not having the strength to hand it to Luke.

Luke blinked with surprise. Was there just a hint of humanity in this demonic monster? "Safe. Fort Mason."

As Luke reached for the envelope, a knife filled Boggs's hand seemingly from nowhere. The Texas Ranger easily deflected the blade.

Biggs gave a brief grunt of pain, closed his eyes, and breathed his last, evil to the very end.

Luke opened the envelope. It turned out to be instructions as to where his sons could locate their father's fortune of gold. Luke was conflicted between the inheritance of Biggs's innocent children versus the price the lawbreaker must pay for the evils he'd wrought. He decided to forward the note to Rip Ford and let others make that decision. Perhaps they'd show some mercy. He caught his drifting thoughts and snapped back to the here and now. "Chief, let's gather the horses and deliver these men to Sheriff Stills."

Three Toes was looking longingly at the scalps of the dead men. Biggs's long dark hair was especially attractive. Memories of the massacre of his family still loomed in his consciousness.

Luke nodded and tugged at his own hair. "Would you kindly tie these men over their saddles? I'll fetch the man on the hill and get our horses, too." He was respectfully leaving the Comanche alone with his emotions and his knife.

The chief was conflicted. He was beginning to under-stand the White man's way, but had decades of tradition in harshly treating his enemies working on his mind. The name Comanche, after all, translated to enemy. He looked at Hester. The man was nearly bald. There was no scalp to take. However, the hated Biggs was a deserving prize. He heard Luke returning with the horses, and moved swiftly to relieve Biggs of his scalp.

"Will you return to your people?" Luke ignored the bloody scene.

Three Toes nodded affirmatively, almost ashamed of taking Biggs's scalp.

"You should take Biggs's horse, my friend. You deserve it for the pain you endured."

With his limited English, Three Toes didn't understand every word Luke spoke, but he got the gist of it. He stroked the bone necklace with the cross. "Powerful medicine, Ghost-Who-Rides."

"Next time we meet, I'll tell you about it, my friend." Luke turned toward Laredo with his funeral procession. He looked forward to Sheriff Stills's reaction and wished that newfangled telegraph had been extended into the Nueces Strip so he could have let Rip Ford know about his success.

An hour later, Luke pulled up in front of the Laredo jail. He saw Sheriff Stills peek out through the front window. Luke had just dismounted and was about to hitch his horse when Stills appeared.

"Luke, looks like you're bringing me more dead lawbreakers. Gettin' to be a habit."

Luke could only absentmindedly stroke his mustache and offer a sheepish smile. He finally offered a sardonic smile. "Saved y'all the hassle of a trial."

Stills walked around the horses, inspecting the bodies. "Looks as though you had help again. Another scalp, too?" Stills noted the arrows in Hester and Burns. "Your Comanche friend?"

"He was a big help, Sheriff." Luke didn't feel compelled to explain how Biggs had tortured the Comanche chief. He was tempted to add that he preferred to bring dead outlaws in, since live ones tended to escape Stills's jail. "There's one other thing. A couple of miles north, there's a barn containing stolen government property. Biggs had been inspecting the contents for someone being investigated up in Austin. I'm going to ride out to Fort McIntosh on my way back to Nuecestown to let the commanding officer know."

Stills nodded that he understood. It also didn't take a mental giant to figure out that the barn contents must be very valuable. "I expect you know there was a hefty reward on Roy Biggs."

"Yes, I know about the reward for Biggs, Sheriff. I'd appreciate it if you would see that it's sent to my account in Corpus Christi. Guess I'll be buying a few more head of cattle. Oh, and you can keep the dead men's horses for your trouble. I did gift one to my Comanche friend."

"You aware of any next of kin?"

"Don't know about the other two men, but Biggs has a couple of young children being held at Fort Mason. I'll see that word gets to them, Sheriff. I did find what seemed to be identification for one of Biggs's companions. One of them is named Cole Hester." He watched as Stills completed filling out the necessary paperwork. He'd thought it best not to mention the Biggs's bequeathment.

"Here you go, Captain Dunn." Sheriff Stills handed Luke a copy.

The star-shaped earthen breastworks of Fort McIntosh set along the banks of the Rio Grande soon came into view. Luke was anxious to get home, but felt duty-bound to let the commanding officer know about the hidden treasure trove of government booty.

"Halt! Who goes there?" the gatekeeper challenged Luke's imposing figure seated on the big gray stallion.

"Texas Ranger Captain Luke Dunn at your service. I'd like to talk with your commanding officer." Luke tipped his hat as a friendly, non-threatening gesture. He sensed that there was a tension and wondered at what might have caused it.

"I'll get you an escort, sir."

Luke waited patiently until the guard reappeared with an enlisted man to escort Luke to the commanding officer. Luke dismounted and followed the soldier through the gate. "Thanks, soldier." They walked a few feet toward the headquarters cabin before Luke ventured to find out what was causing the perceived stress. "Y'all been having trouble here? I get the feeling that y'all are on some sort of high alert."

"You'll have to ask the lieutenant, sir."

Luke wondered at that. He expected a higher-ranked officer, at least a captain. In any case, the garrison didn't appear to be at full strength.

They arrived at the commanding officer's cabin, and the escort knocked on the door. "Sir, Texas Ranger Captain Dunn to see you."

"Let the Ranger in, soldier."

The escort stepped aside, allowing Luke to step inside. "Lieutenant? Name's Luke Dunn. Pleased to make your acquaintance."

The lieutenant stood and extended his right hand. "I've heard about you, Captain Dunn. I'm Lieutenant Myers."

"All good with the Army, I hope." As he answered, Luke noted that the lieutenant's left hand was heavily bandaged.

The lieutenant offered Luke a seat across from his desk. "Laredo seems to be reasonably peaceful these days, at least according to Sheriff Stills. I understand you delivered some deposits for their cemetery." Myers forced a smile at his dark humor. "I thought there wasn't any funding for Texas Rangers these days. What brings you to Fort McIntosh?" He leaned forward as if more interested in what Luke might have to say.

Luke smiled. "I'm here to alert you to a well-hidden storage barn a couple of miles north of Laredo that contains material stolen from the Army and the Indian agencies. I found it as a result of tracking some of the men involved in the scheme to defraud the government. I'll be alerting the folks in Austin when I get back to Corpus Christi. I do suggest that you consider posting a guard since, as word gets out, others may wish to steal the property. As to the Texas Rangers, after I rode with Captain Callahan back in '55, they were defunded, but I was asked by Rip Ford to stay on in a Special Ranger role."

The lieutenant seemed to grasp Luke's message. "To be honest, Captain Dunn, my garrison is pretty lean right now. I don't feel that I can afford posting guards to this barn you've discovered. We've been experiencing a resurgence of Lipan Apache attacks in the surrounding territory. One of my patrols was nearly wiped out last week and the tension here is high."

"I'm sorry to hear that, Lieutenant. If it'll ease your mind any, I've heard rumor that the political folks in Austin may fund a couple of Texas Ranger companies soon."

"Rip Ford was out here not so long ago. If he has any influence, I expect they'll find the money. I do appreciate you letting me know about the barn. I'll try to do what I can, Captain. Meanwhile, I wish you a safe journey back to Corpus Christi. Do keep your eyes peeled for those infernal Apache savages." He offered Luke an informal salute from his seat.

"Thanks, Lieutenant. I expect I'll be heading home. I hope your hand heals well. Dealt with a bad wound to my hand a couple of years ago, and you'll find that exercising it is important." He tipped his hat, turned, and exited. Soon enough, Luke was on the road back home, ever vigilant for the possible lurking Apache. He considered that some of Roy Biggs's fortune might be put to good use funding Texas Rangers. He rightly figured it a worthy outcome.

EIGHTEEN
GOOD NEWS FROM AUSTIN

NORMALLY, Luke would be passing the time singing Irish ballads, though sung in an increasingly Texas accent. With the lieutenant's warning weighing on his mind, he decided that loud noise wouldn't be such a great idea. The silence was deafening, but worse could lure the mind too easily and make a traveler lapse into inattention, even daydreaming.

He looked forward to getting back to Elisa's loving arms and great cooking. She'd be relieved to know that Roy Biggs would never be a threat again. If he didn't know better, he'd be tempted to think that lawbreaking on the Nueces Strip had been stopped. Of course, he knew better. Rustlers and hiders, mixed with the usual cast of malcontents, thieves, and murderers, would be around to keep him busy so long as he cared to try to bring justice to the region. He prayed that he'd be finding a bit more time to spend on the ranch. With the reward from bringing Roy Biggs to justice, he and Elisa could buy more cattle as well as increase their land holdings. Last but not least, he looked forward to playing with his sons, Peter and John. They'd be old enough in another couple of years to begin to participate in the chores inherent in life on a working ranch. There'd be small tasks at first, but Luke hoped to instill the love of life and hard work that he'd learned growing up in County Kildare as well as a sense of God-inspired right and wrong that would ever color their lives as they grew up.

He'd purchased plenty of dried beef and venison before leaving Laredo, so he had no need to build a fire. The hot summer temperatures, however, were causing him to consume his water a bit faster than he'd have preferred. He missed hot coffee, too. He might chance a small fire as he got closer to San Diego and the beginnings of the home-stretch to Nuecestown.

The road was mostly straight, curving left or right depending on terrain and meandering arroyos. With trees few and far between, a traveler could see quite a distance. He approached mottes of live oak or mesquite cautiously, as hidden dangers might be lurking.

Luke was about four days from Laredo when he found himself approaching a live oak motte. It was about three hundred or so yards out. He'd seen it on earlier travels, but something gave him pause to be extra cautious. He drew the Colt rifle from its scabbard and moved toward the motte.

Sitting as he was, a big man on a big horse, Luke dismounted. Big Horse wouldn't mind the lightened load, and it made for a smaller target if Luke's intuition proved true.

Luke froze. He reached down and removed his spurs. The less noise he made, the better. He saw that at least three saddleless ponies stood on the far side of the motte. Apache? Kiowa? Comanche? It was too soon to tell, but

Indians of some tribe seemed likely. He kept Big Horse close. If Comanche were around, they'd surely covet his stallion.

He was drawing closer and grew ever more curious as to why he'd not seen or heard any signs of life other than the ponies. He returned the rifle to its scabbard and drew one of his Colt Navy revolvers and a knife. If anything were to happen now, it would most likely be at close quarters. The hair stood up on the back of his neck. Something wasn't quite right.

Luke reached the motte and was taken aback by what he found. Three Lipan Apache bodies were staked out naked in the blazing sun. The work was fresh, as the vultures hadn't even begun their telltale circling. Luke shooed off a couple of coyotes.

The Apache had been tortured before having been shot. His instincts told him it was the work of Mexicans, though it could've been drovers from a nearby cattle drive. They strongly begrudged the Apache inclination to steal their livestock. Still, these Apache had ranged pretty far north, especially given that Callahan's Texas Rangers had run the tribe out about three years earlier. Luke was surprised that the ponies hadn't been taken. It seemed as though whoever did this deed wanted the bodies to be discovered. A warning? A threat? Luke scanned the horizon. Nothing to be seen. He figured that he likely missed the actual event by an hour or so.

He drew out a small shovel from his bedroll. He'd long ago found the tool invaluable for extinguishing fires, digging channels around his bedroll during rainstorms or, as in this case, burying the dead. He freed the three ponies and began the task of burying the victims. It wasn't pleasant, but it was the right thing to do.

After burying the dead Apaches, he took a break and

actually built a small fire. There wasn't much of any wood around, so he used grasses and a few live oak twigs lying about. The grass made for a smoky fire. Importantly, Luke finally enjoyed some hot coffee.

Walker Carson limped gingerly along the road to Laredo. He'd turned his ankle, and his horse had pulled up lame. Carson had also been on the receiving end of a brave bank teller's bullet and, though it only grazed him, it added to his woes. The teller's shot had caused Carson to drop the bag of money. He'd escaped with no loot. It seemed as though life could hardly get any worse. He was ever-frustrated with the ill-fated life paths he seemed to take.

Chased off a barely profitable ranch at the age of sixteen where his father was foreman, Carson was the fifth of eight children. His older brothers and sisters had each been run off in turn as they became more costly to feed and not so willing to work hard. He'd never known his birth mother, as his father's women tended to run off after a child or two. Seemed the environment for women, even Carson's sisters, was physically and mentally abusive. Carson's father was a perfectionist so far as his cowboy profession, and Carson wished he'd been as attentive to perfection with his relationships. Every now and then, his father would go on a drunken bender, and when he did, he'd get angry with himself and take it out on whichever woman was gracing his doorstep. Carson would go off and join his brothers tending horses any time he saw his father come home boozed up. The sisters would try to protect their mother and would occasionally be struck themselves for their trouble.

Carson had droved for a ranch, but got fired after

picking a fight with a trail boss over some petty slight up on the Shawnee Trail. Actually, it wasn't so petty, as he'd gotten up in the middle of the night to pee, lost his way, and accidentally urinated on the trail boss's tack. After cleaning the saddle as best he could, he was summarily discharged.

The word gets out fast, as once fired by a trail boss, it was next to impossible to get another job. The reaction by that trail boss to his honest accident had marked him for life in the cattle drive community. Carson thought seriously about retaliating against the trail boss, but he wasn't up to that quite yet.

Jobless, Carson grew desperate. He didn't see any means of making a living. He tried his hand at being a farrier, but a horse's hoof to his ribs put an end to that. He tried to get hired as a barkeeper, but he tended to be a tad argumentative and rub the clientele the wrong way. With no income, he found himself hungry and a mess to look at. Here he was at age eighteen turning so desperate as to start robbing banks. Now, he was limping along on a scorching hot day on a dusty road in the middle of the Nueces Strip. Could it get any worse for Walker Carson?

He saw a live oak motte off in the distance. Some cool shade would bring welcome relief to his ailing body from the burning rays of the summer sun. He wished he could walk faster, but the ankle and heat simply wouldn't allow it.

Carson had walked to within a couple of hundred yards of the motte. His ankle hurt like hell. His horse began to get a bit skittish.

He'd just about halved the distance when a voice behind him startled him nearly out of his pants.

"You looking for something, friend?" Luke had his rifle

at the ready. "Turn real slow like and keep your hands where I can see them."

Carson obeyed.

"I'm Texas Ranger Captain Luke Dunn. Appears you've had some trouble." Luke had become the master of understatement when the situation suited it. "What's your name?"

Carson found himself face to face with a man a half-foot taller and pointing a rifle at his midsection. To make matters worse, the sun reflected from a Texas Ranger badge. In his travels, he vaguely recalled having heard of some Ranger bringing tough justice to the Nueces Strip. It'd be just his luck to fall into that particular Ranger's clutches. "Um...name's Walker Carson. I'm traveling to Laredo, Captain. Had a bit of a scrap in San Diego, sir." He quickly recognized this as a time for respect, not swagger.

"What happened to your horse?" Luke asked.

"Pulled up lame."

Luke deduced that the steed had been ridden too hard for too long. It appeared otherwise to be a healthy horse. "Where's your water?"

Carson couldn't admit that he'd escaped without any. His mind was racing to concoct a plausible story. "Somebody shot at me and put a hole through my canteen. It wouldn't hold water no how."

Luke's instincts were now working in overdrive. This character had obviously been up to no good. There was no way the man would make it to Laredo with no water. "I'd be happy to help you back to San Diego."

This was the last thing Carson wanted to hear. There was no way he was going back to face his crime. "I'm scared to go back. Just as soon keep heading toward Laredo, if it's all the same to you."

Luke was sizing the man up. In his current condition, he didn't appear to be a serious threat. Whatever he'd done had apparently been bungled. "So tell me what really happened."

Seemed Carson couldn't fabricate a story if his life depended on it. He was exhausted and hurting. "I've been down on my luck. I tried to rob the bank in San Diego." He let that sink in. "Lucky to escape with my life. Teller shot me, I turned my ankle, my horse went lame, and I didn't get any money."

Luke figured he was finally hearing the truth. He could arrest the man for attempted robbery or bet that he'd learned his lesson. Visions of getting back to Elisa and Heaven's Gate ran through Luke's mind and influenced his decision to give Carson a second chance. Perhaps it would change the man's life. Luke lowered his rifle. "Tell you what, Mr. Carson, I'm inclined to give you a second chance. If you'll mosey over to that motte over there, you'll find a pot of coffee sitting on hot coals. You're welcome to a drink. Set a spell in the shade while I see to your horse."

Carson couldn't believe what he was hearing. It'd been so long since life had given him a break. "Thanks…thanks very much." There wasn't much else to say. It felt good to sit in the shade of the live oak.

Luke checked out Carson's horse. The problem turned out to be caused by a loose shoe. Ever handy, Luke secured the shoe properly. He was truly getting into the role of being a sort of good Samaritan. Now, he had to decide how to share his water. He walked over to where the Apache paraphernalia still lay near the freshly dug graves. There appeared to be at least one serviceable water skin. "Carson, the water in this thing isn't the greatest, but you'll find at least two cisterns between here and Laredo where you can fill it up."

"Captain Dunn, I'm ever beholden to you."

"Mr. Carson, you can thank me by never ever doing something that'll put you in my gunsight again." Luke scratched something on a piece of paper from his saddlebag, folded it, and handed it to Carson. "Give this to Sheriff Stills. He owes me for clearing some lawbreakers out of Laredo. By this note, I've asked him to give you a job."

Carson was overwhelmed and grateful nearly to tears. He'd been given a gift that he dared not mess up. They chatted a bit while Carson sipped coffee.

Soon enough, it was time for Luke to resume his travels. "Mr. Carson, rest your bones for a bit. Be sure that fire is out before you leave." Luke walked over and mounted Big Horse. He tipped his hat at Carson. "Safe travel, Mr. Carson."

Luke headed toward San Diego, leaving Walker Carson to whatever fate awaited him. Luke thought on what had just transpired. He figured that Walker Carson thought short-term like most young men and didn't cogitate on how to shape his future. The young man hadn't the experience or imagination to come up with legitimate solutions to meeting his living needs. The kid had been in danger of turning to the evil side of life's ledger, of becoming a predator rather than a protector. Luke hoped that the note to the Laredo sheriff would help set Carson on the right path. In a sense, Luke saw it as part of bringing law and order—justice if you will—to the Nueces Strip.

San Diego was a small town on the northern reaches of the Nueces Strip and consisted of a few houses, a school, a small but serviceable saloon, a modest stable, and a ramshackle building that served as post office, town jail, and erstwhile bank. The town served as a commerce hub of sorts between Corpus Christi and Laredo. Travelers were welcome to freshen up and even spend a night or two. Their money and company were more than welcome.

Luke hadn't a drop of water remaining in his canteen, and Big Horse desperately needed a long drink. They were a hangdog-looking pair riding into San Diego. First stop would be the stable. Luke could wait, but not his beloved stallion.

"Howdy, Ranger. You missed the excitement a couple of days back. Some idiot tried to rob our little bank. Got shot for his trouble." The stable hand was chock-full of information.

"So he escaped?" Luke looked downward so the stable hand couldn't see his smile. He also was being careful that Big Horse didn't drink too much too soon.

"We ain't got no sheriff no more." The young man was giving Luke a visual once-over. He noticed Luke's badge. "You that Luke Dunn fella we've heard so much about?"

Luke gave him the vertical nod. "You've found me, son."

"You really killed Bad Bart Strong and Dirk Cavendish and Roy Biggs? That all true?"

Luke sighed. "Where can I get something to eat and drink, son?"

The stable hand calmed a bit. "Just up the main street a bit, sir."

"Well, if you'd be kind enough to properly take care of my horse, there'll be something extra in it for you."

"I'd be pleased to, sir."

"You can call me Captain Dunn. I'll be back later." Luke headed to the saloon. He really needed food and water before investigating the attempted bank robbery.

There were perhaps half a dozen patrons in the saloon as Luke took a seat at an empty table.

The barkeep sauntered over. "Can I help you...sir." That was invariably the effect of spotting the Texas Ranger badge. "Er...welcome to San Diego."

"What grub are you serving today, barkeep? I'll take whatever you've got and some water."

A few minutes later, the barkeep reappeared with food and water. "My name's Sam, Captain. Have you heard the news about the Texas Rangers?"

"Been away in Laredo, Sam. What have you heard?"

"Rumor has it that Rip Ford is forming up a couple of Texas Ranger companies to bring law and order to the frontier."

"That's welcome news, Sam. I'll look forward to hearing more when I get back to Nuecestown." Luke sat back and closed his eyes for a moment. It was crystal clear that he'd have a big decision ahead. Ranch duties would be expanding as they used the bounty money he'd receive from killing Roy Biggs to acquire more land and buy more cattle. "Say, I hear y'all had a bank robbery here?"

"Oh, that. Young fella messed it up pretty bad, captain. He bolted from here hurt and with no money. You gonna chase him?"

"I expect he may not be worth chasing, Sam. If nobody was hurt and no money taken, I've got bigger prey to hunt. Besides, I need to find out about those Texas Ranger companies you've heard about."

Luke had already heard that the US Army was beginning to pull troops from many of the forts in Texas to go and fight Cheyenne, Lakota Sioux, and Arapahoe up in the northwestern plains. Texas could not afford to have its frontier, especially around the Comancheria, opened up to marauding Comanche and Apache, Mexican bandits, and outlaws. The state was in debt, but they had been forced to find the funds for law enforcement. Justice still needed to be meted out on the Nueces Strip.

Elisa wouldn't be pleased with him heeding his call to duty. It would amplify his indecision between being a rancher or lawman. He treasured her unwavering support of his decisions. In addition to her pregnancy, she had a lot of responsibilities at Heaven's Gate. They were blessed to have Jaime and Julia residing nearby in their old cabin.

NINETEEN
THORPE'S DECEIT

IT WAS DUSK. The archway at the entrance to Heaven's Gate stood tall before him. He was already sensing the sweet bouquet of Elisa's perfume, and he could almost feel her body pressed against his. Oh, how he yearned for her.

He rode Big Horse at a canter up the trail to the house. In the growing darkness, he managed to sneak past the cabin and ride up to the house. He could hear Peter and John babbling as Elisa cooked. He smiled. The aromas of her cooking wafted from the house, overwhelming the aromas of the prairie. He dismounted and began to sing an old Irish ballad that she loved. *"Tis the last rose of summer, left blooming alone; All her lovely companions are faded and gone; No flower of her kindred, No rosebud is nigh, To reflect back her blushes, And, give sigh for sigh. I'll not leave thee, thou lone one!..."* Luke's singing trailed off as his sweet Elisa appeared in the doorway.

"To pine on the stem..." Elisa sang the next line as she came running from the gallery and leaped into her man's arms. "Lucas! Lucas!" She buried herself in his very core. "Oh, my love, I've missed you so."

Luke bent down and found her lips with his. It was a forever kiss until Big Horse broke the spell by nearly knocking them over with a nudge. Luke looked up and saw two little sets of eyes peering from the window. "It's so good to be home, my sweet Lisa."

"Well, Lucas, you're just in time for dinner. Go stable Big Horse and clean yourself up." She looked wistfully into his eyes. "And hurry."

Luke was half-torn with wanting to sweep Peter and John into his arms, but Elisa pointed to the barn. Luke stepped back, smiled broadly, and fully took her in with his eyes. Her belly had grown since he'd left to pursue Biggs. Another Dunn would soon be joining their family. "I'll hurry." He led the stallion to the barn to unsaddle, curry, and feed, all the sooner to get back to Elisa and the twins.

Horatio Thorpe had settled into temporary quarters in San Antonio. He'd been greatly relieved to have extricated himself from any need to deal with his wife back on the plantation. Burying Gascon had taken a heavy toll on Martha, but not enough to achieve the relief Thorpe had hoped for. He desperately wanted to be free of her, but that might have gained the ire of his remaining son, Edward. For whatever reason, that bothered Thorpe. Edward had his own life as a lawyer in Philadelphia, yet Thorpe held out hope that he'd yet take an interest in eventually joining his plantation operations.

He was still struggling with the summer heat and humidity. Even as he ate a piece of pecan pie, he pondered his need to lose weight. Even his newer clothes were straining more and more to accommodate his ample girth. He needed to get his anxieties under control or he'd eat himself to death. A knock at the door brought him out of his languid state of mind.

"Who is it?" Of course, he knew it was Samuel. He'd brought him here rather than leave him to handle his office in Austin.

"Message for you, Master Thorpe."

"Come in, Samuel." Thorpe was nearly wedged into an armchair. It would have been a struggle to get out of the chair to answer the door.

"This is from the telegraph office, Master Thorpe." He handed the message to his master. He looked for a split second at Thorpe. Rumor had it that he'd had a slave whipped to near death during his visit to bury Gascon. Samuel wondered whether that was true. He could never ask.

Thorpe waved Samuel away. "Thank you, Samuel." He looked at the folded message in his hand. He loved the efficiency that the telegraph was bringing to Texas. He'd tried to envision the opportunities that the telegraph and the railroads were going to mean for his business ventures. He opened the message.

> *TO: Mr. Horatio Thorpe, San Antonio. STOP*
>
> *FROM: John Smith, Austin. STOP*
>
> *Biggs dead. STOP*
> *Inventory lost. STOP*

Thorpe gasped and dropped the message. He needed air. Struggling, he leveraged himself from the chair and staggered through the French doors to the balcony.

John Smith was Thorpe's inside man in Rip Ford's office

in Austin. His real name was Pete O'Rourke. He was anxious to reach out to O'Rourke to find what else he might know. It couldn't be done by telegraph and he didn't feature traveling back to Austin.

"Samuel."

The house slave reappeared in the doorway. "Yes, Master Thorpe."

"Send a telegram to Smith. Tell him to get down here pronto."

"Yes, Master Thorpe." Samuel bowed ever so slightly and departed.

Thorpe took a deep breath, wiped his brow, and decided to feed his anxiety with some local cuisine. Given how hot it was, the hotel restaurant qualified as local enough. He soon found himself at the door to the dining room. Thorpe paused at the entrance and scanned the room. It was ornate in the gaudy Spanish style with rich mahogany furnishings highlighted with reds and golds fitting of some sort of European palace. He was actually pleased with himself that he'd paused before being seated as he spied none other than Colonel Henry Kinney and a couple of dinner guests. Upon being seated, Thorpe gave the maître d' a silver dollar to deliver a pricey French wine to Kinney's table.

No surprise that the colonel stopped by Thorpe's table on his way out after dinner. He knew Horatio Thorpe on sight, as did most folks of any wealth and influence in Texas. "The wine was delightful, Mr. Thorpe. You certainly have a fine taste in wines. We thank you."

"If you're in San Antonio for a spell, Colonel Kinney, perhaps we might meet concerning some business matters. My sources tell me that your port in Corpus Christi is truly flourishing these days." He quite naturally ignored the fact that he'd refused to meet with Kinney a couple of years earlier as he felt that commerce in the colonel's city wasn't yet vibrant enough to justify business deals. He also saw it as an opportunity to discuss a certain Texas Ranger that was wreaking havoc with his business endeavors. In fact, he figured the colonel might even have sampled Scarlett Rose's charms at some point in his travels.

Colonel Kinney wasn't going to go out of his way for Thorpe. While Thorpe was one of the very wealthiest men in Texas and held inordinate influence over state legislators, Kinney knew who he was dealing with this time and had leverage given his knowledge of Thorpe's shady dealings. "Thank you again for the wine, Mr. Thorpe." He purposely didn't acknowledge Thorpe's inquiry about meeting.

The snub wasn't lost on Thorpe. As Colonel Kinney's business dealings had grown, so too had his own power and influence over the Nueces Strip. Thorpe made a mental note to take Kinney down a peg or two by rerouting certain raw goods shipments away from Corpus Christi. He figured a little trade war just might get the colonel's attention.

Lieutenant Belknap finally arrived at Fort Mason. He'd been away far longer than anticipated and had much to report on to his commanding officer. He hoped the major would be pleased, even bemused at his encounter with the naval ship captain in Corpus Christi. Word had spread quickly about the exploits of the small group of defenders that had repelled a large rebel Mexican force, so Belknap had become a bit of a folk hero among his military peers.

"Lieutenant Belknap reporting, sir." He stood at attention before the major. Belknap was lean and tanned. Fighting desperados, rebels, and Indians had seasoned him physically and mentally. He had gained great confidence, and that showed in his bearing.

"At ease, Lieutenant." The major returned his salute. "I've been hearing about you, Lieutenant." He tried to contain a smile. "You've gained an impressive reputation, if that Texas Ranger Captain Luke Dunn is to be believed."

Belknap had no idea that Luke had sent any reports. "Thank you, sir. He was a pleasure to serve with...er, under."

The next hour was filled with Belknap describing his exploits and answering the major's questions.

At last, the major stood and indicated the end of their session. "Lieutenant, I do congratulate you. I'm recommending your promotion to captain. Until that becomes official, you are heretofore a brevet captain." The major handed Belknap the captain's bars. The brevet was temporary until the official promotion was formally submitted and approved by higher authority.

"Thank you, sir."

"Now, Captain Belknap, are you ready for a new assignment?" It was a rhetorical question, of course. The major handed him a folder. "Congratulations. You're to rendezvous with the 2nd Cavalry and deploy to the Utah Territory. With your Comanche experience, Captain, you should do well against the Paiute savages."

Belknap's promotion was tempered by the new assignment. He saluted the major and left to inform his men.

With O'Rourke on his way from Austin, Thorpe was impatient to learn who had killed Biggs and what had happened to his valuable inventory. He now wondered whether he could trust Lieutenant Myers at Fort McIntosh.

Thaddeus Brown, his erstwhile partner in thievery, was out of the picture. Brown had worked with Myers, including giving the lieutenant handsome kickbacks for protecting the storage barn. Thorpe was distrustful enough to think the lieutenant might now take some of the loot for himself. He desperately needed to hire someone to move the goods, but was running out of people he could trust...even for pay.

His network of connections with the darker side of San Antonio were not so robust as in Austin or even Houston. He hoped O'Rourke might have a suggestion as to whom he might hire for the Laredo matter. To add to his concerns, he still awaited a response to the apology he gave the French trade minister for his son Gascon's misdeeds. He had a couple of boatloads of raw goods ready to set sail. He could sell them in New York or Boston, but wouldn't fetch nearly so good a price.

To further compound Thorpe's woes, he'd learned that a couple of Texas Ranger companies were being funded and would be led by Rip Ford. These companies were going to clean up the Comancheria and eventually the Nueces Strip. It would create a far more challenging environment for Thorpe's illicit schemes. It also meant that his latest nemesis, Texas Ranger Captain Luke Dunn, would be getting additional resources. The damnable Texas Ranger had done quite well without the help of an additional one hundred thirty men. Thorpe faced the very real prospect of his life being made miserable. He began to cut a piece of pecan pie, then thought better of it and started to devour it straight from the pie tin. Maybe it was time to return to his plantation. How much longer would his wife linger?

Three Toes passed through the campsite area where his family and small band of Penateka Comanche followers had been massacred by Biggs and his cutthroats up near the Pedernales River. He stayed mounted on his pony and stared mournfully at the graves. He began to feel as though the spirits were calling him. What indeed would the Great Spirit have him do?

The chief dismounted and decided to camp at the site and absorb the strong spirits he was feeling. For all he knew, it was the spirits of his own people that lingered there near the escarpment.

He stood at a pool of water and stared at his reflection. He hadn't seen his reflection in many moons. The mountain lion's claws and Roy Biggs's knife had disfigured his once handsome bronzed face.

Three Toes set up a small camp. Perhaps he'd stay more than a single night. The sun was creeping lower toward the horizon, so he had about an hour of good daylight left. The reddish glow of the sky was a harbinger of good weather. A light breeze wafted through the trees along the banks of the Pedernales River, and he found the sounds of rustling leaves and rushing waters relaxing. As if on cue, a smallish deer walked into the clearing before him. An arrow quickly delivered a bountiful dinner and leftovers for his travels.

After dining, he sat and stared into the dying flames of his campfire. How many years did he have ahead of him? Would he be a survivor of the White man's ravages? Could he adapt? He was thus caught up in a near-trance when he heard the faint sound of voices. They sounded like women, and they were undoubtedly already alerted to his location, thanks to the fire.

Two women and a teen boy walked cautiously into his campsite. From their appearance, they were hungry and very tired. Had they been warriors, Three Toes's scalp might already have been adorning a lance. He motioned them closer. "Bird Woman?" He thought he recognized one of the women as having belonged to Long Feathers's band.

"Three Toes?" she whispered.

"Come. Eat and drink."

The three joined the chief around his campfire as he added wood and put some venison on the spit he'd fashioned. "From where do you journey?"

Bird Woman stared intently at Three Toes. She saw the same scars he'd seen in his reflection earlier. "We left Camp Cooper on what they call the Brazos River. Our people were sick and dying of White man's disease. Our warriors were gone. The Texas Ranger Ford attacked us at Plum Creek. Killed many." She wondered at Three Toes's scars. "What happened to you?"

He forced a smile at the young boy. "What is your name?"

Bird Woman spoke for him. "His child name is Laughing Crow."

Three Toes understood. The boy wasn't permitted to talk directly to a Comanche chief. "Listen well, Laughing Crow." He turned his attention to the two women. "I have had many adventures since you last saw me at Camp Cooper. My family and warriors were all killed by White men while I was away. I was attacked by a mountain lion and killed it with my knife. The men who killed my family captured and tortured me."

"How did you survive?" He had the rapt attention of his audience.

"I have a very good friend who has strong medicine. Stronger than the Great Spirit. My warriors called him Ghost-Who-Rides. He is a Texas Ranger who respects our people. We have protected each other." He paused in thought. "He is a friend."

Laughing Crow's eyes grew as big as saucers as he tried to imagine someone with such strong medicine. Visions of a man on horseback floating like a ghost through the air danced in the young boy's mind.

"It is all true."

None would have doubted.

Three Toes turned his attention to the other woman. She was younger than Bird Woman and strikingly beautiful. He looked so intently at her that she averted her eyes. "Who are you?"

She looked at Bird Woman, who nodded her approval. "I am Cactus Flower. I was to wed Wolf Slayer, but he died of White man's disease."

Bird Woman spoke up. "Camp Cooper is empty. A few Penateka are moving north to the Red River."

Three Toes thought a few moments. "You are welcome to join me. I wish to plant a new family." There was no beating around the proverbial bush in the Comanche culture, especially in these dire times. Three Toes had effectively offered a marriage proposal.

Bird Woman and Cactus Flower agreed to his proposal. It turned out that Laughing Crow was the son of a warrior who had been killed in a battle with marauding Kiowa. The boy was also welcomed into the new family.

Three Toes slept with the two women lying on either side of him, sharing the warmth of their bodies against the evening chill. He awakened before sunrise and touched Cactus Flower. She was about to speak but he put his hand gently to her lips. "Come with me," he whispered.

They walked off toward the river and sat in the grass looking up at the stars. They looked at each other searchingly for what seemed a long time, before her gaze softened. He wrapped an arm around her and brought her to him. They laid back, and Three Toes mounted her. He remembered the first times with his wives, so strove to be gentle with Cactus Flower. Soon she was swept up in his passion and locked him to her with her legs. Their beings were lost in the moment.

Lovemaking ended, they lay back in the grass listening to the river and the sounds of the woods. She turned to him. "Why do you wear White man's sign on your necklace?"

"Is gift from squaw of Ghost-Who-Rides. It holds great power."

Cactus Flower seemed to accept his explanation. It was just as well, as Three Toes knew no more.

The chief walked her back and slipped back in beside Bird Woman.

Bird Woman opened one eye. She watched him fall back asleep. She smiled. She would have a turn.

"Dammit, O'Rourke. You took forever to get here!"

O'Rourke took a deep breath, rolled his eyes, and strolled easy-like out onto the balcony. "I can't just instantly up and leave, Horatio. Ford could get suspicious." He plopped himself in the chair opposite his corpulent host.

"I hope she was worth it. Can I order you a drink? Care for some pecan pie?"

"Water...a glass of water would be just fine, Horatio." He glanced at Thorpe's prodigious gut and smiled inwardly as he wondered how many slices of pecan pie the man had already eaten that day. "Guess you heard about the legislature finding the money to fund Texas Ranger companies."

Thorpe sneered derisively at the thought of a newspaperman and politician like Rip Ford pulling together companies of roughneck lawmen who were no better than brigands. Worse yet, his nemesis Luke Dunn would likely be involved. He disrespected Ford and hated Dunn. "I must rid myself of that son of a bitch Dunn before they have a chance to form those companies, O'Rourke. Every man I've sent against him has been on the losing end of the task."

"Is this why you called me to travel all the way to San Antonio?" O'Rourke crossed his arms as if challenging Thorpe.

"Well, I did wonder if you might know someone who could actually get the job done, but I invited you about another matter."

O'Rourke relaxed a bit. "Not sure I can help you with the Dunn problem. As to Ford, the Ranger companies have already been raised, and he chased a passel of Comanche out of Texas after a battle at Plum Creek. What else did you have in mind, Horatio?"

"We had an incident in Laredo." Thorpe floated the comment out rather nonchalantly. It belied the intensity of the problem.

"What happened?"

"I sent three of my people down to check on some inventory that Thaddeus Brown had stored for me. With Brown dead, I needed to be sure my merchandise was still intact. Figures that your friend Rip Ford caught wind of it and sent that damned Texas Ranger Captain Dunn to follow my men."

"And?"

"Dunn found the storage barn, killed all my men, and turned the bodies in to Sheriff Stills. Then, the son of a bitch went out to Fort McIntosh and told Lieutenant Myers about it. Of course, Myers already knew."

"And your problem is?" It was almost a rhetorical question.

"Damn, O'Rourke. Isn't it obvious? Too many people

know about the place and are likely going to help themselves to all or part of it. It's thievery, dammit!"

For Peter O'Rourke, the air was thick with irony. Thieves stealing from thieves. He couldn't contain a slight chuckle. "What do you expect me to do, Horatio?"

Thorpe was a touch exasperated. "I'll pay you handsomely to retrieve my merchandise and store it in a safe place."

"What if it's gone when I get there?"

"I must know." Thorpe chewed thoughtfully on another bite of pecan pie. "Are you up to it, O'Rourke?" His voice was low and almost pleading. He tried not to sound desperate. Uncertainty flew in the face of his obsession with order in his life, and Laredo represented considerable disorder. It had been bad enough to have lost a couple of wagon loads of goods when Thaddeus Brown and General Truax were captured by that damned Texas Ranger near Nuecestown and there was the arson fire in the warehouse in Austin. He needed to start selling off inventory before he lost it all. But that was secondary to finding out what he still had and protecting it.

"Five thousand plus the equipment and men to haul the stuff, Horatio."

Thorpe blinked. It wasn't that he couldn't afford it. His hired help seemed to be getting incrementally more expensive. "Deal. Samuel will get you a bank draft for half. You'll get the balance when the work is done."

"Pleasure doing business with you, Horatio. See you in a couple of weeks." He saw himself out. He checked with Samuel, who handed him an envelope with directions to the barn in Laredo and a bank draft for two thousand five hundred dollars. He cursed that the draft had been written before he'd named his price. He could have negotiated for more. "Deceitful son of a bitch," he whispered under his breath.

"What's that, Lucas?" She looked at the envelope Luke was fondling. "Are you going to open it?" They were sitting on opposite sides of the table, and she playfully rubbed her foot against his shin as she urged him to open the mail.

"I'm just thinking."

"I know, love. I can smell the wood burning from across the table." She laughed semi-playfully.

"There's a big decision inside this envelope, Lisa. I'm certain of it. A very big decision."

Across the top of it was the Texas Ranger logo and Rip Ford's name and address. Ford had by now sold his newspaper and had been pressed into service by Governor Runnels. As senior captain, Ford had been given wide latitude in recruiting men and setting strategies for quelling the Indian problem north of the Brazos River. He had recently led Rangers against hostile Comanche up north in the Battle of Little Robe Creek up on the Canadian River as well as at Plum Creek, so he was primed to take on a newly emerging threat from Mexico in the person of Juan Cortina.

"It's about the Texas Rangers, isn't it, Lucas?"

Luke nodded. He tore open one end of the envelope and pulled out an official-looking document. He read it carefully while Elisa fidgeted in anticipation. He finally passed it to her.

She read it as carefully as Luke had. "You're going to do it, aren't you?"

The air was pregnant with Luke's silence. He was still conflicted between his duties. There was a growing ranch that needed his attention, the twins plus a baby on the way, and an expanding regional population that desperately needed law and order. Ford's letter had included reference to another threat south of the Rio Grande in the person of Juan Cortina. Keeping Mexican bandits and revolutionaries at bay was nearly as challenging as keeping Apache and Comanche in check. At least, White man's disease and encroachment of ranches and settlements was depleting the tribal populations.

"You must, Lucas. You know you must."

Luke was ever so grateful that Elisa shared his passion for justice on the Nueces Strip. Perhaps it had been her dealings with life's realities in the form of attacks by Comanche, outlaws, and wild animals. She'd seen far too many loved ones fall victim to the wild and crazy uncertainties of the frontier.

He nodded. "I'll let Ford know."

"Mr. Ford's list of Texas Ranger equipment is impressive, Lucas. Sounds like he's putting together a military operation."

Luke appreciated Elisa's awareness of these things. "Yep, he seems to be focused on mobility and firepower. I expect some bad folks are going to rue the day they met any Texas Rangers."

"You going to get another Sharps? I'm kind of partial to the one we have here." She could joke a bit about that now as she thought back to using it to defend against Roy Biggs.

Luke smiled and took a long sip of coffee. "Those things will stop a buffalo in its tracks. You've seen what it can do to a human." He recalled Elisa killing Biggs's horse and then blowing the man's hand to pieces. Of course, the recoil nearly destroyed her shoulder. And there was the matter of what the paid killer Berne Culthwaite had done in nearly killing Luke with a Sharps. "I'll keep my new Colt rifle, too. Takes too long to reload the Sharps and it's tough to use while galloping on horseback." He looked up at the partially destroyed rifle on the mantel, an ever-present reminder of that Berne Culthwaite incident. He'd keep a couple of knives, too, as they were considered ubiquitous to any man on the Nueces Strip or anywhere on the Texas frontier for that matter. A man on the Nueces Strip without his weapons might just as well be naked. He appreciated that Elisa could defend herself. She was a strong woman, a perfect wife and mother to any man but especially to a man such as himself. And he never forgot what a wonderful love partner she was. "Lisa...let's take a walk down to the creek."

She responded to the invitation...both his words and his eyes. He was eating her alive visually. What was it about men? It was a rhetorical question for her. "Shall I get a lantern?"

"Got stars and moon tonight." He grabbed a couple of blankets and his gun belt. The gun wasn't very romantic, but this was still the Texas frontier.

Elisa made sure the twins were sleeping, as they quietly headed to the creek.

They passed the spot where they'd first sat together taking in the starry sky and talking of the future. Luke was leading them down to the creek itself. It was a right chilly early autumn evening.

"What are you up to, Lucas Dunn?" She knew very well as he pulled her tightly to him at water's edge.

"You're not afraid of a little chilly creek water, are you?" He'd swiftly stripped out of his clothes and begun to relieve her of hers.

She hesitated partly from wondering what had gotten into him to think of skinny-dipping in frigid water. This was a new side to her husband. A bit adventurous and certainly different. Before she could protest, he'd pulled her into the creek. She clung to him to absorb his warmth as fully as possible.

"I thought..."

"That cold affected it?" He laughed, picking her up and carrying her to shore. He wrapped her and himself in the blanket.

Being carried in his well-muscled arms was titillating to say the least, but nestled in a blanket under her man was even more pleasurable. "Oh, my, Lucas Dunn." She gasped loudly as paroxysms coursed deeply through her. The shivers were not from the chill air.

As they lay in the blankets, Luke pointed to the sky. "See that constellation? That's what most call the Big Dipper. If you line up those two stars in its cup, they point to the North Star. I use it as a guide at night on the prairie."

She looked at where he was pointing and then back at Luke. "That's interesting, Lucas." In the fading ardor of their recent passions, his observation hadn't exactly seemed romantic.

He gave her a broad smile. "Guess you misunderstood. You're my North Star, Lisa Dunn." He kissed her deeply.

TWENTY
BLOOD LUST

THE RIFLE STOCK had been hand crafted with intricate carvings and even some turquoise inlays. It was almost a museum piece. Quinn Maguire slid the rifle back into its bead-decorated fringed leather scabbard. He'd only needed a single shot from this showpiece Sharps rifle to bring down his prey. No point in wasting ammunition.

Now came the toughest part of the job. To collect the bounty, he had to haul the body to a place where its identity could be confirmed. He'd need to find a post office, jail, or Army fort. Fortunately, his prey had his own horse, as Maguire detested the prospect of a dead body draped behind his own saddle.

He rather appreciated that he'd shifted his killing ways from outright crimes of passion to legitimate...and legal... bounty hunting. Every now and then, the quarry would be misidentified and innocent men would become his victims. Accidents did happen.

It took him another day to reach Nuecestown. Maguire rode slowly into the little town and quickly found the jail. By pure chance, Bill Meaney had come up from Corpus

Christi to make repairs to the roof. It wouldn't do to have prisoners being rained on indoors. Maguire dismounted, hitched his horse, and looked up at Meaney hammering away up on the roof.

"Excuse me. Are you the law around these parts?"

Meaney looked down and took in what was apparently a bounty hunter and his prize. "Yep. Sheriff Bill Meaney at your service." The sheriff noted that the man wore a wide-brimmed black hat and was reasonably well-attired. He couldn't help but notice the Sharps in the fancy scabbard. He deduced that the man was a professional at his craft.

"Name's Quinn Maguire. I wanted to collect bounty on this here Randall Watts fella."

"Hang on. Go ahead inside, and I'll be right with you." Meaney was semi-annoyed at the interruption, but it was part of his job. He climbed on down. He was turning the Watts name over in his mind, as it didn't sound familiar. He hoped he wouldn't have to validate it with some other law enforcement authority, as it would delay Maguire's bounty and not get the man out of his hair. Soon enough, Meaney dusted himself off, took a careful gander at the body draped over the horse, and walked into the jail.

Maguire had grabbed a seat across from the desk. "Cozy little place you've got here, Sheriff."

"We've got a larger jail in Corpus Christi. If I don't have Watts's information here, we might have to go to Corpus."

"I'd really hate to have any delay, Sheriff. I've got business back in San Antonio."

"I'm sure you know the process, Mr. Maguire. We have to be sure before we go handing out Texas's money." Meaney pulled a sheaf of papers from the desk drawer and began to rifle through them. He was grateful he'd the presence of mind to alphabetize the wanted posters. "Looks like you're in luck, Mr. Maguire. Randall Watts was wanted for rustling and mail robbery." He read through the flyer. "Hang on. I need to check something." Meaney got up and strode outside to the horses. Maguire followed at a short distance.

"Is there a problem, Sheriff?"

"Flyer describes a long scar on Watts's cheek and yellow hair. This man has no scar and dark hair. Seems we have a problem, Mr. Maguire."

"I called out his name before I fired, and he responded by shooting toward me." Maguire started to become just a tad disconcerted. "It had to have been him."

"This his gun?" Meaney reached into the man's holster and drew out a revolver. He examined it. "This gun is fully loaded. You say he fired at you?"

"He had a rifle, Sheriff. I must have left it back where I shot him."

Too many suspicious things simply weren't adding up for the sheriff.

"Look here, Sheriff. His rifle scabbard is empty." Maguire pointed to the scabbard mounted alongside the saddle. Indeed, there was no rifle.

Meaney looked inside the scabbard. There was plenty of gun oil evidence that a rifle had been kept inside. He thought on the victim. The man could have darkened his hair as a disguise, but where was the scar?

Of a sudden, Maguire had an idea. He walked over and tugged at the rear of Watts's pants. A scar on the man's butt was revealed. "You were looking at the wrong cheek, Sheriff." Of course, the man's butt end stunk to high heaven as he'd soiled himself upon being shot.

Meaney laughed. "Dang! Who would've figured?" He smiled at Maguire and headed back inside. "Just have to do a bit of paperwork. It'll take about an hour. You can wait here or take a walk around Nuecestown."

Meaney emerged an hour later to find Maguire sitting on the front step to the jail. "You been waiting here all this time?"

"Checked out the ferry. Nice little town y'all have here, Sheriff." A tour of Nuecestown didn't exactly take much time.

Meaney handed him a piece of paper. "We don't carry cash around here, Mr. Maguire. You take this to the bank in Corpus Christi or San Patricio, and they'll give you your due."

Maguire shook his head resignedly. "Figures. Guess I'll head to Corpus Christi, Sheriff. Thanks for taking care of this matter." He tipped his hat. "Do you by chance have any posters on fellas that ain't been caught? I'm sort of enjoying this bounty business." He tied the dead man's horse to the hitching post and looked back at the sheriff.

"Matter of fact, I've got a couple, but I can't guarantee that the bounties haven't already been collected." Meaney wondered that Maguire had decided to go to Corpus instead of San Patricio, but he decided not to question the change in destination.

Maguire took Meaney's posters and was soon on his way.

For his part, Meaney was left wondering what got the man involved in bounty hunting in the first place.

Luke kicked back in the chair on the gallery, trying to relax and think about his next steps. Elisa had fed him especially well that morning, and he felt as though he needed to pursue lawbreakers to keep his waistline trim. Chores around Heaven's Gate were simply not enough to offset her fine cooking. So he yielded once again to his sense of bringing justice to the Nueces Strip. He'd sent a message back to Rip Ford accepting the role of recruiting a company of Texas Rangers to help clean up the region. He figured he'd enlist Bol Richards, as his history with the Texas War for Independence would attract the sort of men Luke would be seeking. He sought men of courage, men of a mind that wouldn't be defeated, who'd keep coming on in the face of seemingly insurmountable opposition. Yet, he didn't seek reckless men. They needed to exhibit a law-abiding steadiness of purpose and performance. A Texas Ranger recruited by Luke Dunn would be committed to justice and be fully loyal to Texas.

Luke also figured to recruit young Walker Carson, whom he'd sent to Sheriff Stills in Laredo. He saw a redeeming value in the lad, despite his ill-fated bank robbery attempt. In any case, the word would spread, and he'd have to select the best couple of dozen men that volunteered. He hoped and prayed he'd be able to pay them with the funds promised from the powers that be in the capital at Austin. His planning was interrupted.

"Lucas...Lucas...it's time!" Elisa's water had broken.

Luke almost fell out of his chair. He paused to ring the dinner bell that would alert Julia that she was needed. As Luke entered the house, he heard her running up from the cabin.

Luke began to warm up some water while Elisa prepared herself for the coming event. Despite delivering the twins barely a year before, she still felt like a neophyte at this childbearing business. She had only just turned nineteen. "How do you feel, Lisa?"

"The baby's pushing and turning, Lucas."

Julia rushed into the room and heard Elisa's description of what she was feeling inside. "The baby must come the right way. *Mi madre* taught me how to turn it to be certain there is no problem."

Elisa flashed a smile of relief as her contractions increased and began to grow more intense. She lay back on the bed. Julia began to manipulate the baby as best she could. It wasn't easy. "It must be a girl, *Señora* Dunn. She has a mind of her own." Julia hoped the humor would break the anxiety.

Luke stood back out of Julia's way but close enough that Elisa could hold his hand tightly...very tightly.

Blessedly, Peter and John were sleeping through the commotion. They'd awaken hungry, and Elisa would have three children to feed.

Minutes passed. There was a brief break in Elisa's pushing. She turned to Luke. "Lucas, get a breath of fresh air."

Conflicted at not wanting to leave Elisa's side, Luke nevertheless decided to step out onto the gallery for a momentary breath of fresh air. Jaime walked up from the cabin. He'd been out on the range when Luke signaled for Julia. "Julia is helping?"

"Yes, thanks. I'm very grateful she's here."

Just then came the plaintive cry of a newborn child. Luke turned and dashed inside. "Is everything all right?"

"*Señor* Dunn, you have a daughter. I knew it was a girl when I had to turn her." Julia beamed, then laughed with joy at having helped bring new life into the world.

Luke looked down at Elisa holding their baby girl already suckling at her breast. "You're beautiful, Lisa Dunn."

Elisa gently pulled the baby from her breast. "Hold your daughter, Lucas." She held her toward Luke.

He was mesmerized at the tiny bundle in his big arms. "Do you have a name for her?" He had chosen the boys' names and was of a mind to let her name their daughter.

Elisa was exhausted, but found the energy to offer up a name. "How about Andrea Ann?"

Julia was just finishing cleaning up and turned with a smile. "What a beautiful name, *Señora* Dunn."

Luke took it all in. "I expect that settles it. Andrea Ann Dunn it is."

With seventy-five dollars bulging in his pocket, Maguire had pretty much settled on his next prize. He'd reviewed the half-dozen flyers that Meaney had passed along and picked out a hider who was wreaking havoc killing and skinning cattle down toward Corpus Christi. The man apparently had the temerity to have killed a couple of head of a rancher's cattle, cut out the brand, and sold the hides to other nearby ranchers. The wanted man was a Mexican, and the bounty was only twenty-five dollars. Still, that was a goodly ransom in 1858 Texas. He set his sights on finding this Jesus Martinez and collecting his reward.

Maguire took his sweet time covering the ground from Nuecestown to Corpus Christi. He hoped to learn more about the fugitive from justice and pick up his trail. Now and then, he'd pass the bones of cattle picked clean by scavengers. He'd be seeking fresh kills that might lead him to Martinez.

He long ago realized that it was the kill he relished. He recalled little of his childhood, though it was more of a function of putting bad experiences from his mind. Both his mother and mostly absentee father didn't spare the rod. Ultimately, his mother killed his father in self-defense as he watched. She was sentenced to a few years in prison. Maguire was then left on his own as a fifteen-year-old and moved from one job to another around the darker parts of

Philadelphia. It was no surprise when he fell in with the denizens of crime in the "City of Brotherly Love." He'd soon gotten into a bit of serious trouble back in Philadelphia when he killed a couple of men during a drunken brawl. He barely managed to escape. What he never expected was that he actually enjoyed killing the two men —the feel of his knife plunging through flesh and muscle, grating against bone, feeling the warm blood on his hands. From Philly, he headed ever westward, leaving behind a trail of bar fights and travel encounters that included an occasional killing. It had become a sort of blood lust sport for him, though he began to feel the hot breath of the law and bounty hunters. In his perverted mind, he figured that becoming a bounty hunter himself would legitimize, if not legalize, his murderous habits.

About three days out of Corpus Christi, he found a half-dozen freshly skinned cattle. The kills were recent enough that he had no trouble picking up a trail.

This Martinez would likely have a helper or two, but that would be manageable. Hiders worked quickly so as to minimize the possibility of being caught in the act. Maguire had studied the wanted flyer. His prey would be about average height, dark-skinned, with long dark hair and a big mustache. There were no unusual distinguishing characteristics.

Maguire had been tracking the hiders for about three hours when he spotted what appeared to be a straggler. He had the foresight to have purchased a spyglass a few weeks back, which greatly facilitated his ability to identify his quarries. He needed to be certain. He raised the spyglass. The man certainly met the description, and he was trailing his fellow hiders by not more than a couple of hundred yards. Maguire figured that Martinez was lagging to be sure they weren't followed, as the man kept low and regularly scanned the surrounding landscape. His only concern would be the sound of the Sharps spooking the other hiders. But he had little choice, as it would be next to impossible to sneak up on Martinez for a knife attack. As it was, Maguire had pulled unnoticed to within perhaps three hundred yards of the hider. He dismounted and slipped the Sharps from its scabbard. He'd have to fire from a standing position to ensure a clear line of sight over the tall grasses.

He nestled the rear bead into the u-shaped front sight at the muzzle of the Sharps, aiming just a bit high to allow for distance. He'd become quite expert at allowing for wind and distance, and this wasn't going to be an especially difficult shot. His prey wasn't moving. It was as though he awaited his demise. Maguire exhaled a bit, held his breath, and squeezed the trigger. A near instant later, his target fell from his saddle.

Off in the distance, he saw what he figured were the remaining hiders take off in a panic. Maguire mounted up, slipped the Sharps back into its scabbard, drew his revolver, and rode over to where the man had fallen. The man was lying on his back and bleeding profusely from a gut wound. Maguire dismounted and figured the kind thing would be to finish him. But first, so long as the man breathed, he had a chance to confirm his kill. "You Jesus Martinez?"

The man struggled to breathe. *"Me llamo...Roberto... Sánchez."* And he died.

Recognizing that he'd made a big mistake, Maguire sought to rationalize. Who'd know, he told himself. In his mind, the damned Mexicans all looked alike anyway. He'd claim this man was Jesus Martinez and get his bounty. After all, most Anglos wouldn't give a hoot, as Mexicans were considered by many to be something significantly lower than human. At least, Maguire didn't have to waste a bullet finishing the man off.

He hoisted his kill over the saddle of the man's horse and tied him in place. Considering his location, he decided to head back to Corpus Christi where he'd already established a sort of trusted relationship with the sheriff.

Luke wasn't going to be doing any Texas Ranger recruiting for a few days. Elisa needed rest and, even with Jaime and Julia helping, there was plenty to do around Heaven's Gate. That having been said, he did manage to send a message to Bol Richards to come visit when he got a chance. He and Elisa were grateful for his *vaquero* and his wife, especially as Julia eased Elisa's need to share attention with the twins. Despite their young ages, Peter and John were bewildered at the increased activity around the house. Up to now, they'd been the center of attention, and they sensed that was changing. Even more challenging, she was faced with having to nurse three children with only two breasts. Julia convinced her to wean the twins a bit early.

A couple of days later, Richards showed up at the ranch. He saw Luke taking a rare respite in his favorite chair on the gallery. He hailed him as he rode up to the house. "Luke! I hear you've got great news!"

"It's a girl, Bol."

Richards looked quizzically. "I meant forming a Texas Ranger company, Captain."

"Oh, that. I received a letter from Rip Ford. Funds have been authorized, and we're to form up a company to clear out remaining Indians and lawbreakers on the Nueces Strip. I could use your help." Luke went on to describe the types of men he was seeking.

"I can help with that, Captain. I've been making connections around Corpus Christi, and there are a few that should meet our needs."

He was in a great mood with the prospect of joining up as a Texas Ranger. "By the way, there's been an incident back in Corpus."

"An incident?"

"Yeah. Some bounty hunter named Quinn Maguire tried to turn in a body of a wanted Mexican called Jesus Martinez...only, it wasn't Martinez. Sheriff Meaney recognized the dead man as Roberto Sanchez. I expect that may be your *vaquero's* cousin. The sheriff went to arrest Maguire, but the man bolted."

"Is Bill chasing Maguire? Who else knows it was Roberto?" Questions swirled through Luke's head. "Dang, but we don't need this sort of thing...not now."

"I think Meaney is forming a posse, Captain. I figure that Maguire fella is long gone by now."

As fate would have it, Jaime came riding up from having tended to stray longhorns out on the range most of the morning. In the course of his riding around the outer reaches of Heaven's Gate, he met up with a couple of his cousins who told him about Roberto. They were going after Quinn Maguire, but Jaime decided it was his duty to let Luke know what was happening. He saw Bol Richards standing with Luke but, knowing his attitude toward Mexicans, fully ignored him and directed his attention to Luke. "*Señor* Dunn, have you heard?"

"Yes, Jaime. Terrible news."

"My cousins have gathered some friends and family to chase the killer, *Señor* Dunn. They wanted me to join them, but I wanted to see you first."

TWENTY-ONE
VIGILANTES

FOR LUKE and pretty much most law-abiding folks, the difference between a vigilance committee and a posse was that the latter was formed and led by a law enforcement officer. He appreciated Jaime alerting him as to his cousins' plans.

"Jaime, I don't think Sheriff Meaney would be very happy with your cousins chasing after Maguire. Can you get them to join his posse?" Luke had visions of Jaime's cousins capturing Maguire and hanging him or worse.

Richards was less than sympathetic. After all, Maguire had only killed a Mexican, and they were subhuman so far as Richards figured. "Heck, Luke, let the bastards do their best."

Luke scowled at Richards. "Bol, that's not what we want from our Rangers. You've got to get your head straight as to our Mexican friends and neighbors. There are good men and bad men from both cultures."

Richards didn't exactly appreciate being scolded in front of Jaime, but had brought it on himself. He decided to strive to be more helpful. "They could likely use my tracking skills."

Jaime acknowledged Richards's offer with a nod, but was still unsure of what to do. "*Señor* Dunn, what should we do?"

Luke was conflicted, as he instinctively wanted to be at Heaven's Gate with Elisa and his newborn daughter. But duty had a strong pull. "Jaime, we don't want vigilantes exacting their version of justice. It turns the law upside down. Can you get your cousins to rendezvous with us?"

"*Si*...I mean, yes, *Señor* Dunn. I'll ask them to meet here."

Quinn Maguire was riding hard. For all he knew, the sheriff had rounded up a posse and was already giving chase. He figured his best chance for escape lay southward, so he set his hopes on making it to Rio Grande City and a possible crossing into Mexico. However, he had a lot of ground to cover and only one horse. His mount was already well-lathered, and he dared not ride the beast into the ground.

He cursed the remote chance that the sheriff would have known the victim of his overly-zealous bounty hunting. Now, he felt as though his kill-for-profit world was beginning to crumble around him. Somehow, he needed to get the hell out of Texas.

It occurred to him that the folks in Mexico might not be too welcoming if they found out he was on the run from killing one of their own. His hope was to cross the Rio Grande, head west, and then dash north into New Mexico.

By now, his horse was struggling. Maguire saw a low-lying building off in the distance and hoped the horse would hold out until he got to it. With any luck, there might be someone with another horse.

His mount was barely walking, when Maguire rode into the small hider ranch. Apparently, the men were out looking to rustle cattle for more hides, so only an elderly Mexican, a couple of women, and some children were to be seen.

Maguire rode slowly up to what appeared to be the main building, essentially a low-lying hovel. He wasn't especially facile with the Spanish language but gave it a try. He confronted the old man. *"Hola!...um...necesito un caballo."*

"No hay caballos."

Maguire looked over at the half-dozen horses in the nearby corral. *"¿Qué hay de esos?"* He pointed to the horses asking rhetorically what those four-legged beasts were.

"No para la venta." The old man sounded firm that the horses weren't for sale.

"Then I'll steal one, Mexican bastard." And Maguire drew his gun and dropped the old man where he stood.

The women stood back aghast at what the gringo had done. They tried to comfort the old man while Maguire quickly picked one of the better-looking steeds in the corral and switched out his tack. He was fortunate that the horse had been saddle-broken. As he mounted, one of the women picked up a gun that had been stuffed in the old man's waistband and pointed it at Maguire. She fired but missed. Maguire didn't, and she fell on top of the old man and the other grieving woman.

"Via con dios, Mexican bitch!" Not a further word was spoken. Maguire laughed heartily as he enjoyed his little episode of blood lust and rode off.

★★

O'Rourke was pleased to take Thorpe's money, but was intent on accomplishing his mission before Rip Ford's Texas Rangers were swarming all over the Nueces Strip. He needed to get to Laredo, load up what inventory he could find, and take the merchandise to Veracruz where it could be shipped out to Thorpe's representatives in New York City. The most dangerous part would be the vulnerability of the slow-moving wagons traveling along the border. In any case, he had to get this job done with all due stealth while not jeopardizing his position spying for Thorpe in Rip Ford's office.

Of course, all plans would change if Thorpe's supposed allies in Laredo had already pilfered the loot. O'Rourke decided to purchase his wagons in Laredo, so he wouldn't be unnecessarily slowed in getting there. He assumed there'd be wagons available and, if need be, he could simply cross the Rio Grande and buy them in Nuevo Laredo. His first stop was to see Lieutenant Myers at Fort McIntosh. He rode slowly up to the gate.

"Halt! Who goes?"

"Peter O'Rourke to see Lieutenant Myers."

"The lieutenant is not here, sir."

"Any idea where I might find him?"

The guard shrugged. There weren't all that many secrets on the frontier. "He's patrolling just north of Laredo."

It didn't take a mental giant to realize that the lieutenant was nosing around looking for Thorpe's hidden barn. "Appreciate the information. I'll see if I can find him."

He turned to ride toward Laredo, but stopped. "Did he take any wagons?"

"Why, yes, sir…yes, he did."

O'Rourke tipped his hat and rode on at a brisk trot. He murmured under his breath, "Son of a bitch."

Seems Thorpe's worst fears were being realized. Still,

O'Rourke was surprised that it had taken the lieutenant more than two weeks to go after the treasure. There must have been some thing or things that distracted Lieutenant Myers. Maybe rumors of Apache attacks had been more than mere scuttlebutt.

"Bill, I hear you might need help going after that Maguire fellow?" Luke, Bol, and Jaime sat on horseback facing the sheriff as he stood in the doorway to the Corpus Christi jail. Luke had been none too happy to leave Heaven's Gate at this time. Jaime hadn't been able to reach his cousins, so Luke had no choice but to try to link up with the sheriff to form up a posse to pursue the murderer. He felt compelled to at least try to get to Maguire before the vigilantes.

"Nothing I can do now, Luke. That Maguire fella is long gone from my jurisdiction."

Luke could sense that the normally level-headed Jaime was beginning to get just a bit hot and bothered by Meaney's response, especially after passing up the opportunity to join with his vigilante cousins. It was a potentially volatile situation. Luke put out his hand palm down to calm Jaime, then looked at Meaney. He shook his head. "Thought we could count on you, Bill."

"Sorry, Luke. Colonel Kinney surely wouldn't have me running off across Texas on some wild goose chase and leave Corpus Christi unprotected." Unsaid was his belief that the killer of a Mexican wasn't worth risking his time, much less his life, for.

Luke wasn't about to waste time trying to convince Meaney. "I'm sorry, too, Bill. You're likely making the right decision, but it's an unfortunate one. We're going to try to catch up with Jaime Sanchez's cousins and bring Maguire to justice." Luke figured there was no point in trying to guilt Meaney into riding with them.

"Jaime, Bol, let's ride." Luke intuitively sensed that Maguire would head southwest toward Rio Grande City. If there was a trail, it wouldn't take long to pick it up. Besides, Jaime's cousins were surely cutting a wide swath through the prairie. In any case, they had rations for a week on the trail. If they didn't overtake Maguire in a couple of days, there'd be no point in pursuing further. They certainly couldn't follow Maguire into Mexico, though Jaime could likely get away with it. It'd be Luke's luck to run into someone who remembered him from the incident with Callahan.

It didn't take O'Rourke long to find Lieutenant Myers, and the officer was none too friendly when he did. He threw caution to the winds and rode straight up to the lieutenant's caravan of five large ox-drawn wagons lined up outside Thorpe's barn.

"Halt!"

He found three rifles aimed in his direction.

"Is Lieutenant Myers here?"

The lieutenant had heard the mild ruckus and emerged from the barn. "This is private property. What's your business?"

"Horatio Thorpe sent me. It appears that you're protecting his merchandise."

The lieutenant had been caught red-handed, and O'Rourke was offering to let him off the hook. The officer could have easily overcome the interloper, but he wasn't exactly up to earning Thorpe's vengeance. Murder of his duly-appointed representative would go far worse than simply pilfering a few pieces of stolen loot.

O'Rourke slid from his saddle and strolled boldly past the lieutenant and his soldiers, taking a seat on a steamer trunk toward the rear of the barn. "Join me, Lieutenant. I'd have a word with you." He waited while the lieutenant thought a moment, whispered something to his men, and walked back to where O'Rourke was casually seated. "You must have heard that Mr. Thorpe wants me to take his valuable goods to Veracruz for shipment. I would certainly pay you for these wagons, though I do need some laborers. I might be able to make it well worth your cooperation, Lieutenant."

Lieutenant Myers stroked his goatee as he thought on O'Rourke's offer. Any lingering doubt in his mind had more to do with the lingering threat of Apache attacks. They'd engaged Lipan Apache four times in the past week, intercepting them as they attempted to cross the Rio Grande. They'd lost two wounded and had killed eight of the savages. "Mr. O'Rourke, I suggest that you will need an armed escort for much of your journey. The Apache have been restless and would like little better than to add to their collection of scalps. I cannot afford to assign soldiers to your mission, but can suggest some folks in Laredo."

O'Rourke was feeling ever more confident that he'd avoided any nasty situation with the lieutenant. "As token of good faith, Lieutenant, I invite you and your soldiers to load one wagon with goods that you might find suitable for your living quarters at Fort McIntosh. In exchange, I'll take the remaining wagons and your guidance in hiring an armed escort. I can assure you that Mr. Thorpe will be very appreciative."

Lieutenant Myers eased back and thought on the offer. Haggling wasn't one of his specialties in any case.

It was time for O'Rourke to close the bargain. "I guess I should add that several troops of Texas Rangers are being formed under Rip Ford. The Nueces Strip will be swarming with lawmen within the next couple of months. There won't be another opportunity like this one."

"You've got a deal, Mr. O'Rourke."

Quinn Maguire took it easier with the horse he'd obtained from the Mexican hiders, but was intent on continuing to put distance between himself and any pursuers. In addition to any relatives of Sanchez and possibly lawmen, he'd now gained the ire of the hiders. He was still a couple of days from the Rio Grande but dead tired. He'd pretty much run out of food and water, so decided to rest and resume his journey at night.

He found a reasonably sheltered spot where a deeply carved-out arroyo meandered through the prairie grass. Maguire figured it'd be a couple of hours until sunset, so got his horse to lie down out of sight. He laid out his bedroll, placed his knife and a revolver next to his hip, and fell asleep as soon as his head hit the saddlebag he used as a pillow. He thought on the four people he'd killed over the past three weeks. Strangely, the reliving of those experiences relaxed him.

"¡Señor Maguire, despierta!"

Maguire couldn't have been sleeping much more than an hour.

"¡Despierta!"

There was just enough sunlight that he could make out three rifles pointed at him. They were in the hands of what appeared to be Mexicans.

"Levántate, Señor." One of the men gouged his ribs with

the muzzle of his rifle and urged him to get up. His two companions were quick to grab Maguire and pull him to his feet.

Maguire stood shakily. This was not good. *"¿Quién eres tú?"* His Spanish was rusty. They hadn't identified themselves, though he wasn't going to push too hard. He was thinking fast now as to how to buy time.

The apparent leader smiled broadly and poked Maguire with his gun. *"Agarra la cuerda."*

Maguire knew enough Spanish to know that the man was calling for a rope.

"Mi nombre es Carlos Sánchez," the man said. He emphasized the name Sanchez. As he spoke, he draped a loop of rope over Maguire's head and pulled it tightly around his neck. One of his companions forced the captive's hands together behind his back and tied his wrists.

One of Sanchez's men led Maguire's horse over. *"Usamos el caballo después de que él está muerto."* He especially coveted the beautifully bead-decorated fringed leather scabbard holding Maguire's rifle. For the present, he seemed content to wait until Maguire's death before taking it.

Maguire had no idea how these men had closed the ground on him so quickly, but that hardly mattered. Bizarrely, he found himself desperately hoping there were lawmen out on the Nueces Strip tracking him and who might show up in the nick of time to save him from his apparent fate.

The leader sneered as he made sure the rope was snug around Maguire's neck, mounted his own horse, and wrapped the other end of the rope around the saddle horn. *"Mataste a mi hermano."*

It was plain to Maguire these were the relatives of the

man he had mistakenly murdered. Turned out the victim was the brother of the Mexican holding the rope.

Sanchez backed his horse just enough to draw the rope taut. He saw the beginnings of fear in Maguire's eyes. With a satisfied smile, he spurred his horse and began a gallop with his victim dragging behind through all manner of sage, rock, and cacti. Maguire quickly became a bloodied mess of cuts and scratches.

He'd gone no more than a couple of hundred yards. He was hovering over Maguire to check his condition and preparing to take him on another gallop when a gunshot echoed across the prairie. Maguire was gasping for air as the rope had constricted his neck.

Luke Dunn's habit of traveling through the night had enabled him to catch up to Jaime's cousins. "¡Alto! ¡Alto!"

The good news for Jaime's cousins was that they hadn't yet killed Maguire, though he was growing ever closer to death's door. Covered with cuts and scrapes, blood seemed to even be oozing from the bounty hunter's pores, and his breathing was labored.

Jaime and Richards rode up behind Luke.

Luke's *vaquero* boldly rode up to his cousin, unwrapped the rope from around his saddle horn, dismounted, and loosened the noose around Maguire's neck. "*Eso es suficiente.*" Jaime spoke the words firmly to let his cousins know in no uncertain terms that they'd done enough. They were not to be vigilantes. "*No somos vigilantes. Señor Dunn, el prisionero es tuyo.*" He was giving Maguire to Luke.

Carlos Sanchez wasn't quite so sure. "*¿Quién es este?*"

"*Es un Ranger de Texas.*" He continued to speak with strong conviction. "*Es* Texas Ranger Captain Luke Dunn. *Es amigo.*" He was mixing English and Mexican a bit, but getting his message across.

For his part, Maguire tried to stand but managed to get

no further than on his knees. Bol Richards rode forward and confronted the beaten man. "I ain't no lover of Mexicans, you son of a bitch, but you're one damned lily-livered skunk of a coward for sure." He grabbed Maguire and hoisted him onto the horse they'd brought around for him. The noose still hung from his neck, and Richards tied the other end to the saddle horn. "Don't go fallin' off, now, ya hear?" Richards laughed at the prospect.

Luke rode over to Jaime's cousin Carlos. *"Muchas gracias.* You can come back to Corpus Christi with us, if you like. *¿Ven con nosotros?"* To seal the truce, he handed over Maguire's bead-decorated fringed leather scabbard that one of the vigilante cousins couldn't take his eyes off of.

The cousins nodded affirmatively, and the group headed northeastward toward Corpus Christi.

For his part, Luke appreciated that so far as possible saner heads had prevailed. Maguire would surely hang for his crime, but the entire episode came too close to having to arrest Jaime's cousins for murder. He also realized that vigilantes would, for better or worse, become part of the Nueces Strip landscape, especially so far as there were inadequate lawmen to bring justice to the region.

That said, the prospect of a large Texas Ranger force under Rip Ford might begin to change that...but Luke knew he was likely being overly optimistic. So long as the world spawned broken people, the law would be broken and some folks would take justice—or their perception of it —into their own hands.

Luke looked forward to depositing Maguire in Meaney's jail. Only then could he get on with his recruiting efforts.

Peter O'Rourke had the good sense to send a courier to San Antonio to let Thorpe know that his goods were in transit to Veracruz. The journey would be a slow one, and it wouldn't do to have an impatient man like Thorpe suffering any sort of anxiety. At that, his deal with Lieutenant Myers meant that O'Rourke was going to pocket a greater profit.

True to his attention to detail and appreciative of Thorpe's obsessions, O'Rourke inventoried all the merchandise. He especially noted the goods that the soldiers took. He'd also paid Sheriff Stills a small token of appreciation to look the other way.

O'Rourke had recruited eight men to serve as armed guards, including an enthusiastic young man named Walker Carson. Carson, like the other hires, had no idea that O'Rourke's cargo had been acquired by fraudulent means. So far as he knew, it was a legitimate job that Sheriff Stills had recommended and paid good money for. O'Rourke even promised them that they'd have no shortage of women in Veracruz. Basics, especially food and sex, transcended any and all creature comforts with these sorts of men.

They found themselves closing in on Rio Grande City, roughly eight days into their journey, when trouble materialized. They'd been on the lookout for Lipan Apache, heeding the advice of Lieutenant Myers back at Fort McIntosh. But this trouble didn't turn out to be Indians.

Seemingly, out of nowhere, at least two dozen heavily armed Mexican bandits appeared. These were Cheno Cortina's men, and they swooped down on the slow-moving caravan with guns blazing.

Much to presidential pretender Benito Juarez's consternation, an erstwhile champion of the people named Juan Nepomuceno Cortina, or Cheno for short, was seeking his personal destiny along the Rio Grande, attacking from his *rancho* base in Brownsville. Society-fracturing cultural conflicts seemed to have become endemic to Mexico, and Cortina fanned the flames as people sought a dynamic leader, a man of destiny. He'd begun with the relatively petty thievery of horses and cattle, and killing of a sheep or two. Cortina was said to have the disposition of a gambler, combined with the abilities of a natural leader. Soon enough, he'd taken to rustling, murder, and generally wreaking havoc in southern Texas.

To describe the scene among O'Rourke's wagons as mayhem would be a gross understatement. "*¡Viva Cheno Cortina! ¡Mueran los gringos!*" Riders descended on the wagon caravan, quickly exposing its vulnerability.

O'Rourke's intuition had told him to go ahead separately and meet the wagons in Veracruz, but he felt obligated to help guard Thorpe's interests. He had the dubious good fortune to be riding as an outrider on the far side of the caravan, away from the brunt of the Cortina attack.

Gunfire seemed to be coming from all directions. Shouting and yelling left no question as to whom was attacking. "*¡Viva Cortina!*" was a constant refrain.

Walker Carson had been posted as a guard in the fourth of the five wagons. He felt several bullets whiz past before he seized the opportunity to leap onto the back of a passing horse ridden by one of Cortina's men, wrestle the man from his saddle, and ride north at breakneck speed to escape the battle. Glancing behind as he galloped northward, he saw none other than O'Rourke, equally desperate to break free of the fight.

They pulled up beside a mesquite motte a mile or so away. Carson was breathing every bit as hard as his horse. He turned to O'Rourke, who had pulled up next to him and was equally breathless and aboard a well-lathered mount. "What the hell was that?"

O'Rourke didn't have a ready answer. "They kept shouting about someone named Cortina. Never heard of him."

Carson took inventory. There were at least four places where bullets had grazed his horse's tack or went straight through his own clothes. There was a hole clean through his hat. He checked on O'Rourke, and he'd fared no better. They each had a canteen of water, but food was back with the wagons. "We better keep on riding, Mr. O'Rourke."

For his part, O'Rourke was dying to know the condition of the men and wagons. They could no longer hear any shouting or gunfire, but it would have been imprudent to go back and see the outcome. He assumed all the men had been killed or captured, and the wagons would be in the hands of Cortina. "Your name is Walker Carson, right?"

Carson nodded. "That's my name."

"I must go back. Can I trust you to deliver a note to someone in San Antonio?" O'Rourke pulled a small slip of paper from his saddle bag, wrote a brief note, folded it, scribbled Thorpe's name on it, and passed it to Carson, along with twenty-five dollars in silver coin.

"I can do that, Mr. O'Rourke. Just glad to be alive."

"Being alive is certainly what we call a beneficial outcome, Walker. Ride safely."

"You be careful, Mr. O'Rourke."

TWENTY-TWO
JOURNEY'S END

THREE TOES FELT that the Great Spirit must have meant for him to be absent from his people when Rip Ford's Texas Ranger companies routed the Comanche up on the Red and Canadian Rivers. He was thoroughly enjoying the intimate company of Cactus Flower. Even Bird Woman had warmed to him. They saw his scars as badges of honor from the trials the Great Spirit had him endure.

The chief was well-practiced at painting stories of his exploits as told in many council meetings. He regaled them with ever-enhanced tales of his hand-to-hand battle with the mountain lion, his enduring of torture by White men, and his leading of raids on settlers. His favorite tales, however, were those about his travels with Ghost-Who-Rides. Young Laughing Crow was transported by dreams of the sorts of adventures Three Toes had with the Texas Ranger.

Three Toes told Laughing Crow of at one time owning six hundred ponies and of having five wives, though he didn't share how he'd eventually been reduced to three wives and thirty ponies. He shared stories of taking scalps and counting coup. Each eagle feather in his war bonnet had a tale to reveal. Even the women were impressed with his feats.

Three Toes's campfire tales were a relief from their day-to-day existence. They stayed on the move. Their safety seemed to depend on not lingering too long at any one place. Every three or four days, they'd move their humble encampment.

For his part, Three Toes was fully enjoying the sexual pleasures afforded by Cactus Flower and, to a lesser extent, Bird Woman. And they were eager to please. There was some inborn spirit, an innate, instinctive drive to propagate the race. The Comanche needed new warriors if the tribe was to have any hope of surviving. They even looked to Laughing Crow, though he was as yet considered too young to participate. Desperation makes for a strange bedfellow, and times were desperate for the Comanche.

Three Toes took long walks in the wilds around the western reaches of the Brazos River. He meditated, pondering on the future of the Penateka Comanche and fighting off yielding to his feelings of hopelessness. He was ever more willing to accept the White man's ways since clinging to the old customs was increasingly untenable. He strove to impart his thinking to his companions, though they had not quite reached his level of openness about the matter. They still hoped that the Comanche would over-come the Anglos and chase them from their forefathers' lands. White man's diseases would be gone, the buffalo would return, the prairies would be fully open and free, and the Comanche would flourish forever across the vast Comancheria.

In his walks, the chief wondered about Ghost-Who-Rides. He hoped he was safe. In fact, the Texas Ranger was ever in his thoughts. He wondered, too, at the cross that hung on the bone-bead necklace around his neck. When Elisa had given it to him, she said it would give him ultimate strength. He pondered that. Could having survived the torture by Roy Biggs and the seemingly random coming upon the remnants of his people be illustrative of this strength? What was so special about it that it was so very meaningful to Elisa and Luke? Still, he wondered, why did he find these crosses in the burned-out remains and lingering deaths of many White man's settlements? How was that strength? Why did the white victims of the Comanche pray in their final moments of life? Perhaps one day, Three Toes would see Luke and Elisa again.

They plodded slowly into Corpus Christi. Luke led the way with a nearly dead-in-the-saddle Quinn Maguire flanked by Jaime and his cousin Carlos. It was a sight to behold. A crowd of several dozen mostly Mexicans had formed along their route to the jail where Sheriff Bill Meaney stood at the doorway ready to take the prisoner into custody.

"¡Cuelgalo! ¡Cuelgalo alto!" resonated with the modest throng. Even the Anglos joined the chorus, "Hang him! Hang him high!" Luke spurred Big Horse a bit toward picking up their pace. It wouldn't do to have come such a long way only to have the law corrupted with mob violence. A lynching wouldn't do at all. Richards inserted a round in his Sharps just in case, and Jaime's cousins rode up to form a tighter cordon around the prisoner. Maguire, despite his semi-stupor, was sweating profusely and feeling quite nervous.

They pulled up in front of the jail. "Greetings, Bill. We brought you a present." Luke handed the reins of Maguire's horse over to Meaney.

"Thanks, Luke." Hesitating a moment, and with one eye to the gathering crowd, he untied Maguire from the saddle, eased him down, and walked him into the jail. As he entered, he looked over his shoulder. "Luke, come in a moment."

Luke looked at the crowd. They were menacing, but under control. "Bol, keep your eye on things out here." He hitched Big Horse and followed Meaney into the jail. "What's up, Bill?"

"There's more than we thought to this Maguire critter. He's wanted for murders in six states. There's going to be some rewards to be collected." Meaney would take a small percentage for doing the work of certifying Maguire's capture and likely his death, and then distributing the proceeds.

Luke glanced over at the bruised and cut-up prisoner sitting on the edge of the cot in the jail cell. "Any federal warrants?"

"Nope. Doesn't appear to be any, Luke."

"Then I expect he's ours to dispose of. He's not in very good shape. In addition to murdering that Sanchez fella, he killed a couple of hiders at their ranch. He seems to have some sort of blood lust possessing the very core of his soul, Bill. He'd kill you as soon as look at you. Anyway, I suggest the reward money be divided among the cousins, as they did the work of capturing the man."

Meaney nodded agreement. "Sounds like the best way, Luke." He made a note so there'd be no forgetting. "Luke, I'm not sure how long I can keep him safe here. Can you watch him while I rustle up Judge Nelson? We do need to keep this all legal-like, even though he only killed Mexicans."

Luke detested the implication of Meaney's final phrase. "They are humans, Bill."

"Sorry, Luke. It's hard to change what you've grown up with. I'll get Judge Nelson. Do you think you can get Maguire safely to the courthouse? We can meet the judge there."

Maguire sat in the cell listening to the dialog. "What's happening?"

Luke turned to him as Meaney walked out to fetch the judge. "Justice is happening, Mr. Maguire. We're taking you to trial. With any luck, we'll keep you from being torn apart by an angry mob."

"Trial? A fair trial?" A desperate tone crept into Maguire's voice.

Luke checked the manacles and escorted Maguire from his cell and out the front door. "Bol, Jaime, we need to escort the prisoner over to the courthouse."

More chants of "*¡Cuelgalo! ¡Cuelgalo alto!*" emanated from the gathered crowd.

The prisoner was wedged between Jaime and his cousin Carlos, while Bol stood in front with the Sharps rifle at the ready.

Luke raised his hand to the crowd. "*Por favor, amigos. Debe obtener un juicio justo.*" He translated his Irish-lilt-tinged Mexican for the Anglos, "Please, please, we must have justice. A fair trial." The crowd calmed just enough that they managed to escort Maguire to the courthouse.

Once there, Luke turned to Richards. "Bol, you and Jaime see if you can distract that crowd with something besides taking the law into their own hands."

Richards walked through the front door of the court-house and stopped in his tracks. He glanced over his shoulder, as the crowd was very distracted. They were enthusiastically concentrated on building a gallows. The crowd was rightly optimistic about the outcome of the trial. After all, Judge Nelson had earned the nickname "The

Hanging Judge." It was well-deserved, to say the least, as mercy didn't seem to be in the judge's constitution.

Roughly twenty minutes later, Judge Nelson delivered his decision. A still-manacled Quinn Maguire was escorted to the makeshift gallows. He struggled briefly but hopelessly in the vice-like grips of Jaime Sanchez and his cousin. The soul had abandoned the man long ago, so there was only the body to dispose of.

The mob grew silent as Maguire was lifted to the rickety platform. They'd try to clean Maguire up a bit, but he still bore the cuts and bruises of having been dragged through the Nueces Strip landscape. Luke looked up at the contraption. He prayed that the cross member would hold the prisoner's weight. A slow, agonizing death would be cruel, even for someone so deserving of torture as Maguire.

"No hood," he whispered, as one of the cousins went to slip it over his head. The cousin backed away, and a second cousin slipped the noose over the man's head and tightened it around his neck. There was no trap door to be sprung, so Maguire had been lifted onto a bench-like device about two feet above the platform.

Meaney looked up at the man. "Any final words, Quinn Maguire?"

"You can all go to…"

No one knows for sure who kicked the bench out from under Maguire. He dangled with his legs kicking for a few moments, as his tongue hung out and his face turned purple. He passed away just as the cross member holding him broke in two. A cheer went up from the crowd. Justice had been served—tinged with vengeance, to be sure, but justice nonetheless.

★★

After watching Walker Carson ride off carrying the message to Horatio Thorpe, O'Rourke turned back toward the scene of the attack by Juan Cortina's men. He figured that the fight against the Mexicans couldn't have lasted very long once his hired guns were eliminated. Any further delay would be that endured by Cortina's men, as they'd be slowed down by the pace of the lumbering oxen hauling the wagon loads of loot. They'd be every bit as vulnerable as O'Rourke had been.

He rode to within a few hundred yards of the caravan. There was really no point in getting any closer. He wasn't going to single-handedly defeat two dozen well-armed Mexican bandits. He focused intently on confirming that Cortina had captured all of the wagons and that there were no survivors among the men he'd hired.

O'Rourke rode over to the scene of the attack. There were a half-dozen Anglo bodies lying around the area, and all were quite dead. The silence was broken only by the sounds through the grasses of a stiff westerly breeze. He saw a couple of coyotes circling. Cowards that they were, they'd wait until he'd left the scene. Even the buzzards watched hungrily as they flew lazy circles over the battlefield.

He dismounted and removed any valuables from the bodies. He had a list of names, but really could do nothing to positively identify, much less remove, or even bury the deceased. He stuffed watches and coins into his saddlebag. He found a couple of nearly new Colt Dragoon revolvers that he confiscated. They looked as though they'd never been fired.

As he arose from plundering personal effects from the last of the bodies and turned to mount his horse, he heard a shot. In the instant he heard it, he felt a bullet tear through his shoulder. He grabbed his gun as he started to drop to the ground but didn't quite make it before there was a second bullet and a third hitting him. He looked down to see blood gushing from his chest. He'd forgotten about the Apache.

O'Rourke was still upright on his knees with his hands dangling helplessly at his sides. Through rapidly glazing-over eyes he saw an Apache warrior gallop in. Before he could fall, he felt the warrior grab his hair. He dangled there a second before the Apache cut through his scalp. He completed his fall, as another savage's rifle ended any lingering misery.

The Apache were quick to grab O'Rourke's saddlebags. He'd inadvertently saved them the trouble of pilfering valuables from the victims of Cortina's men. The true scavengers had taken the prime booty. The coyotes and buzzards could have the rest.

Meanwhile, Cortina's men heard the shots and kept on moving. They knew the Apache were active in the area, and there was no point in risking men to be certain of their presence. So far as they could tell, no one was following, and that was all that mattered. It was about survival of the fittest.

Carson never looked back as he rode as straight a line as he could toward San Antonio. He barely stopped for the necessities of food, sleep, and bodily functions. He figured Horatio Thorpe was likely someone important, and he might see more money with delivery of O'Rourke's note. Of course, whomever Thorpe was would be none too happy about the loss of the wagons with their valuable cargo. Had Carson known of the demise of Peter O'Rourke, he might have been doubly concerned at Thorpe's possible reaction.

He had no idea of the importance of the message writer to Thorpe's schemes. After all, O'Rourke had been the plantation owner's direct spy into the strategies of the Texas Rangers.

Carson thought back to the second chance Luke had given him. Now, he found himself living on the edge, a precipice if you will, of what the Texas Ranger had warned him to avoid. Though Sheriff Stills had recommended that he join O'Rourke's caravan, he'd been clueless to the shenanigans that underlay the entire scheme. He was unaware of the payoffs and bribes that enabled the caravan of goods to leave Laredo, much less that the goods being transported were stolen. And he couldn't know that none of the generous money trail could be traced back to this mysterious Mr. Thorpe. Had Walker Carson known what he was headed for, he might have changed course and sought the Texas Ranger. Ah, but such is fate.

It was late when Luke finally turned up the trail into Heaven's Gate. Jaime, having spurned the entreaties of his cousins to go to Mexico with them, rode with Luke. They talked about plans to expand the ranch and possibly hire another *vaquero*. Additional properties had come up for sale, and Luke and Elisa would surely spend some of his meager Texas Ranger pay on more longhorns and a few more acres. While it wasn't a common practice, he promised Jaime that he'd cede a small plot to Julia and him for farming purposes.

They avoided talk of the nastiness of the hanging of Quinn Maguire. It wasn't the sort of event that folks dwelled upon except as saloon talk. Justice of sorts had been served, but Maguire's victims would never know true justice and their kin could forgive but never forget.

They rode quietly into the barn, trying not to awaken Luke's children. Once the horses were cared for, they felt free to part ways and join their wives. There was romance on both of their minds, as he and Jaime had wisely picked bouquets on the ride from Corpus Christi. For Luke, it also meant enjoying time with newborn Andrea Ann and their toddler twin boys. Luke strode up the front steps to the gallery. He slipped off his boots. No Irish ballad this time. He knocked softly and entered. "Lisa?"

Elisa started for a second at the softly spoken but yearning greeting before seeing her man standing in the doorway. "Lucas!" she whispered. She placed her finger to her lips. "The children are sleeping."

She stood back a moment and took him in. She could barely contain herself.

"And I...I've missed you, my dear sweet Lisa," he whispered. He pushed the handful of wildflowers toward her.

A longing feeling coursed through her body as she'd so missed him, so craved his touch. Now, here he was, safely home. She buried herself in his strong, loving arms. "I've missed you, Lucas."

The bouquet scattered to the floor. In but heartbeats, her nightgown dropped as well, and she stood wantonly naked before him. There before the fireplace, there on the mountain lion skin Three Toes had gifted them, there...Luke barely slipped from his pants.

Elisa and Luke locked in a lovers' clinch...a heated fiery embrace...exploring hands...passions freely flowing.

They lay silently later, their ecstasy assuaged...for the moment. Legs still intertwined. Luke's fingers gently danced across her soft, milk-laden breasts. "Surely, I dream..." Luke's soft words caressed her heart. She began one by one to unfasten the buttons of his shirt. She took in the aromas of her man, the trail dust, the gunpowder residue, a bit of horse lather, leather and, of course, sweat.

Elisa pushed him onto his back, slid one leg over his hips, sat astride him, and took him again deep to her core. With passion unbounded, ardor fully released, they soon fell asleep in tender embrace.

Two little pairs of eyes peeked from a nearby doorway.

Thorpe wished that newfangled telegraph extended further south. He had plenty to tend to, and decided to spend no more than another week in San Antonio. He needed to be closer to the seats of power in Austin or he'd jeopardize the remaining sway he held over the Texas Legislature. He knew Sam Houston had won the race for governor and was too much of a straight shooter for Thorpe's tastes. He needed someone in the executive role that could be bought.

He was pondering this when Samuel knocked. "Master Thorpe?"

"Come on in, Samuel." He immediately spotted the glum expression on his slave's face. He'd rarely seen Samuel other than smiling and, at the worst, emotionless. "Do you have news for me?"

Samuel handed him a telegram. The "newfangled" system was working quite efficiently after all.

"Thank you, Samuel. You can go."

Thorpe pivoted in his chair, so as to face the balcony and the breeze wafting in through the opened French doors. He'd been working a bit at losing some of his ample girth, but getting up and walking was still a struggle. He opened the telegram.

Horatio ThorpeSTOP
San Antonio, TexasSTOP

We regret to inform you that your
wife, Martha Giddings Thorpe,
succumbed to illness on this day,
October 20, 1859. Funeral services to
be held upon notice from you.STOP

Dr. Carlton SwiftSTOP

Thorpe was momentarily stunned. He'd been hoping the consumption would take her sooner than later and that Gascon's death might hasten the end, but he was nevertheless somewhat saddened by the loss. He'd need to leave San Antonio post haste, as it wouldn't do to dally, given the importance of appearances.

He figured that Edward, his only remaining child, would likely find his way home to bury his mother. It was time to have a conversation...*the* conversation...with Edward. Thus far, he'd been disinterested in plantation life and in politics.

Luke and Elisa shared a morning cup of hot coffee out on the gallery. The late October weather was still warm, but there was just a bit of a chill in the evenings.

Thoughts of Luke's homecoming the night before lingered in Elisa's thoughts. Peter and John played at their feet, and Luke held baby Andrea Ann. It was a perfect picture setting. "This came for you while you were away, Lucas." She handed him an envelope.

Luke carefully tore it open while wondering what more

Rip Ford could be wanting. With Bol Richards's help, he'd already recruited about a dozen men for the Texas Rangers per Ford's request. He pulled the letter out and slowly unfolded it. He read it and passed it to Elisa. "Go figure, Lisa."

"I don't understand." She was perplexed. "I mean, I like what Mr. Ford is proposing, but your role seems to be best when leading men on missions to bring lawbreakers to justice."

"So he's asking me to raise the Texas Ranger company, but doesn't want me to lead it. I'm to be a special agent on occasional missions that best use my individual skills. Seems I'll still be a Texas Ranger captain, just not bogged down with worrying about a couple of dozen men. I wonder what sorts of missions he has in mind and what's occasional?" Luke looked down at Andrea Ann, and then over at Elisa. "Seems as though I've got a decision to make, Lisa. In any case, I'm thinking occasional might mean more time here at Heaven's Gate." As if on cue, a tumbleweed rolled by on a stiff autumn breeze. He wondered where this decision would take him, where was the journey's ultimate destination? Texas Ranger? Rancher?

TWENTY-THREE

WINDS OF WAR

WALKER CARSON RODE into San Antonio only to find that Thorpe had departed apparently with some haste. He found Samuel finishing up packing his master's belongings. "I am Walker Carson and I have a message for Mr. Thorpe that I must deliver personally. Is Mr. Thorpe returning soon?"

"No, sir. His wife passed and he's headed for the funeral back on the Magnolia plantation. Likely be back in Austin in a couple of weeks."

Carson thought the black man was rather more articulate than many folks of that race that he'd encountered. "Do you work for Mr. Thorpe?"

Samuel smiled. "I am owned by Mr. Thorpe." He quickly surmised that this man likely wasn't familiar with slaves or slave labor. As likely, he hadn't even heard about the free state versus slave state controversy that had been racking the nation. "Your news is important?"

"It's from Mr. O'Rourke."

That told Samuel a lot. O'Rourke was on an important mission and this Carson fellow was probably not totally aware of the circumstances. If it was typical of business dealings with Mr. Thorpe, it wouldn't do to send the message via the telegraph. There were no secrets on the wires. "We don't expect him to be coming back here. You might go to Austin to find him, Mr. Carson."

Carson sighed. Seemed his mission wasn't over quite yet.

At the crack of dawn, Luke hitched the mules to the wagon with the intention of making a run for supplies in Nueces-town. He tied Big Horse to the back, and Elisa and the children piled in. She sat next to Luke with Andrea Ann in her arms, while the twins entertained themselves with a horny toad in the wagon bed.

Soon enough, they pulled up at the little general store. Luke climbed down and hitched the team before helping Elisa from the rig.

Bernice and Agatha, surely having a sixth sense about these sorts of things, appeared as if from nowhere to see the baby and busy themselves fawning over Elisa and the boys.

"She's beautiful, Elisa. And she has your mother's eyes." Bernice squatted down to better see Peter and John. "My, but these boys are growing. They'll soon be handsome men like their father." Compliments were flowing freely, and Elisa couldn't help but blush.

"Lisa, have you seen the new church?" Luke pointed up the road a way. "Looks like Pastor Rucker has been busy."

"Will y'all have time for a bite?" Agatha was anxious to learn more about the life at Heaven's Gate and what Luke had learned of the world at large. Seems that these sorts of visits to town became occasions for a bit of community social life. "We've got a surprise, too."

As if on cue, Scarlett Rose appeared with little Margaret in tow. She smiled friendly-like at the twins and hugged Elisa and Luke. "I've missed y'all so much. Y'all really must come see me in Corpus Christi."

Once Luke and Elisa had bought their dry goods, including a new dress for Elisa, they moseyed over to the boarding house to enjoy Bernice's and Agatha's hospitality and hear about Scarlett's endeavors.

Coincidences seemed to be the order of the day in Nuecestown, as Sheriff Bill Meaney came riding into town. He headed straight to Luke. "Good to see y'all. My, but the Dunn family is growing. You're going to have a bigger family than your cousins up the road."

"You have time to join us for midday meal, Bill?"

When folks on the Nueces Strip had an opportunity to share community, especially over victuals, the moments were seized with great enthusiasm. The more folks that gathered, the better. Even Doc strolled over from across the street and joined in.

"I'm so proud of Luke. Rip Ford asked him to pull together a Texas Ranger company and serve as a special agent Texas Ranger." Elisa beamed at her man with unbounded pride.

"That's good news, Luke. Guess with Sam Houston becoming governor, there's going to be a bigger role for the Texas Rangers. I've heard that there'll be nearly a thousand of y'all across Texas in no time. With much of the Army pulling out to fight Indians up north, the folks on the frontier will need the protection."

"It's a lot of territory to cover, Bill."

Doc had been quiet up until now. He was the only resident of Nuecestown that read the newspaper. The news was often delivered quite late, but he enjoyed having knowledge of what was going on in the world beyond

Texas. "Have y'all heard about that John Brown fella back east? Son of a bitch was tryin' to stir up the slaves. He made some big raid of a federal armory in Harper's Ferry up in Virginia."

"What's he hoping to do? These anti-slavers are stirring up a lot of hate and discontent these days." Bill Meaney had strong feelings about slavery.

Luke was chewing thoughtfully as he enjoyed Bernice's cooking. He looked at Elisa, who nodded. Luke generally wasn't inclined to express his opinion on these sorts of matters. "I've heard tell that someone named William Wilberforce has achieved an end to the slave trade in the British Empire. Now, mind you, that didn't stop slavery. Many of my friends and some of my family were slaves to British lords in Ireland. I've seen men whipped by overseers for simply stealing a loaf of bread for their starving families. Not much difference between that and slavery." Luke let that sink in.

"What's your point, Luke?" Meaney took the bait.

"You have to ask yourself whether it's right for one man to own another. Is there some greater good that comes by it? I have a cousin who owns some slaves to help with crops. Is he right to own humans?"

"Didn't know you felt that way, Luke. Must have been rough in Ireland."

"I joined the Irish rebels to fight back against the Brits, Bill. Now I fear that all this turmoil being stirred up by the politicians may lead to violence here." He paused for effect. "Big violence."

Doc was beginning to wish he hadn't brought up the subject, though he was fascinated by the conversation. "Luke, you saying we shouldn't allow slavery?"

"Would you want to be a slave, Doc? Would you want to be whipped or chained in a stock? In Ireland, we fought for freedom from the British. Shoot, America fought for freedom from the king. Yet here in America, we keep folks enslaved. They have no freedoms. Where's the justice in that?"

"What if it came to neighbors fighting neighbors?" Elisa wasn't inclined to hold back her feelings, either.

Luke nodded. "Good point. Far as Texas is concerned, we've got to wonder how Sam Houston feels about the issue. Most slaves are on the plantations in the eastern part of Texas. Those plantation folks are few in number but have lots of political clout...you might say it's too much influence."

"According to Colonel Kinney, that Horatio Thorpe fellow owns a huge plantation, Luke. He has half of Austin's politicians dancing with him," Meaney said.

"Little wonder he breaks the law, but we can't pin anything on him," lamented Luke.

Doc wasn't quite ready to let go of the slavery topic. He had wrapped his jaws around it like a gator on its prey. "So, as the plantation owners go, so goes Texas and Governor Houston be damned? Sounds like that's what I'm hearing." Doc had strong feelings for sure.

The conversation had taken a decidedly emotional turn. "Y'all enjoying my ham?" Bernice sought to change the subject.

Luke laughed, and that changed the mood of the gathering.

Everyone looked around the big table at each other. The winds of conflict over the slavery matter were beginning to blow. It remained to be seen how the economic and political dynamics would play out.

Much to Bernice's...and everyone else's...relief, the conversation turned to lighter topics like ranching and weather.

"Edward, it's been a long time, son." Horatio Thorpe chased after his son as they left the gravesite. He gently but firmly grasped his son's elbow until they were at a halt side by side. "We must talk."

Edward had arrived that morning and had been very obvious in avoiding contact with his father, except as necessary among other folks attending the funeral. Try as he might, Thorpe had not been able to wrangle time alone with him. "Must we?" Edward asked.

"There's much to discuss, Edward." Thorpe strove to not show irritation with his son's behavior.

Edward sighed and rolled his eyes. "I'll meet you in the library. Give me a few minutes." He knew his father couldn't possibly understand his need to grieve. He considered how his son of a bitch father only cared about himself, indulging his lascivious personal desires and his power over others. As soon as he was old enough to see that, Edward had made a conscious effort to avoid him. He'd vowed to never be like his father.

The library, like most of the house, was ornately decorated in beautiful oak and mahogany woods with plenty of artwork on display from paintings to statues. The book collection was sizable, though Edward doubted his father had read very many of them. In fact, he'd likely read far more of them than his father. There was a large, well-cushioned reading chair with plenty of surrounding light from lamps. A secretary desk stood in the center of the room.

Edward had arrived first at the library and opened the door in response to Thorpe's knock. "What would you discuss, Father?" He knew what his father would propose, but feigned being oblivious to it.

"Good to see you, too, Edward. Sad about your mother's passing."

"A lot you cared." Edward couldn't contain his bitterness over the way his father treated her...and everyone else. "She's far from you now." He watched for any sign of emotion on his father's face. "Find any slaves to screw while you're visiting?"

Thorpe slapped him across the face. "Enough of that." He regretted the slap, but regretted more having been goaded into it.

Edward smiled. He knew his father all too well. "So, I suppose this is about me taking over Magnolia?"

"At least you remember what we call this place. It's paid for everything you've gotten, boy. Never forget that."

Edward wanted to add that it had paid for his father's depredations as well. "Yes. How could I forget, Father? You've always taken great pains to remind me."

Continuing the acrimony wasn't getting Thorpe anywhere. "Why should I let you run this place?"

Edward's eyes fully took in his father. He was looking at a tall, grossly overweight man who struggled to walk and find clothes that fit. "Who else would run it?"

"I'm considering selling it. There's an ill political wind sweeping the country, and Magnolia with its nearly two thousand slaves might become a liability." Thorpe was always concerned with appearances so was alert to the drift of public opinion. Turning his assets into cash would be wise so far as giving him the flexibility to get out of the line of fire were conflict to arise. Of course, the hope would be that the cash would maintain its value until he had a chance to reinvest it in properties and businesses elsewhere.

Edward knew his father was talking about the slavery issue. It was the first time he'd found himself agreeing with him. "So, do I have a role in this plan?" He almost referred to it as a scheme.

"I may not have been the father you'd have liked, Edward but, in deference to your mother, I'm not going to deprive you of your birthright. I assume you prefer living back east in Philadelphia. You will be able to live quite well on your share of the proceeds from the sale of Magnolia."

Relief spread through Edward's body. He almost wanted to say that his father might not be so bad after all. On the other hand, he was half-tempted to turn him down on principle. "I'm listening." It was said as respectfully as he could muster.

"I'm going to stay in Austin a while. I have my attorneys seeking buyers for this place."

Edward was by now dying to know what his share would amount to. "Do I need to stay here?"

"No. I'll send money to your bank in Philadelphia once the sale is complete."

"Thank you, Father."

"I need to return to Austin tonight. I wish you safe travel, Edward." Thorpe half-smiled as he exited the library. "Oh, in case you were wondering, I'm giving you one-third of the proceeds."

Edward was surprised at his father's generosity. It was more than he had expected. Then again, he was sole heir if anything happened to his father. He ruefully watched as the corpulent figure waddled down the hall to the master staircase.

Thorpe turned back once again before descending. "Help yourself to anything that has personal meaning to you, Edward."

Edward nodded. He wondered about the slaves. Surely, they'd figure out that Magnolia was for sale. Then again, they were chattel and would convey with the property.

★★

Carson was waiting when Thorpe arrived in Austin. Samuel had ushered the young man into his office, and so he sat and waited. He was a bit taken aback when Thorpe finally walked in. He hadn't expected such a physically imposing man.

"Who are you and what's your business, young man?" Thorpe ensconced himself in the chair behind his desk.

"My name is Walker Carson, sir. I was employed by Peter O'Rourke to help guard a shipment of materials to Veracruz. The caravan was attacked by men of the Mexican rebel Juan Cortina. O'Rourke and I escaped. He asked me to get this message to you." Carson handed Thorpe the note O'Rourke had scrawled. The paper was in bad shape and the writing smudged and barely legible.

"What of Mr. O'Rourke?"

"He went back to check on the caravan. I don't know what became of him as I've neither seen nor heard from him."

Thorpe feared the worst. "Well, I appreciate your dedication, young man." He fumbled through a small purse. "Would you be willing to do something for me? I'd pay you, of course."

"I expect so, Mr. Thorpe."

"I need to know what has happened to Mr. O'Rourke and to my merchandise. As you might have suspected, it was a valuable cargo." Thorpe wasn't anxious to throw more money at this problem. Normally, he'd simply cut his losses. However, O'Rourke was a valuable asset, given his ties to Rip Ford. "I'll pay you two hundred and fifty dollars to get me the answers."

"I'm your man, Mr. Thorpe." He watched as Thorpe counted out the money.

Thorpe gave Carson half. "You'll receive the balance when you return with answers, Mr. Carson." He actually found the energy to get up and escort Carson to the door.

As Carson exited, Thorpe looked down and noticed his vest wasn't stretching so tightly as to pop any buttons. Seemed as though he was actually losing a pound or so. That thought raised his libido enough to decide to visit one of his local brothels, which in turn got him thinking about Scarlett Rose and that damnable Texas Ranger that kept frustrating his intentions.

Thorpe decided perhaps it was time to take matters into his own hands. Much as he detested long travel and found Corpus Christi not civilized enough to suit his style, he would have to deal with the whore and the Texas Ranger.

Captain Belknap had just completed an arduous journey all the way to Utah. His men were exhausted, not so much from the distance traveled as the terrain traversed. The mountains, majestic as they were, took their toll on man and beast, forts and settlements were few and far between, and water was an ever-more precious commodity.

Belknap had no sooner arrived than he had received orders to return to Texas. Rumor had it that there were fears of some sort of a slave uprising. As he'd been led to understand it, nearly a third of the inhabitants of Texas were slaves. Given the emotional temperament of the day, if the slaves were to mutiny, there'd be all hell to pay.

He resigned himself to another four weeks of travel. It was most difficult to tell his men. They'd been fortunate to not encounter any hostile Indians during their journey, but there could be no guarantee that such luck would continue.

His orders were to head to Austin, but he fully anticipated being sent east toward the Sabine River. If there were to be an uprising, it would most likely be in eastern Texas among the plantations.

The message arrived in Thorpe's office just a couple days after Walker Carson had headed south on his mission.

A US Army patrol out of Fort Ringgold had found O'Rourke's body lying on the prairie north of Rio Grande City. It had been riddled with bullets and scalped. There'd been a crumpled piece of paper in his pocket that linked him to none other than Mr. Horatio Thorpe of Austin, Texas. It was a bad-news, good-news situation. So long as the caravan of merchandise hadn't been linked to him, the death of O'Rourke didn't matter a hoot to Thorpe.

Thorpe's anger, born out of frustration, knew no bounds. He vented, throwing whatever he could lay his hands on against the wall, floor, and even the ceiling. He was so crazed that Samuel feared he'd have heart failure. He finally stopped and leaned with both hands on the desk while trying to catch his breath. The deep purple color began to recede from his face. He began to collect himself.

He walked over to his desk and pulled open a top drawer. Inside was his rarely used but well cared for old Walker Colt revolver. It was in mint condition. This one had been a gift from his father. The gun also brought back the memory of having gifted a Colt 1851 Navy revolver to his ill-fated son Gascon. He went to the closet, rummaged around, and found the gun belt and holster. The belt didn't fit.

"Samuel!"

Samuel quickstepped into Thorpe's office. He was startled to see his master carrying a sidearm. "Yes, sir, Master Thorpe?"

"I need a carriage with a trustworthy driver and enough supplies to get me to Corpus Christi. The driver will also provide the usual services." By that, Thorpe meant cooking, camp set up and break down, caring for the horses, and soliciting prostitutes. He'd be well paid. "I plan to leave in the morning."

"Yes, sir, Master Thorpe. I'll do it immediately."

"Oh, and Samuel, I have some legal papers to be delivered to my son Edward." He looked out the window in thought. "And last, you are to see the man whose name is written on this card, as he will have something important for you if for some reason I don't return." He laid a card with a lawyer's name printed upon it on the desk. In a way, it was also a test of Samuel's trustworthiness.

"I can't imagine you not returning, Master Thorpe."

Thorpe appreciated the sentiment, even from a slave. As Samuel left the room, Horatio Thorpe's thoughts drifted to future dalliances with Scarlett Rose. He was determined to own her or die trying.

The morning and his departure were as yet several hours off. In the interim, he'd have to make do with the brothel up the street, which boasted of the very best whores in Texas. He'd certainly be the judge of that. He looked at himself in the full-length mirror standing in a corner of the office. He confirmed at least in his own mind that he was losing weight. He put the gun away for now. He wouldn't be needing it for what he was up to for the evening. Before he walked out the door, he took a swig of whiskey. It made him feel even better.

Luke and Elisa were enjoying another of her fine dinners. He knew he'd gained a pound or two since he'd been home. Work around the ranch wasn't quite enough to offset the quantity of food Elisa was cooking for her man. She made the very best cornbread in the entire world, and that was a vice he simply couldn't shake.

They were about to turn in for the evening when the sound of a horse galloping up the trail toward their house reached them. They heard the door to the cabin open, as Jaime made certain there wasn't some threat riding in. A stranger to him was riding in, but wasn't showing any aggressive behavior. With all the Texas Ranger recruiting Luke had been involved with, Jaime figured this was likely related to that activity.

Luke peeked out the front window and thought he recognized the rider. As the man grew closer, the face seemed more familiar. Luke stepped out onto the gallery with rifle at the ready just in case. "Walker Carson?"

"Yes, sir, Captain Dunn." The young man was amazed that Luke had remembered. "I apologize for showing up so late. I got a bit lost."

"Well, come set a spell, and tell me what brings you here from Laredo."

Carson dismounted and grabbed the seat Luke offered.

Despite the late hour, Elisa brought out a couple of cups of coffee. "Would you care for a bit of cornbread?"

Luke stood and introduced the visitor. "Elisa, this is Walker Carson, the young man I told you about that I'd met up with near San Diego. Walker, I'd introduce the children, but they're bedded down."

"Thank you, ma'am," Carson said with a smile. "I'd take great pleasure in some cornbread."

"So, tell me what's happened to bring you here," Luke said.

Carson went on to describe the work he'd gotten involved with through Sheriff Stills in Laredo, up to and including having met Horatio Thorpe. "I was on an errand for Mr. Thorpe, when I learned in San Antonio that Peter O'Rourke had been killed by Apaches near Rio Grande City. All of Mr. Thorpe's goods had been stolen by Juan Cortina's Mexican rebels."

Luke smiled. He fully appreciated the information Carson was providing, as it solidly linked Thorpe to the merchandise in Laredo. "I don't expect that you knew Mr. Thorpe's merchandise was stolen from the United States Government?"

Carson's jaw dropped. "No!" He pondered that a moment. "Guess that's why Mr. O'Rourke was paying money to Lieutenant Myers at Fort McIntosh and to Sheriff Stills. Dang, Captain Dunn, I feel like such a sucker!" He used the "dang" word in deference to Elisa who was listening in.

"You know anything else, Walker?"

"I know that Mr. Thorpe's wife died and he's selling his plantation. I heard a rumor in San Antonio that he's left Austin and is headed to Corpus Christi. I've heard that the man is obsessed over some woman of ill repute he'd met in Laredo."

Luke knew that could only mean trouble. "Appreciate the information, Walker. If you care to ride into Corpus Christi in the morning, see a man named Bol Richards and tell him I said to sign you on as a Texas Ranger. He'll help you get outfitted."

Once again, Walker Carson found himself trusted and respected by this Texas Ranger. "Why, thank you, Captain Dunn." He got up and walked over to his horse. "Oh, and thank you, Mrs. Dunn, for the cornbread. Dang best cornbread I've ever eaten."

"We don't have a place to put you up here in the house, but there's a comfortable corner of the barn for you to bed down tonight. It'll be warm and dry. Feel free to feed your horse. Breakfast is at dawn, and then you can be on your way to Corpus."

Elisa watched thoughtfully as Carson led his horse to the barn. She turned to Luke and took his hand in hers. "Seems like a young man finding his way. We ought to invite him to one of Pastor Rucker's Sunday sermons." Thinking of the retired colonel-turned-pastor and the strength of her own faith, she touched the beaded amulet that Three Toes had gifted her with. She wondered whether he had yet begun to understand the meaning behind the cross she'd given to him. Luke had shared the story of the chief's capture and torture, how he'd rescued Three Toes, and that the Comanche chief was convinced that the silver cross on the bone-bead necklace had some sort of great power.

Together, Luke and Elisa stood a while longer, sharing the starry night illuminating the vast prairie before them. The reflection of the moon on the prairie grasses turned them into slivers of shimmering silver so far as the eye could see.

Thoughts of her friend Scarlett possibly being in danger gnawed at Elisa. "Should we worry about this Thorpe fellow?" She drew closer to Luke. She didn't want this Thorpe concern to be a distraction, even though it was. Nor had it occurred to her that Thorpe might have evil designs on her husband.

"I'll make sure Sheriff Meaney keeps an eye on her. In the meantime, there's lots to do here at Heaven's Gate with winter knocking at our door." Luke knew that the weather on the Nueces Strip could be a fickle mistress. He had a few cattle that needed to get to market, and he had to be sure plenty of feed was stored away for horses and cattle alike. Elisa had talked him into acquiring a couple of hogs as well so, combined with plenty of chickens, Heaven's Gate featured quite a menagerie.

Luke strove to put ranching out of his mind and focus on the moment. "The night sky is amazing, Lisa." He smiled as his eyes shifted from taking in the sky to looking down at her. "Like you." His hand reflexively caressed her reddish golden locks.

Still holding hands, they crossed the threshold into the parlor. As romantic thoughts floated on the air, baby Andrea Ann let it be known that she was hungry. Elisa looked up tenderly into Luke's deep blue Irish eyes. "I'll be along shortly, Lucas. Don't you be falling asleep on me." She winked seductively and gave Luke a brief glimpse of her bare breast as she prepared to nurse Andrea Ann.

Luke grinned. Life seemed so very good.

Father John had felt compelled that morning to go visit Mrs. Nugent. She'd been seriously ailing of late, and the priest had learned that she might not have many days left. She lived a long way from Corpus Christi, even beyond little Nuecestown. He'd be taking the ferry to cross the river and reach her humble cabin.

He gave his horse its head up the road toward the ferry. He'd ridden this road before. He turned his Rosary round his fingers, as he prayed and generally took in the beauties of nature surrounding him.

Father John's white collar nearly popped off as a bullet tore through him. He was just about dead when he hit the ground and the sickening impact of falling those couple of feet from his horse took the remaining life from him. In but a heartbeat, his day of faith-filled joy under bright sunny skies stretching across the horizon had turned dark, had turned to death. He'd never even had a chance to draw his pistol in self-defense, never been able to engage his attacker. It had been an ambush, pure and simple. His blood pooled under him and then was sucked into the dry Nueces Strip soil.

A lone rider pulled up. His rifle muzzle was still warm. He scanned his surroundings. Nobody around. He tossed a gold coin beside this man of the cloth. Payment? Reparation? The sound of horse's hooves soon faded into the distance.

ACKNOWLEDGMENTS

Book writing simply doesn't happen in a vacuum. The author provides the creative talent and crafts the stories, but there's so much more that demands acknowledgment. I've been blessed with many friends and family who have supported my writing of the Tumbleweed Sagas. My wife Carolyn's reviews and encouragement were a huge help along with very important tech support from our sons Mike and Matt. Other supporters have included Cara Miller, Jim May, Ernie Angell, and cousins Jim & Cindy Holmgreen and Johnny Dunn. Many more friends have contributed support at some level to the creation and publication of *Nueces Deceit*, be it encouragement or advice.

Naturally, I am major grateful to the great folks at Wolfpack Publishing. The team they bring to publishing is first rate from promotion to editing, cover design, narration, and the myriad tasks that lead to successful book sales.

Most of my authoring has occurred in my office as decorated to channel my inner Texan, but my creative juices have often been inspired and imagination stoked in cafés and coffee houses across America. My favorites were Hester's Café & Coffee Bar in Corpus Christi, TX; Nueces Café in Robstown, TX; Java Ranch Espresso Bar & Café in Fredericksburg, TX; PAX Coffee & Goods in Kerrville, TX; Ragged Edge Coffee House and Bantam Coffee Roasters in Gettysburg, PA; 1889 Coffee House in Helena, MT; Dunn Brothers Coffee in Rapid City, SD; Postmasters Coffee &

Bakery and Brio Coffeehouse in Waynesboro, PA; Birdie's Café and American Ice Co Café in Westminster, MD; Deja Brew Coffee House, New Oxford and Deja Brew at Miney Branch, Carroll Valley, PA; and Baltimore Coffee & Tea Co., Frederick Coffee Company & Café, and Dublin Roasters in Frederick, MD. I must admit to also frequenting a few Dunkin Donuts and Starbucks around our fine nation. The décors and easy listening music in these fine establishments combined with savory cups of coffee tended to set me in the right creative frame of mind.

Last but not least, I'm especially thankful for the many folks who have read and enjoyed my books.

I do believe it's important to acknowledge how the old west represents the brave pioneering spirit of settlers that met the challenges and transcended mere survival to enable America to achieve exceptional growth. The settling of the American frontier west is replete with tales of leveraging freedom for individual achievement. I hope you'll agree that reliving our past—even through history-based fiction—often has the effect of pointing the way to an ever-brighter future. Might we be up to it? I hope that the inspiration I've drawn from my having walked the very earth my characters have trodden coupled with my extensive historical research will enable readers to fully experience the grit, adventure, and passion of my characters while sensing aromas of gunsmoke, trail dust, leather, and bluebonnets.

A LOOK AT BOOK FOUR
NUECES BLOOD

Blood spills freely on the Nueces Strip.

Texas Ranger Captain Luke Dunn's life is forever entwined with the rough and tumble prairies of the Nuecestown, Texas. As the nation edges toward the War Between the States, danger lurks at every turn, from prairie fires and blizzards to floods, stampedes, desperate killers, and relentless rustlers.

With each ride, death could be reaching for Luke's reins. Known as "Ghost-Who-Rides" to the Comanche, his determination to uphold justice is tested as paid killers plot to rid the Strip of his unwavering pursuit. New threats to justice emerge, and a fierce showdown is imminent.

As Luke hunts down Horatio Thorpe and a succession of hired guns, can he navigate a treacherous landscape where loyalty is scarce, and bloodshed is inevitable?

AVAILABLE JANUARY 2025

ABOUT THE AUTHOR

Award-winning author Mark Greathouse's love for the Western genre draws upon his deep family roots and love of the outdoors, honed from teen years spent hiking the Appalachian Trail and family travels across America's frontier. He hopes his work reveals his passion for America's western history.

A member of Western Writers of America and the Wild West History Association, Mark also contributes articles on the history of America's west to Western-themed magazines. He was recognized as a 2024 Finalist in the Western genre by the American Literary Book Awards for his sixth Tumbleweed Saga, *Nueces Truth: Texans Face War's Realities*.

Mark began writing full time after a successful career as a business executive and later as an entrepreneurial investor and advisor. His service as president of several business and community nonprofits led to their extraordinary growth. He holds a BA in English and MBA in marketing.

Mark also donates time and books annually to support wounded military warriors. He was a Boy Scout leader (Eagle Scout) and served on a local school board earlier in life.

www.ingramcontent.com/pod-product-compliance
Lightning Source LLC
Chambersburg PA
CBHW011515240626
47154CB00010B/3032